Charles Donnel Gibson

My Lady and Allan Darke

Charles Donnel Gibson

My Lady and Allan Darke

ISBN/EAN: 9783337107277

Printed in Europe, USA, Canada, Australia, Japan

Cover: Foto ©Andreas Hilbeck / pixelio.de

More available books at **www.hansebooks.com**

MY LADY
AND ALLAN DARKE

MY LADY

AND ALLAN DARKE

BY

CHARLES DONNEL GIBSON

New York

THE MACMILLAN COMPANY

LONDON: MACMILLAN & CO., Ltd.

1899

Norwood Press
J. S. Cushing & Co. — Berwick & Smith
Norwood Mass. U.S.A.

To the Memory of

THE WISEST, KINDEST, NOBLEST MAN

I HAVE EVER KNOWN

MY FATHER

CONTENTS

CHAPTER I

CHAPTER II

CHAPTER III

CHAPTER IV

CHAPTER V

CHAPTER VI

CHAPTER VII

CHAPTER VIII

CHAPTER IX

Contents

MY LADY AND ALLAN DARKE

I

THE LAST OF THE OLD LIFE

THERE comes a time when imposition becomes unbearable, even when the tormentor is a young and pretty girl, and one's cousin into the bargain ; which latter fact justifies more summary and effective punishment than may be inflicted in other cases.

Therefore, when my cousin, Dorothy Farnsworth, crowned a prolonged course of petty annoyances by thrusting a morsel of an old last year's chestnut bur down my back, so that it tormented me grievously, I turned on her and chased her to the orchard, where her breath failed from running and laughter together, and she was fain to let me catch her. She looked so winsome, all flushed and panting from the run, that if she had been any other than my cousin, I could not have resisted the temptation to kiss her. But my cousinship had made it impossible to punish her in that way, — I wonder whether girls do ever regard such treatment as punishment ! — having done it so often in the earlier stages of our acquaintance; so I contented myself with gently boxing her pretty ears, and then drew her down beside me on the fallen trunk of a great apple tree.

I put an arm around her waist (merely for her support), and the witch rewarded me by slapping my back, so that I could have cried aloud but for shame's sake. She knew exactly where the remains of that bur ought to be — and they were where she had expected. I clinched my teeth and took a tighter grip of her, in necessary self-protection. So held, she could not strike again, at least, not in the same place.

"It wasn't there, Dolly," I said, lying bravely.

The rogue laughed, and tried to wriggle out of my grasp.

"Are you quite sure of that?" she retorted, with a malicious twinkle in her eye. "I thought I felt it beneath my hand, but no doubt you know better than I. At least I'll be sure to find it next time."

"There is not going to be any next time," I returned, with great inward fear lest I should find the assertion untrue. "I am going to keep you here as a sort of hostage for your own good behavior, until you promise to stop playing me such tricks."

It was a very wrong way to go about getting such a promise, as I ought to have known. I have learned better since then.

"I won't promise anything under compulsion," she pouted.

"You certainly won't promise any other way," I retorted. "You will have to stay here with me until you do it."

"Never!"

"Never — what? Never stay? You cannot help yourself."

"Never promise."

"I am sorry," I returned, trying to make my tone a regretful one. "But I will have that promise, if we have to sit here till sunset for it." It was then scarcely nine o'clock in the morning.

"I am sure your arm will grow tired," she insinuated.

"So will you."

"Yes, of your company," she retorted. "Still, I have endured so much of it of late that a little more will not be any great matter. One becomes benumbed after a certain amount of suffering."

"That's consoling and hopeful for both of us,"

I said. "I am glad you will not be unnecessarily uncomfortable."

A pause; then —

"Let me go!"

"Couldn't think of such a thing."

"What will mother say?"

"Say I did quite right to protect myself."

"She won't. I'll tell her!"

"So will I."

"She won't believe you."

"Oh, yes, she will, when you corroborate my story," I replied very comfortably, and thought I had her there.

"I won't. I'll contradict anything you say!"

"Very well. Then I'll tell her that I have been misbehaving outrageously, and that you were trying to reform me. She will know how much of that to believe: I remember she has been acquainted with you for several years."

"But that would be true; I couldn't deny that," said Dorothy, casting her eyes down demurely. Unfortunately for her, they would not stay down, and when she looked up at me we both burst out laughing.

"Come, Dolly," I said, after we had quieted down. "Be a good girl — for once; it would be such a thrilling experience for you! I'm really in earnest. Pick out some other fellow for those little attentions of yours; there's plenty of better game than I afoot in this neighborhood."

"Most true, indeed; but none so convenient," she laughed. "Really, Allan, you have become as much a necessity to me as my pin-cushion."

A pin-cushion probably would not object to burs, but I did. Hence I resented the comparison.

"That is absurd, Dolly. What did you do before I came? I never laid eyes on you until six weeks ago."

"All the worse for your eyes. Did you ever see anything nicer to look at?"

I never had, if the truth must be told; but I had no intention of owning the fact to her. The question was too impudent; I only laughed and refused to answer.

"Whose fault was it that you never saw me before?" she went on reproachfully.

"Mine, of course. But I had no idea what I was missing, you know, — especially in the way of burs and other such little tokens of affection, — and ever since then I have been trying to make up for lost time."

"It is only more time wasted," she answered.

"Really? Is that true, Dolly?" I asked. "Don't you intend to love me any more?"

"Really, I ought not," she replied, looking down shyly. Mistress Dorothy was a most accomplished coquette, as I had found out long before this.

"Ought not what, Dolly?" I whispered.

"To love you any more — than I do."

Then the minx lifted up her head, and laughed in my face.

"What a fool you can be, Allan, when you set about it," she remarked, with cousinly candor. "Or are you trying to make me one?"

I saw another chance.

"When I was a boy, Mistress Dorothy —"

"When you were a boy!" she interrupted. "And pray, Master Allan, when did you outgrow that affliction?"

I was five and twenty, and felt all my years. I would not condescend to discuss such a question with a chit of seventeen.

"When I was a boy, Mistress Dorothy," I resumed, imperturbably, "one of the first things I was taught about hunting was, that there is no use shooting at a dead duck."

"Oh, and you think I am like a dear little duck? How nice!"

I was disgusted at finding the point of my retort (of which I felt rather proud) apparently lost on her, though I was quite sure she understood it perfectly.

"Dolly, you are really too frivolous for a sober-minded young man to associate with," I remarked, with as much severity as I could muster. "I fear you will injure me."

To give more emphasis to the remark, I withdrew several feet from her, and left her sitting by herself. She rose slowly to her feet, with a look on her face that I knew meant mischief, and came close to me.

"And what becomes of that promise, Master Allan?" she said, laughing. Another slap on that abominable bur brought me to my own feet in a twinkling. I had forgotten both the bur and the promise; her words reminded me of the one, her action of the other — and both to my sorrow.

She fled incontinently, and I followed as best I might, determined to take some notable revenge when I caught her, as I doubted not I should do in the end. She was running toward the house, where she knew she would be safe. I had almost caught up with her when we both narrowly escaped bowling over my cousin George, who stepped out from behind the hedge, holding a packet in his hand.

"Stop, you two mad people, before you injure some one," he cried, waving the packet. "Allan,

I have a letter for you. It comes from Virginia, and is marked 'in haste.' I was about to look for you to deliver it, thinking it of importance."

Dorothy stopped beside him.

"It looks dangerous," she remarked, peering over her brother's shoulder. "Some official order, no doubt. It may be the King has named our grave and reverend cousin Governor of Virginia; how proud I should be to find myself cousin to a Governor! Or perhaps 'tis your death-warrant, Allan; open it quickly!"

She little knew how near it would come to being so.

I took the packet and broke the seal. I had recognized the hand, and expected no great matters, only tidings from a friend at home. Tidings there were, indeed, and such as to cause my face to flush with excitement.

"What is it, Allan?" demanded Dorothy, who had been watching my face with lively curiosity.

I looked up from the letter and spoke to both of them.

"A summons to Virginia," I said. "The Indians have broken out again, and the frontier settlements have suffered grievously. The Albemarle Riflemen are among the companies that go to chastise them, and I must hasten home unless

I wish to be left behind. I do not know that I can catch up with them now, for we are not used to waste time in starting on such occasions. The post is so slow in bringing the news, but I will try to reach them."

"Not so slow, this time," said George, who had glanced at the letter. "The letter is dated only a week ago."

"Even so—a week for the letter to reach me, and a week for me to reach them; I shall be late in any case."

"We will do the best we can to speed you," said George. "I will go to get the horses ready to lose no time."

"Indeed, yes; I must start this morning."

Dorothy had been a listener thus far, but now she must speak.

"And pray, Master Allan, what have you to do with the Albemarle Riflemen?" she asked, with a pretty air of disdain.

"Mistress Dorothy Farnsworth, I have the honor to be a lieutenant in that honorable body," I responded, making her a ceremonious bow.

"A lieutenant! *You?*"

"Even I, unworthy though I be in your eyes."

"A lieutenant! Lieutenant Allan Darke: that sounds very well," she murmured. I fancied she

looked at me with more respect than she had hitherto shown me. "But I supposed they enlisted
only men," she went on, with a return of her old
impudence.

"Not having the advantage of your years and
experience, they imagined that I was a man," I
returned. "I hope the Indians may not find me
less."

"The Indians! You are going to fight the
Indians! I had forgotten that."

"By Jove, so had I, for the moment!" I exclaimed. "I have no time to lose. I must beg
your indulgence, Dolly, for deserting you, but I
must pack my things."

She slipped her hand into mine, and walked
with me to the house without further remark.
She was a curious compound of child and woman,
with many of the affectionate little ways of the
child, together with a large share of the wider
sympathy of the woman, when she chose to let
it be seen — which, in truth, was seldom, she having hardly yet outgrown the youthful shame at
having emotions.

George had already told his parents of my intended departure, and things were in train to allow
me to set out quickly. I tossed my clothes reck-
lessly into my portmanteau, at great risk of ruin-

ing the whole of them, and had almost completed the work when George burst into my room with a crash, panting from his quick run up the stairs.

" Allan, I have an idea that may save you much time in getting home," he exclaimed. " Ride with me down to the Cape, where there are often vessels bound for Baltimore that have stopped for shelter or some other reason. If you can persuade the master of one of them to stop on his way up the Chesapeake, and let you off, you can reach home in half the time, and with almost no trouble. The fare may be rough, but you won't mind that for a few days. It will probably be only a question of price : those masters are always ready to pick up a few shillings more. Even if we find no vessel there, it is only six miles added to your journey."

"It is a good plan," I said, after a moment's thought. "The very chance is well worth the risk of the extra miles, for I confess I don't fancy the prospect of riding such a distance in the haste that I must make."

" Good, I'll have my own horse saddled in five minutes. I know many of those fellows, and may be of use to you," and he shot out of the room as noisily as he had come into it.

I shook hands with my uncle, and kissed my

aunt; they had both come to like me well during my visit, the first I had ever made them, and were as sorry to see me go as I was at the necessity that constrained me. But when I came to Dorothy, she surprised me by putting her arms around my neck.

"You can have the promise you wanted, Allan," she whispered; "and I am sorry about the bur."

Her unwonted tenderness moved me so that I could only say, "Thank you, Dolly, dear," as I kissed her. Then I looked deep into her eyes; and though they were bright with a suspicion of tears, there was no such expression in them as I almost feared to find — only affection, honest and cousinly. She was sorry for the loss of a congenial playfellow, and feared a little for his safety: that was all.

If I had stayed longer with them, I might have come to fancy myself in love with her (surely man could have no better excuse, I thought!) and might have persuaded her to match my folly. Which thing would have lost me the greatest joy of life; for, though I knew it not at that time, there was but one woman in the world for me, and she was not my cousin Dorothy. Wherefore I had occasion many times thereafter to thank God that when I rode away

I left no seed of earthly love implanted in my pretty cousin's heart, and carried none away in mine.

Neither did I dream, then, that this was the closing chapter of my old life, nor that I was about to enter new scenes that would alter the whole course of my existence.

II

A LAND OF MADMEN

A SLEEP of utter exhaustion was broken by
the glare of the morning sun striking fiercely
through my eyelids, and burning upon my face.
I sat up and looked around, bewildered, and
unable, for some time, to recollect where I was.
My surroundings speedily reminded me. In front
lay the sea, still in great commotion from the
storm of last night. The surf pounded thunder-
ously upon an even flat beach of dazzling white
sand that stretched straight away on either hand
as far as I could see. At my back lay a great
dune of sand nearly fifty feet high and some
hundreds of yards in length; similar dunes fringed
the beach above and below where I stood. Upon
the sea not a thing was visible except the curl-
ing crests of the waves as they neared the shore;
on the land, only the beach and the dunes. Of
the vessel that had brought me, there was no
sign. If she had been driven aground, it must
be miles away, for not even a broken, useless

piece of plank seemed to have been cast up from her, If the sea was running last night as it did this morning, I could not understand how I had escaped those giant breakers; and I felt sure that if the darkness had not hidden the prospect that I had to face, my courage and hope would never have sustained me through the struggle.

The top of the dune behind me would afford a larger vista, and some living thing might be visible there. On the seaward side it was too steep to climb with either ease or safety, so I rose and walked down the beach toward the lower end of it. I felt as though I had been pounded in a mortar: every muscle ached profoundly, and my joints seemed to creak like wheels that lacked oil. The hot sun had already dried my clothes, but I was hungry and thirsty, and as weary as though I had not slept for days.

I reached the end of the dune, and as I rounded it I came face to face with another man who was coming from inshore. We were equally surprised at the encounter, but he did not hesitate a moment before levelling in my direction the gun that he carried.

"Stop where you are!"

His weapon was a convincing argument, and I was unarmed. I stopped promptly.

"Who are you?" he demanded, in a curiously monotonous tone.

"A castaway," I answered. "I was blown ashore here last night and had just started in search of assistance."

"Sit down on the ground, and fold your arms!" I hesitated, and was on the point of speaking. "Sit down," he repeated, "or I fire!"

There was not the variation of a semitone in his voice; it seemed best to obey. He lowered his gun, and sat himself on the slope of the dune, holding the weapon ready for instant use.

"What is your name?"

"Allan Darke."

His hands clinched on the gun, and he started to raise it, but after a moment's hesitation he replaced it on his knees.

"What name?"

"Allan Darke," I said.   I longed to ask why my name affected him, but thought I had better not seem too curious at first or irritate him.

"Where did you come from?"

"New Jersey, last; from Cape May."

"Where do you live?"

"My home is in Virginia, though I have not been there for some little time."

"Why not?"

"Because I have had business that has kept me travelling most of the time. Good heavens, man," I broke out, impatiently, "I'm hungry and thirsty and worn out — a shipwrecked man. Give me something to eat and drink, and then I will answer as many questions as you please to ask, but for God's sake spare me your catechism until then!"

He stared at me for some minutes without a word. His face, entirely devoid of ruddiness, though of rather dark complexion, was like a mask in its entire absence of changing expression: like a stone mask in its fixedness. In all the time that I knew him afterward — in pleasure, pain, anger, fear, excitement — it was as immovable as granite. Laughter might issue from his open mouth, or a cry of pain or rage, but not another muscle of his face ever moved. Not only his features, but his voice also, as I learned, was blessed (or cursed) with the same quality of unchangeableness. It was rather a pleasant voice, at first hearing, but when he spoke for any length of time the awful monotony of its tone became almost maddening.

At length he pointed inland, keeping his eyes on me watchfully.

"Go before me in that direction. If you turn, or attempt to escape, I shall shoot."

I arose obediently, and moved in the direction indicated.

"I certainly don't want to escape until I have had something to eat and drink," I remarked as I passed him. "May I ask who you are, and where I am?"

"No. The Master will tell you what pleases him."

So, he was not the Master. There was hope in that, in spite of the saying, "Like master, like man." It could not be that there were two such people in the world, I thought; and there was no reason why I should be treated like an enemy or a criminal — unless, indeed, I had stumbled on a band of criminals. But even then they could have no reason for harming me, for they were welcome to the little money I carried if they would give me food, and forward me on my way; and as for fear of my betraying them, I felt sure of my ability to convince them that I could not do that, since I had not the slightest idea of my whereabouts, except that I had come ashore many miles below Fenwick's Island. Besides, I was ready to give them every assurance of my absolute silence.

A short distance from where we had met, we came to a road, apparently little travelled, and at the end of this, about a mile inland, I saw a grove of trees. I was too weary to walk fast, and though my captor did not hurry me, the way seemed long enough before we entered the well-trimmed woods. A short distance ahead I could see buildings of some kind, and I rejoiced at the prospect of food and rest. In time we met a number of negroes, who stared at me curiously; and now my captor, bidding me halt, called several of them to him, and whispered to them. A moment after, I heard light footsteps approaching me from behind : forgetful of the command not to turn, I faced about, and saw three of the negroes close to me. Before I had time to think, even if I had suspected treachery, they had sprung on me : in a twinkling my hands were drawn backward and tied behind me, so that I was perfectly helpless.

"What does this mean?" I cried, struggling furiously, as my captor approached me. "Is this the way you treat strangers?"

"It is the way we treat such as you," he returned calmly, as he handed his weapon to one of the negroes to carry. "Go on, now!"

"Where to?"

"Where I tell you: straight ahead to that house you can see."

"I won't move until I know what this means. If you intend me evil, I may as well die here," I said stubbornly.

"You will not be harmed—yet," he replied, with a little laugh. "And if you refuse to go, you shall be whipped until you learn to obey. Constantine, get me a whip."

I looked at his expressionless face, and could see no relenting. Suddenly I remembered that there was some one in authority over him. He had spoken of the Master, and though the conduct of the servant augured ill for my treatment by his superior, there was yet a chance of better treatment.

"Very well," I said. "I will go on. But if I live, you shall pay for this some day."

He laughed again, and his laugh was as stony as his face.

"If you live! We shall see." The prospect was not pleasant to contemplate.

He came close to me. "I will show you how unnecessary it was for me to call the negroes, if I had chosen to tie you up myself," he said.

Placing a hand lightly under each of my arms, he lifted me high as his arms could reach, then tossed me several feet in the air, and caught me as I descended.

"You see I am fairly strong," he remarked, holding me just off the ground. "I could easily lift you with one hand, if necessary. You will understand that it is not well to trifle with me: beware how you do it!"

I was as a child in his grasp; he set me down lightly. The exertion did not seem to have affected him in the least. I was silent, knowing not what to say, or what manner of man this might be. He led me to a side entrance and placed me on a bench, with one of the negroes on guard, and disappeared for half an hour. When he returned he said:—

"Come! The Master says you are to be fed before your trial."

I wondered what he could mean, but did not attempt to guess. I was really too tired and hungry to think, except of food; and besides, the whole matter would be plain in a few hours. More than sufficient for the day was the evil already encountered.

They led me to a pleasant room where a table was spread, and placed a good meal before me. My hands were untied, that I might eat in comfort, but behind my chair stood a negro with club raised. The situation was not reassuring, though I knew they would not strike unless I should offer to rise from my seat. At last I laid down my knife and fork with a sigh of satisfaction, feeling equal to encountering anything.

"Are you ready?" said my captor, who had watched me silently.

"Yes."

"Place your hands behind you." I did so, and they were again tied, though not so roughly as the first time.

"Now come to the Master." He led me through a number of passages to a great square hall at the front of the house. Evidently the owners were well to do, for the building was a large one, though by no means new, and the furniture was massive and finely carved. But when we entered the hall, I met the greatest surprise of my life.

Seated at the far end of the hall, I saw a figure, —an old man, to all appearance. He wore no wig, and, contrary to the fashion of the time, his beard had been allowed to grow. It flowed magnificently down his breast, and though his complexion was comparatively fresh and full of health, the hair and beard, both of which were perfectly white, gave him a most patriarchal air. His was one of the most imposing presences I ever saw. He could be stern, but I knew at the same glance he could be just. No treachery, no murder, lurked in that face. My spirits rose on the instant, and I was sure that in a few minutes I should be released and cared for.

Close by him, but a little farther back, sat a girl of about twenty, evidently his daughter. She was not beautiful, according to the standard of the schools, but, rather, she was imperial. Her height almost equalled my own (which is well above the average), and her bearing was majestic. As for her features, they were irregular. Her eyes were the best part of her face : great, honest, truthful eyes, able to flash in anger or melt with pity or love ; eyes that looked through one, and seemed to search out every little baseness in one's heart and rebuke it. And the face was one that could express every shade of emotion and feeling, while in general it maintained the strong appearance of her father's. In spite of its irregularities, it was a handsome face. Yet the nose was somewhat upturned, the mouth was large, the cheekbones too prominent. Afterward, I came to know that she was rarely beautiful, though almost every feature transgressed the accepted laws of beauty. The bearing of the lady and her father reflected conscious power, both mental and physical.

As I was led into the hall, it was evident that these were to be my judges. My captor stopped me in the middle of the hall, and took his place beside me; and though I was absolutely void of conscious offence toward any one, those two pairs of stern eyes made me almost feel as though I must have done them some great wrong. There was a positive accusation in their gaze. At last the old man broke the silence — a long silence.

"Your name, sir, if you please?"

"Allan Darke."

I saw his hands, which lay along the arms of his chair, clinch hard on the leather cushion.

"Is that your own name, or the name of him who sent you?"

"Nobody sent me. My name is Allan Darke," I said.

"Where do you live?"

"When I am at home, at my plantation of Chilton, in Virginia. It is well known all over the province."

"Were you born there?"

"Yes; my family have been well known there this hundred years or more. In Heaven's name, what does this mean, sir?" I burst out. "Am I supposed to be a criminal on trial? If so, I demand to know upon what charge, and by what authority?"

The man who stood behind me seized my shoulder and shook me roughly.

"Answer what is asked, and else be silent — or it will be the worse for you!"

Bound as I was, I turned on him fiercely, forgetting my helpless condition. I was thoroughly angry at his insolence, as any one might have been in a similar case, and was in no mood to count the cost of my rashness. Instantly, he clinched with me, and in another moment I should have gone heavily to the ground; but the young woman arrested him with a single word of reproof.

"Burton!" He released me instantly, and stood stolidly beside me. "Stand aside!"

"Yes, My Lady."

Discipline seemed to be paramount here. He walked to the other side of the hall, much to my relief, as his grasp was no child's play. The man had muscles of iron.

The master took up the inquiry.

"I beg you to pardon the violence of my servant," he said courteously. "He is zealous in my service, and does not think of consequences where my interests are at stake."

I bowed as politely as my condition allowed.

"I appreciate his faithfulness, though I should prefer to see it exhibited in some other way," I said. "I really do not see any occasion for such violent measures as have been taken with me — with your approval, I suppose."

The Master's face darkened. "Your excuses may be heard later," he said. "Meanwhile, be kind enough to answer my questions. You will not lose by it, in the end."

"But why — " I began. He held up his hand, and I stopped short.

" All that afterward, if you please."

I waited, since I must. He was the Master, in more ways than one, and resistance was useless.

"How and when did you come here?"

"I was blown ashore last night, as I told your servant."

"Why did you come?" He asked the question as though my previous answer had not covered the same ground.

"Why? Because I could not help myself, as I told you. Do you suppose people get shipwrecked on purpose?" I burst out.

He rose from his seat; the girl moved forward, and laid her hand on his arm, whether for support or restraint, I could not tell. Old as he seemed, his eyes gleamed fiercely with the fire of youth.

"Allan Darke, tell me the truth! Why did you come here?"

I paused, and looked long at him before answering. If the man was mad, he surely did not look it; and certainly his companion seemed sane enough.

"I have told you the truth," I returned, with a sort of dumb despair.

It seemed bootless to press further my explanation in the face of this determined suspicion. Yet, had I but known, I should have seen that this weak protest confirmed my captors in their hideous mistake.

He resumed his seat.

"Are you really Allan Darke, of Chilton?" he asked again. He returned to this one idea with a curious persistence.

"Yes."

"I do not understand your plan," he said thoughtfully. "I do not see why you should admit your identity, and yet deny your purpose — "

"I tell you I had no purpose," I persisted.

"But that is nothing, since we know it," he proceeded, without heeding the interruption. "I should have expected you to have sufficient courage to abide by the consequences of your actions. I regret that you have not. I could even find it possible to doubt that you are Allan Darke, in spite of your assertion — " He stopped short, as though he found himself saying more than he had intended. His manner was perfectly judicial; there was not even a trace of excitement about him.

"But you have made it evident that you are; and such being the case, there is nothing to do but to decide what is to be done with you."

"For God's sake, sir," I broke out in a last attempt to cut this mystery, "what do you mean? You say you know me, and my plans and purposes, and you speak as though I were some escaped criminal, or as though you had known me before. There is some horrible mistake here, and I cannot imagine what it is. I swear to you that I am an honest man, wrecked much against his will on your shore — and I do not know even where that shore is, or who or what you are. On my own part, I have nothing to conceal from you or any other man; if you are not so fortunate, I assure you I am the last man in the world to try to ferret out your secret, or to betray it if I should happen upon it. Your secrets are nothing to me; if I knew them, gratitude for succor received would prompt me to aid you to conceal them, especially if you will only help me to reach the mainland and proceed on my business, which is of great importance. I wish you no harm, and would gladly forget your very existence, if you wish, provided you will only allow me the chance. I swear it on the honor of a gentleman!"

"The honor of a gentleman!" he repeated, in cutting tones, passing by my earlier words as if they were the babble of an impostor. "The honor of a gentleman! I should have expected a slighter oath from you, under the circumstances. Again, I regret that it is so. But it makes it only the more necessary for us to take our own course without regard to your assertions. And first, for your own satisfaction, and to make it plain that we are not deceived, I may tell you that I know perfectly who you are, and why you come here. I cannot imagine what clew you could have found to lead you here after all these years; but you made a great mistake in following it alone. God has worked for me hitherto, and this time He has not deserted me. He delivered you into my hands, and, until my servants are less faithful and less vigilant than I believe them, your rash attempt can profit you nothing. You should have remembered that we were desperate men, likely to stop at nothing that would assist us to gain our point and preserve ourselves safely!" He seemed to wish to hurt me by a sneer, but his words fell harmless on my ear, since I could not make out their meaning. "I advise you, for your own sake, to repeat no more your silly story; it will do nothing to improve your plight."

He gave me no chance to answer, but turned to my original captor. "What shall we do with him, Burton?"

The graven image at my side answered impassively.

"Let him die."

I turned quickly to glance at his face, forgetting its immobility. Then I looked at the girl, whose eyes were opened wide in astonishment or horror.

The old man turned to her. "What say you, my daughter?"

Her eyes were watching me, though she answered her father.

"You know that I am ignorant of all the circumstances, except that he is an enemy. I cannot imagine what necessity could demand the death of any one, so I hope that at the worst he may be kept a prisoner. Surely, in our situation, it would be easy to keep him so without hurt to us; and surely you would not wish to take a man's life."

The old man gave me a sharp glance as she finished, probably wishing to see the effect of her words on me, though I could not guess his object. He nodded gravely in answer to her.

"She speaks wisely and mercifully," he said. "My remaining years must be few; probably I shall not live many months longer. After I am gone, this man will be powerless for harm, and I would not go down to the grave with *any* man's blood on my soul." Again the look he cast at me seemed to have some special meaning; again I felt at a loss to fathom it.

Burton interrupted him. "It is either his life or—"

"It shall be neither!" responded the old man. "I understand and appreciate the reasons for your opinion, but I cannot approve it, and I am sure you did not expect that I should. He must not be harmed, but he must not leave the island."

"His parol, father?" queried the girl.

The Master laughed ironically.

"I would neither offer nor accept parol in the case of such a man who comes sneaking into my home to do me harm," he said sternly.

"Sir!" I cried, astonished and stung to the quick by the contempt in his tone.

"Sir?" he returned calmly, eying me as though I were an insect under a magnifying glass.

"If you were a younger man," I burst out, taking a step forward, and trying to feel for the place where my sword ought to be.

"You would challenge me, no doubt," he interrupted, with a sneer. "I think not. If I were your own age, you would not be so anxious to fight with me. There was a time when I could hold my own, with sword or pistol, against any man in the colonies. I have had my little affairs of honor, and lost no honor by them; but I was always careful that they should be with *gentlemen.*"

A sort of stony quiet came over me. All the world and the whole course of events were combined against me. I was sure mine was a case of mistaken identity; but there was no way to right it at present. Even if I could have produced incontrovertible evidences of the truth of my story, I doubted that the Master would believe them, holding as he evidently did to some false notion.

The girl whispered to him again. Low as she spoke, I heard her.

"At least ask him, pray!"

He looked unwilling, but finally consented.

"Mr. Darke, will you give me your word not to attempt to leave this island during my life? It will not be for long," he added softly.

The girl clasped his arm affectionately, but he did not look at her.

"Sir," I answered coldly, "you are inconsistent. You refused to accept my assurance that you had made a mistake about me; you have just declared that you considered me unworthy to offer a parol, and insinuated plainly that my position as a gentleman was not sufficiently good to entitle me to challenge a man of your standing."

I spoke with some bitterness, as the situation warranted.

"Will you give me your word, sir?" he repeated, entirely unmoved.

"No, I will not!" I returned, with considerable heat, quite justified, I think, by the circumstances. "I shall escape if I can; and when I do, I assure you I shall return with means to demand explanation and satisfaction for this treatment."

"Very well," he answered, undisturbed by my threat. "You may understand that you are a prisoner within the limits of the island. You will be watched; as long as you act peaceably you will not be harmed; but any force you may use will be met by force, and it will be your own fault if you suffer by it. If you have any complaints to make of your treatment they will be heard, and the matter gone into. You and yours have done much to bring sorrow upon me, but I have no wish that you should suffer more than is unavoidable. I know your course has been taken under a terrible mistake. You consider yourself justified in seeking my life and happiness by any means, no matter how secret or vile. The error that has led to this attempt is but natural, perhaps, yet I must take care that its consequences become no worse. Burton, you will give instructions to the slaves to this effect. Mr. Darke can live in the south cabin. You will see that it is properly furnished, and will supply him with whatever provisions he may need. Make him as comfortable as the case allows. He will miss many conveniences and luxuries, but at least he will be better off than in confinement. Loose him, and take him away!"

I resolved to make one last appeal, and turned toward the girl.

"Madam, I believe you can be just as well as merciful. I ask only for justice. Will you not beg your father to afford me some plain explanation of this matter?"

I spoke with the utmost earnestness, but it seemed to make no impression on her.

"I know nothing of the matter as yet," she answered. "I trust to my father's judgment, and I am sure that what my father does is right."

"Very well," I answered sullenly. "You all refuse to give or receive explanation. At present I am helpless, among a colony of lunatics, as it seems; but some day I shall call you all to account for this outrage. The law —"

The Master smiled.

"*I* am the law here," he said calmly, while My Lady colored high with indignation, and returned my gaze with much scorn. Burton grasped my shoulder with a grip that left dark marks upon it for many a day thereafter. But the Master merely said, again, —

"Loose him, and take him to his quarters."

Burton loosed his grasp with manifest reluctance, and untied my arms as slowly as he dared while they were watching him. The others sat perfectly still, and my last sight was of My Lady standing with her hand on the old man's shoulder, gazing after me with eyes that seemed to scorch my heart, innocent as I knew myself.

III

THE "south cabin," as the Master had called it, was a solidly built cabin of logs, containing two small rooms. The roof and sides seemed to be in good condition, and the windows were large and numerous enough to promise abundance of light and air. A little distance behind it stood a great pile of cut wood, apparently intended for the use of the mansion, and more than sufficient to last me for many months, even though I should keep a roaring fire going continuously in the fireplace. The furniture was plain and rude but quite extensive enough for comfort; bedding and cooking utensils were there, and a rough closet contained a stock of provisions. The place seemed ready for occupancy at a moment's notice, and I wondered how many prisoners had been housed there before me. Incidentally, I also wondered how long they had been there, and what had become of them in the end.

Burton showed me, in a surly manner, where

the various articles were stowed, and turned to go. "Wait a moment!" I exclaimed. "Now that you people seem to have settled everything to your own satisfaction, can you not tell me what all this means?"

He laughed grimly.

"What is the use of keeping up the play now?" he said. "You need no telling, and even if you did, you have come to the last man from whom you would be likely to get it. You will find no confessions here, I promise you, and no cringing. You may consider yourself lucky that you are living. I wish I had blown your cursed head off when I met you on the beach. I should have done it in a moment, if I had supposed the Master would be so weak as to spare you. But he always was tender-hearted, and he has grown more so during these late years. For my own part, I should like nothing better than to hang you up to the nearest tree, or blow your brains out where you stand."

"But why?" I queried.

He stamped his foot savagely, and made a threatening motion.

"Don't try me too far," he said, "or I shall forget my orders and twist your neck now. Stay where you are, and ask no questions, and you will be safe enough for the present; try to escape, or go on provoking me, and your life will not be worth a penny."

"Do you mean that I must confine myself to this hut?" I demanded, with heat. "Because I won't do it."

The words raised his anger; he glared at me fiercely, but his orders were to spare me, and he mastered his rage.

"No; you may wander where you please, within the limits of the island. But mind, no attempts at leaving. You were not wanted here; but now that you are here, you are too valuable a possession to be parted with lightly, though you may be mislaid some day," he added ironically.

He was hopelessly inimical; I turned away without further question, and began to examine my belongings. He lingered for a few minutes, and then, finding that I intended not to notice him further, walked rapidly away toward the mansion.

As soon as he was at a safe distance, I dragged a stool to the open door, and sat down to survey my surroundings and ponder on my strange situation. The cabin was placed about half a mile from the mansion, near the edge of a grove of large trees that covered some twenty acres. On all sides lay fields and pasture lands. Southward, about a mile distant, a great wood stretched for more than a mile east and west; I could not guess its depth. Northward lay the house, with more woods at a considerable distance beyond. To the east lay the sea and the dunes, as I had good cause to know; and westward I could see more water, a mile or so from the hut. In this direction there was a clear view down to the shore, whereby I knew that the absence of dunes, which would have hidden it, indicated calmer water. On this side, then, must lie some inland bay or sound, and probably the mainland would be not many leagues distant. There must lie my best chance for escape; for I was enough of a woodsman to be sure that if I could land there with half an hour's start, my captors could never find me, even though they dared pursue me. It was not at all likely that they would so dare; they were probably without influence on the mainland, since their one idea seemed to be concealment and having nothing to do with the outside world. It only remained to find or make a conveyance, and then to escape the vigilance of my keepers. Patience and perseverance would certainly provide the opportunity, and I resolved to snatch at any and every chance, however desperate. I was utterly destitute of tools or weapons, but I was young, and, as I flattered myself, not without ingenuity. The Master was too old to interfere; however numerous the slaves might be, they could not spend all their time in watching me, nor could Burton, though he evidently hated me enough to make such an occupation an enjoyable one.

I arose and took a survey of my immediate surroundings. The grove in which the hut stood had not been touched by the axe; the cut wood must have been brought from the more distant growth to the south. A few yards away, a spring provided an abundance of water, and the sea, little more than a mile distant, promised a bath whenever I desired. It was as pretty a neighborhood as any one could imagine wherein to pass a few weeks or months of solitude. If only I had not felt myself a prisoner, I should have enjoyed a short sojourn there immensely; but, with the usual perversity of human nature, the feeling that I was a prisoner took away all possibility of enjoyment.

It is hardly worth while to go into a detailed statement of my doings for some weeks, for they were much alike from day to day. It became my custom, after breakfasting, to put some provisions in my pocket, and set out to explore the island, returning about dusk. As the island measured only some seven miles long by two broad, it did not take long to become fairly familiar with its general outlines, and I began to study it in detail. I tramped the woods until I could almost find my way through them blindfold, and felt sure that if I should attempt to escape at night, not one of my pursuers could thread them more easily than I could. I studied the outlines of the shore, and made intimate acquaintance with every curve of the beach, every indentation, every shallow and sand-bar; for wherever the state of the water indicated a bar, there I either waded or swam, until I was thoroughly acquainted with its depth and dimensions. No knowledge would come amiss, and I neglected nothing that suggested itself; for I was resolved that a single attempt at escape should be final. Every day I spent some hours on the beach: now on the seaward side among the dunes; now looking toward the distant mainland, searching vainly for an approaching ship or boat that I might signal to my rescue. If one had ever come within a mile or so, I should have attempted to swim off to it, for I was a good swimmer, as might be imagined from the circumstances of my first landing. But day after day passed without a single speck of white heaving in sight. The island seemed to be planted in a deserted sea, and I began to wonder what part of the world I could have stumbled upon, though I thought I knew my whereabouts within much less than a hundred miles. I had not supposed it possible to find so deserted a spot on the whole coast, from Boston to Savannah.

My first idea, of course, was to get hold of a boat in some way; failing that, to construct a raft. I had no difficulty in discovering where the boats were kept; a large boat-house in which a number of small boats were stored, stood on the shore of a little inlet about a mile from my cabin, and about the same distance from the mansion. I knew that Burton would take precautions to prevent my getting at them; but I was hardly prepared to find that two stalwart negroes guarded the boat-house by day, and were relieved by two others who watched all night. A small sloop was moored to the wharf; but she was secured not only by ropes but by chains, and the amount of rust on the chains indicated that it was long since the little vessel had been used. Even the small boats were seldom taken out, except for pleasure, for whenever fresh fish was wanted, some of the negroes dragged a great seine. Also, in my wanderings, from time to time I caught a glimpse of a negro at a considerable distance behind me, and felt sure that a constant watch was kept over my movements. Sometimes I tried to elude my followers, but rarely with much success; if I threw one of them off my track, it was not long before another one appeared in some other direction. A few times I detected Burton himself engaged in the pursuit. It was irksome to feel that my every movement was spied upon, though when the ludicrous side of the matter struck me, I would laugh aloud at the mistake they were making, and at all the trouble and anxiety they were wasting on a man who could not harm them if he would, and who would have been only too glad to forget their very existence. And then, when the burst of laughter was over, the cruelty and injustice of the thing would strike me afresh, bringing a feeling of intense irritation; so that sometimes I felt disposed to go straight to the boat-house and fight my way to freedom, or be killed. It was fortunate that I had no weapons, or there is no guessing what folly I might have committed.

When the day was clear, I had no difficulty in making out the mainland from the westward side of the island, apparently some four or five miles away. On this side lay my best chance of escape, for there seemed nothing to hope for to seaward.

I could not doubt that this side would be watched more carefully than the other, and, in case of escape, this place would be the first to be looked after. On this side a desperate man might try to escape by means of a raft, or even by swimming, since the opposite shore was not more than five miles away, as nearly as I could judge, and might possibly be reached in this way. But eastward, or to the north or south, nothing but a boat would serve; and all the boats, which were kept on the inland side, were too well guarded to give me any hope of seizing one of them.

In the course of my wanderings I frequently met with negroes working in the fields or woods, and always stopped for a few minutes to chat with them. I knew that whatever tale might have been told them, they could not possibly cherish the same feeling of animosity against me as did the white people. In a land where a man has only enemies, even the toleration of the lowest may have its advantages, and it was not for me to neglect any possible chances. If I could find a disaffected one among them, he might be of infinite use to me. But I am bound to acknowledge that from first to last I never found one who would not rather have cut off his right hand than do anything that seemed likely to injure the Master.

At first they were very reticent, though never uncivil; but, after some weeks, finding that I seemed perfectly harmless, they became to some extent more friendly, and some of them even seemed pleased to have me stop and speak to them. I early discovered that they had been warned to give me no information, and to watch over my movements when they met me. They did their utmost to keep me in ignorance of the place and the people, but an uneducated man is seldom a match for an educated one at such a game; and such a strait as mine was a matter to improve one's acuteness immensely, so that from isolated hints, unknown to them, I deduced many things. I learned to remember and combine disconnected remarks in a way that years of practice would not have accomplished under less pressure of need. Among other things, I gathered that they were entirely ignorant of the cause of my detention, and doubtless they wondered about it as much as I did. But even those who liked me best were wonderfully faithful to the Master, and neither artifice nor promised reward could draw one syllable of direct or intentional information from them.

"Who owns this plantation?" I asked a friendly negro one day.

"Massah."

"Yes, I know that; but what is his name?"

"Massah," he answered stolidly.

"But hasn't he a name?"

"I s'pose so."

"Well, then, what is it?"

"Doan' you know, sah?" he asked cautiously.

"No; I never heard him called anything but 'the Master.'"

"Me no more," he affirmed. I could not decide whether cunning or stupidity dictated the reply, though I could hardly believe the statement, and tried another way to ferret out the desired information.

"Is the young lady his daughter?"

"Yes." His face lighted up at the mention of her.

"What is her name?"

"My Lady."

"But that isn't her name," I objected.

"'At's what we call her."

"Then what does the Master call her?"

He only looked at me distrustfully, and turned back to his work. I walked away, discouraged.

There seemed to be no objection to my wandering all over the island at any time of day or night; even the precincts of the great house were not forbidden, and I fell into the habit of walking over to the mansion in the still spring and summer evenings. I would station myself somewhere within good seeing distance of the front rooms, and through the open windows, evening after evening, I watched the Master and My Lady, though I was careful to keep far enough away to prevent any accusation of eavesdropping, in case any one should be watching me. I would never have believed that a few weeks of semi-solitude could cause such an intense longing for cultivated companionship as I suffered; and even this distant observation of my captors was an immense solace to me.

It was beautiful to see the affection of those two. It displayed itself in every look and gesture. The very way in which My Lady, in passing, would put her hand on her father's shoulder or his arm, proved the tender solicitude that she felt for him. The very way she bent over him, like a protecting angel, even when she did not touch him, and he hardly knew of her presence until she had passed by, was enough to excite the envy of a man who felt himself an exile among a hostile people. He seemed to be an old man, though his complexion — probably due to his quiet and temperate style of living — was almost that of a boy, with its clear red and white and smooth skin. The way the color came and went on his face would have excited the envy of most of our Virginia belles. Yet there was nothing effeminate about him; his change of color would be plainly caused by the vivacity of his conversation, which was unrestrained by the training that men living in less solitude acquire early in life. He must have been strong and bold and active when he was young.

Frequently during those evenings I heard My Lady singing, and it was a vast delight to me when I saw her move toward her harp in response to the Master's request. Though I could not hear his words, her voice had a penetrating quality that bore it out clearly into the trees where I was accustomed to stand, and I could distinguish her words plainly. Sometimes the songs were old ones, with which I was perfectly familiar; sometimes they were strange to me, yet always they were such as suited exactly the compass and quality of her voice, and there was in them an accent of feeling, of meaning, that is so often lacking in well-trained voices. She sang only such songs as answered her mood at the time, and she sang them as though they had been written on the moment, and for the temper she was in at the instant.

There was one song, especially, strange to me, but plainly an old one to her, that she sang more frequently than any of the others. From the Master's behavior while she sang it, I judged that it was an old favorite of his own. He seemed to ask for it often, and I heard it so many times that both the words and the air became indelibly impressed on my memory, like the nursery songs that our nurses sing to us over and over when we are children. The first two verses were in a plaintive minor key, as though the singer were filled with regrets for the long-lost days of youth, and when she sang them, the Master was wont to shade his face with his hand, and sit motionless.

When autumn is adorning
　　The mountain sides with gold,
And clouded skies give warning
　　The year is growing old;
When oak leaves turn to amber,
　　And chestnut burs unclose,
There blooms without my chamber
　　A single crimson rose.

Just one; but from its growing
　　In lonely splendor there,
New beauty gathers, showing
　　A hundred times more fair,

A thousand times more precious
Than all the blossoms strewn
On clusters tall and gracious
In brighter days of June.

Then the air changed to a triumphant major key, full of patience and hope, full of satisfaction, and the Master would sit up and gaze at My Lady, with all his soul in his eyes, and watch her as though she had brought back to him the love and promise of his youth.

So, when my youth is stricken,
And frost of age appears,
My soul, perchance, may quicken
To bloom of early years.
One's heart need not be blasted,
And hope need not be fled,
Though summer flowers are wasted,
And summer days are dead.

And I thought I could read his secret thoughts. To him, My Lady was the rose, growing in lonely splendor and bringing back the memories of his youth. The words seemed to describe her exactly. Even by reason of the lost golden days of his youth, she was a thousand times more precious to him; through her his soul was reawakened, his youth restored, and for a little space he dwelt in the past and the present at once. By his face I knew that some part of that past, at least, had been a most happy one; and I could readily understand how happy, if My Lady was like her mother, as seemed most likely. The symbolism of the song was self-evident, and I envied the Master both his dreams of the past and his joys of the present.

Then, sometimes, it would come home to me how I was cut off from human intercourse, and by whom. My proper place should have been by My Lady's side, an honored guest of the house. Yet absolutely without reason that I could discover, they had cast me out from their presence, and made me the lowest of all human things on that island. I could not even go to my own place and dwell among my own people.

And at such times the sweetness of My Lady's singing brought with it a bitterness that I tasted long afterward, and the evil more than outweighed the good. I returned, however, to gaze at them again and again, and in watching them I grew to feel as though they were friends whom I knew well, yet could not reach, and sometimes it seemed as though I could almost read their thoughts. While I watched them, I entered into My Lady's tender care for the old man's health and happiness, and fully sympathized with his

love for her, his pride in her. So much so, that
sometimes I shared in his interest in her, that is,
until I remembered the estimation in which they
both held me; and then I would awake to the real
state of things, and curse — perhaps I had better
not say what I cursed. They were my enemies,
my tyrants, and they detested and despised me —
or, at least, the man they took me to be. I ought,
by rights, to have hated them in return, but what
I saw during those evenings disarmed me, and I
could only feel greatly grieved that I could not
prove to them that I was really their friend. I
knew they could not have many friends, living the
lonely life they did, and I felt a great desire to let
them know that they were losing the chance of
one who could be as devoted to them as they were
to each other.

But they never afforded me an opportunity.
The Master rarely went far from the house. Despite his fresh and youthful complexion, he walked
like the old man that his whitened hair and beard
proclaimed him. His strength was unequal to
support him any distance ; when he walked in the
neighborhood of the house, he leaned heavily on
the arm of My Lady or of Burton. I almost
began to feel a respect for the latter, when I saw
the care he took to protect the Master. And

though in my wanderings I frequently met My Lady riding across the country or walking on the beach, she gave me no opportunity of addressing her, passing me at as great a distance as she could, not even throwing a glance in my direction after the first sight of me; while her face was invariably set with such an expression of indifference or contempt that it would have been a far bolder man than I who would have ventured to address her uninvited.

IV

A FIRST ATTEMPT — AND FAILURE

I HAD flattered myself that my ingenuity would discover or contrive a means of escape; but when two months had gone by without offering a single chance, I began to doubt. My jailers were more acute and more careful than I had counted on, and there seemed to be no relaxation of their vigilance.

The very first necessity was some means of transport to the opposite shore of the sound. A boat was not to be looked for, and I had no means of constructing a raft (even if the watch kept on me would not have prevented its construction, or have discovered its existence before I had opportunity to make use of it), or of propelling it if I had been able to make it. I had at least the consolation of believing that my captors had relaxed their watch to some slight degree, so that I could occasionally move about for a short time at night without being spied upon, and at length I resolved to put into play the only means that suggested itself. It was desperate, but less so than swimming, which seemed the only other alternative.

I had no means of felling a tree, my only edged tool being a common table knife of poor quality; and though the watch on me had become less apparent, it was still too sharp and too constant to allow me to make any manifestation unknown to the watchers, even had I had an axe. But certain pasture grounds near the stables were fenced in with common snake fences. The rails being merely piled, and not fastened, a rail or two was not likely to be missed. Late one night I abstracted a large, round rail, and carried it down to a certain spot on the shore, some two miles distant from my cabin, and there concealed it among the tufts of marsh grass where I could easily find it at any hour. I dared not repeat the theft that night, fearing to arouse attention, for the cabins of the negroes were only a short distance from the pasture ground. I even restrained my impatience for four nights afterward before I ventured to repeat the operation. Then I had my means at hand.

The next day I selected and cut off a number of long strips of tough vines, and got them to my cabin unnoticed by winding them about my body beneath my coat. Rope, I had none, and these were to supply its place.   And now I had only to wait for a night that should be dark, yet clear, so that I could guide my course by the stars.   While I waited, how often and how wistfully I gazed across those miles of water at the faint blue-green line that I knew meant the mainland and freedom, if I could once touch it !

The night I looked for came at last ; I knew the weather signs, and made my preparations while it grew dark.   I had ground my table knife — my only weapon — upon a stone, until the rounded tip was worn off into a sharp point, making it a rather formidable instrument for either attack or defence at close quarters.   I tied the knife securely with a small vine, and fastened the other end of the vine around my waist beneath my clothes, leaving some five feet of loose vine, so that I could use it freely, or even drop it, without danger of losing it.   The knife and the loose part of the vine were thrust inside my shirt.   I left my coat in the hut, carried the rest of the vines in my hand, and started for the shore as soon as it was dark enough to conceal my movements ; and though I had no reason to believe that I was watched, I went cautiously, and by a circuitous route, to the place where I had hidden my two precious rails.   I was immensely relieved to find them undisturbed, for there was always the possibility that some one might stumble upon them; and their mere presence in such a place would have aroused suspicion.

Each rail was a chestnut log, about four inches in diameter, stripped of the bark, and well dried and seasoned by years of exposure to the weather. My first task was to connect them at the ends by strong pieces of vine, so that they lay half a yard apart; after this I placed them close together, and tied them fast in another place by fresh pieces of vine. The rest of my vines I fastened on the logs securely, for use in case one of my bindings should break. I proposed to use the rails as a certain means of support when necessary, swimming with only one arm, while the other clung to the rails. In case I became exhausted, a few strokes of the knife would sever the second set of bindings;. I would then slip between the rails, with an arm over each, and float quietly until strength returned, the first set of bindings holding the rails together at a convenient distance. I kept on my shirt and trousers, but tied my shoes fast to the tiny raft.

It must have been about nine o'clock when I carried the rails down the beach and waded noiselessly into the quiet water. There had been little wind all day; there was hardly a ripple on the

face of the sound : only a slight short swell of the
tide, that was more restful than otherwise, and did
not obstruct my progress in the least. It was
with a feeling of great thankfulness and as great
elation that I finally bent forward and struck out
for freedom. I had at least seven hours before
me in which to reach the farther shore before the
dawn would give my captors opportunity to see
me; and, even if I should not have quite attained
my goal, the chance of spying a man's head on
that great bay was a remote one. If I ever succeeded in touching the shore, I had perfect confidence in my ability to take care of myself against
any odds the islanders could bring.

I had resolved not to hurry for some hours; it
seemed better to husband my strength until the
last, so that if I had not yet reached the shore
when the day broke, and if the pursuers caught
sight of me, I should still be able to make a dash
for liberty. So I swam on at a moderate pace for
more than an hour, as nearly as I could judge,
much pleased to find that the trouble of towing
the rails caused neither such hindrance nor such
delay as I had expected. From time to time I
relaxed my muscles by turning on my back. In
this position I could see the stars, my only guides,
even better than before; and as I moved slowly

forward, they seemed like kindly eyes watching the progress of a tiny atom in a waste of water. They sent me the first friendly glances I had seen for months, for during my captivity they had only mocked me ; and I blessed them as much for their kindly aspect as for guiding me so certainly.

After some time, however, a slight breeze arose, and swept the water into a series of ripples and slight swells that washed over my face, and made swimming in this position not nearly so pleasant, though it did not interfere with my progress. At last, the monotony of the motion and the sound of the little waves threw me into a dreamy state in which I almost ceased to think, but swam on steadily and mechanically, careless of the things that were past, or of the things that were to come.

Suddenly I roused from this state with a start, for a sound came to my ears that was different from the regular plash of the waters. I stopped swimming to listen, and to this stopping I owed my life; for, a moment later, a mass of blackness shut out the stars from my view, and something heavy and solid grazing my shoulder with great force, drove over my little rails with a crash that seemed to fill the night. The blow on my shoulder numbed my arm ; the rails that had been supporting me were suddenly driven from my slight hold. Instinctively I threw up my other arm and grasped wildly at the thing that had struck me, caught hold of something that yielded under my weight, and down I went beneath the water.

Such a mishap is nothing to a swimmer; in a few seconds I returned to the surface. But to my intense astonishment the stars had vanished, and the ripple of the waters sounded afar off. I threw out both hands, and both touched what felt like wood; I raised one hand over my head, and feeling the same substance above me, I realized instantly what had happened. A heavy dug-out canoe had been driven at me and over me; when I grasped the edge of it, the thing overturned, and I had risen beneath it. As long as the air lasted, I could breathe in the space between the bottom of the overturned boat and the water quite as comfortably as outside.

The exact state of affairs flashed upon me in a moment. My escape had become known; I had been followed; and the canoe had been driven rapidly forward with the intention of striking me on the head. By my stopping to listen, my assailant had missed his stroke, though my bruised and aching shoulder testified to the substantial accuracy of his aim. I had no doubt as to his identity. The Master could not follow me thus; the negroes would not dare.

For some minutes I kept perfectly still, revolving plans of escape; but none offered. If I should be discovered, there was little doubt what my fate would be, alone there in the water with a single man whose strength was fourfold my own; with my bruised shoulder I could not hope to reach either shore, and a successful struggle for the possession of the canoe was out of the question. I knew Burton must be swimming about in search of me, if by any chance I should rise to the surface; so the minutes dragged slowly away, until at length I felt him touch the canoe. Then he attempted to right it, and for a moment I held it, so that with all his weight it could not turn. But I knew that contest could not continue, and with the utmost caution, but as rapidly as possible, I worked my way along until my head was at the bow of the canoe; and then, still keeping hold of it, I let myself sink, and rose noiselessly on the outside. I could see him, not ten feet away, struggling with the refractory canoe, which turned over easily as soon as I released my hold on its sides. He had a paddle in his hand which he tossed into the canoe, and then climbed in. It was full of water, but, being a dug-out, and some three inches thick, it bore him bravely. The ends had a rise of more than a foot above the midships, which concealed my head.

I glanced around for some sign of my trusty rails, which I knew could not be far off; if I could have found them, I should even yet have attempted to reach the mainland. But the night was too dark; there was no sign of them, and I dared not leave the shelter of the canoe to search for them. Meanwhile, Burton was industriously bailing with what I took to be his hat, and the canoe began gradually to rise in the water. This had the advantage of concealing me more perfectly, while at the same time it brought the crisis nearer; for what was to become of me when the canoe was clear, and he started homeward? I knew well that with my wounded shoulder I could not hope to swim such a distance — about two miles, as I estimated it.

I could hear his monotonous voice grumbling and swearing at the accident (as he plainly believed it) that had upset him, and at the slowness with which the level of the water fell. The canoe was still, as I judged, nearly half full, when suddenly he gave a loud exclamation of disgust, and, moving to the other end, began to paddle. And then I saw how my enemy was to be made the means of saving me, after his recent attempt at murder. For, with the canoe half full, as it was, he could not suspect the cause of some extra resistance to his progress, as he must inevitably have done if he had stopped to empty the boat. I had only to cling where I was, and make him tow — or rather push — me ashore.

And this he did, grumbling exceedingly at the labor it involved. At a distance from shallow water that I knew I could cover easily, while he paused to rest his overstrained arms, I let myself sink and swam straight away beneath the water until my lungs felt ready to burst. When I rose again, I could make out my enemy and his canoe some distance away, a mere indistinct dark mass against the lighter horizon and the sky. So I felt mightily relieved, knowing that if the canoe was so nearly hidden from me, my head would be quite invisible to him, for I was careful to swim low in the water.

It was nearly two hours later that, bruised and weary, I reached my cabin. I was footsore, also, for my shoes had gone with the lost rails, and shells and sand-burs and stiff marsh-grass make havoc with unaccustomed feet. I threw off my wet clothes and dropped upon the bed — too nearly exhausted to think or to care what I should do on the morrow. I wanted rest, only rest !

Burton gave me a curious, startled look when he met me the next day, which I answered with one of defiance. But he said not a word as to the events of the night before; and for my own part I concluded that if he was willing to let sleeping dogs lie, so was I. I hoped for better luck next time, and that the sleeping dogs would continue to sleep. Although I was quite ready to undertake all risks that might be necessary, I was not desirous of incurring any more than must be. My first attempt had proved that I had no fools or sluggards opposing me, and that escape was a more difficult and more dangerous proceeding than I had counted on. Yet it seemed to me that I had been as cautious and as secret as any man could be.

OUT OF THE DEEP

In my survey and study of the island in search of chances of escape, I had naturally thought more of the possibilities to the westward, across the sound, than of the chances to seaward. The route by the sound I had already tried, with disastrous results, it is true; yet one failure did not mean utter defeat, and I had not abandoned the hope of ultimately making my escape by that route.

To go by sea was more difficult. Swimming was out of the question for such a distance; to escape by this way would require a boat and some small store of provision. The latter I was certain of being able to procure. Indeed, the supply of food furnished me was so generous that I need have had no difficulty in saving half of each day's allowance, while still making ample meals; and a few days of such saving would have seen me plentifully supplied. But the boat — there was the rub! Try as I would (and I racked my brains with the problem day after day) I could devise no means of coming at one. There was more than a sufficient supply close at hand, of all sorts, from the twenty-ton sloop lying idly at the wharf down to the lightest canoe; but as far as I was concerned they might as well never have been built. I knew very well that every one of them that I could possibly handle alone was guarded night and day. The lighter ones, in fact, were kept in a boat-house under lock and key, as well as under guard.

Though no scheme suggested itself whereby I could get one of them, I clung to the idea that, sooner or later, my chance would come. I simply could not force myself to believe that these people could allow me to roam the island at will, and yet be able to confine me to it for an indefinite length of time. The chapter of accidents is a long one. Whatever precautions they might take, there must surely come a time when some lucky chance, or some oversight of theirs, would place the means of escape in my hands. At least, so I firmly believed.

Meanwhile, it behooved me to neglect no point of knowledge of the locality that might be of use in helping that chance forward. Though I expected help of some kind, I could not guess from which side it might come. Hitherto I had devoted most of my time to the western shore, along the sound, and I had learned it pretty thoroughly. Now I began to study the seaward side with equal care, beginning at the southern point (since Cape Charles, toward which I had been travelling when I fell into my great misfortune, lay in that direction) and gradually working northward.

During my study of this coast, too, I often caught sight of men who were evidently watching me; but I had now grown so used to this constant surveillance that it had almost ceased to annoy me, and I paid little attention to it. Sometimes the spy was Burton, sometimes one of the negroes. They took slight pains to conceal themselves or their purpose; but they never intruded upon my loneliness, nor thrust themselves upon my attention, so that, for the most part, I entirely forgot their presence. Thus I spent the best part of a week studying the peculiarities of the east coast, and so impressed them upon my mind that I could have drawn an accurate map of the whole shore in a few moments. No unusual incident disturbed me until I had come to within half a mile of the northern point, where a sand-bar ran out seaward a few hundred yards at right angles to the shore line.

Nearing this one morning, my attention was drawn to a slight depression in the sand, some fifty feet wide, and running back nearly to the line of the dunes. It was a very slight depression, of no seeming importance, except that the sand seemed to be somewhat finer ground than along the rest of the beach ; but it was rendered noticeable by the fact that the footprints of some late passer turned aside on meeting it, and skirted the edge of the higher part, instead of crossing it. At sight of this I stopped to gaze at the tracks, wondering why they should change direction, until it suddenly struck me that the maker of those tracks had probably approached the dune in order to pick up something, — a shell, a stone, perhaps a piece of driftwood. So, smiling at my own stupidity, I walked rapidly forward in the line I had been following, close to the edge of the water.

For a few steps all went well enough. I noticed that my feet sank deeply into the moist sand, so deeply, in fact, that it made each step more difficult than the last. Each time I raised a foot, the motion seemed to sink the other one deeper than the first, until, when I was almost exactly halfway across, I suddenly realized that I was utterly powerless to extricate the last foot I had put down. A little irritated, somewhat amused at my predicament, but still not at all alarmed, I pressed the other foot deeper into the sand in search of the firm ground I felt sure must be somewhere beneath me. It went down easily six inches deeper than I had yet reached — and stuck there.

This was serious. I had not even a staff on which to throw my weight while I raised myself. I stooped, and pressed my hands against the surface, hoping to support part of my weight on them while I withdrew my feet, for I believed that if I could get one foot to the surface, the other one must follow. But my hands helped me not a whit; indeed, they sank into the yielding sand as easily as my feet had done. I withdrew them, and even that slight motion seemed to plunge my legs deeper. I was already sunk for some little distance above my knees.

I began to feel a vague disquietude, though I was still far from realizing the full peril of the situation. It was awkward and stupid to let myself be so caught, but I knew that one of my guardians (as I was in the habit of calling them to myself), some one of my watchers, must be near, and he would either pull me out or tell me what to do to help myself.

I called, and called again, but heard no answer;

then I shouted loudly: still no response. After keeping this up until I began to grow hoarse, I decided to desist; I should surely be missed, and search for me would be begun immediately, I knew. I was entirely too prized a possession to be lost. Even the fact of my position as a captive began to have a certain value just now; all I had to do was to keep quiet and wait with what patience I could muster; it would be tiresome, but it was the only sensible (or possible) thing to do.

Thus I reasoned, foolishly.

And then, looking downward, I saw that during those few minutes I had sunk six inches deeper, and it suddenly dawned on me what the matter was.

For a moment the thought was so appalling that I could only gasp; then a mighty terror rushed over me like a strong tide, and awful shudders rent me, and left me weak. I knew my situation and its hopelessness unless help came quickly. It was my first experience with quicksand, but I knew well enough what to expect; whether I struggled or not, a slow sinking into its horrible maw, inch by inch, until it should reach my chin, my mouth, my nostrils, and then — one last awful choking effort for breath. For a few moments more two dreadful staring eyes would gaze above the surface, and then oblivion, complete obliteration from the face of the earth.

I looked around despairingly. The sun shone brightly; the surf rolled in without ceasing, and broke placidly within a few yards of me; some gray-backed gulls chased one another in play close by my head. Did they know already that they had nothing to fear from me? Everything spoke of life and the joy of living, except to me. To die; to die thus, watching slow death crawling remorselessly up from feet to head, inch by inch; to measure its approach almost to the second, looking forward always to the terrible, slow suffocation at the last! I had the fantastic notion that my feet and legs were already dead, and I seemed to feel dissolution creeping upward.

"Oh, my God, is there no help?" I cried, turning my face toward the sky, as though the days of miracles had not ended ages ago. I looked for none, yet my involuntary exclamation was natural enough.

"None!" said a quiet voice near by.

I gave a great start, and a shout of relief, in spite of the word, and turned my head in the direction of the sound.

He was sitting on the sand, with his back

against the dune, eying me curiously: my watcher, my jailer, my enemy, my would-be assassin — Burton. How long he had been there, I could not guess; perhaps almost from the moment I was securely caught.

"Are you enjoying yourself?" he inquired, after some moments, during which I had been gazing at him in astonishment.

"Enjoying myself! Man, don't you see what danger I am in? Help me out of this, and I shall be eternally grateful to you."

"— because I am!" he went on, as though I had not spoken.

"You are — what?" I asked.

"Enjoying myself," he returned.

"How?"

"Watching you struggle," he answered. "It is many years since I have seen anything that gave me so much pleasure."

"I am glad that I have been able to afford you some entertainment," I said ironically. "But don't you think the thing has gone far enough, now? If I sink much deeper, I fear I shall be past helping."

"I am entirely of your opinion," he remarked coolly. "I think another foot will make it inevitable."

He seemed to measure the distance from the surface of the sand to the top of my head.

"Well, it won't take long to sink that much, if it keeps up as at present," I said. "So hurry up, and get some planks, or a rope — unless you know some way of getting me out without them."

"Getting you out!" he shouted, in apparent astonishment. "Getting you *out?*"

"Yes, of course; you don't suppose I want to stay in this horrible place, do you?"

"Getting you out?" he repeated. "Who said anything about getting you out?"

"Confound you!" I cried. "Don't you see how fast I am sinking? Throw me something that will bear my weight!"

He put his hand in his pocket, and drew out a pipe and some leaves of tobacco.

"Yes, I see how fast you are sinking," he said, beginning to crumble the tobacco between his hands. "You are going down at about the rate of an inch a minute, I should judge. That will allow us about half an hour of conversation before you disappear for good and all."

He produced a tinder-box, and proceeded to procure a light for his pipe.

"This may be your idea of a joke," I cried angrily; "but it is a very poor one, and it has gone far enough.   Get some means of lifting me out of this!"

"Now, what sort of an idiot are you, I wonder?" he remarked, after a few meditative puffs. "Is it possible that you really expect me to assist you — you! — out of the trap into which you have so obligingly walked?"

"Of course I do!" I shouted; "and quickly, too!"

"How prone to error are the young and impulsive!" he mused aloud. "Now I knew that you were a very foolish young man, or you would never have come to seek us on this island, knowing how much reason we had for suppressing any one who attempted to pry into our affairs and what happened thirty years ago.   Why could you not let sleeping dogs lie, after they had slept so long? . . .   And I knew that you were impulsive, else you would not have walked into the middle of a quicksand, when it lay right before you so plainly that you could not have helped seeing it; in fact, I saw you stop and inspect it carefully before you measured its strength against yours. I hope your curiosity is satisfied now?   If not, it will be before long."   He laughed.   "But to really expect that *I* should help *you* out of it! Alas! alas!   My opinion of your common sense has lowered considerably during the last ten minutes, Mr. Darke."

He seemed truly sorry for me, as he said. It angered me intensely, being in no mood for jesting.

"I don't care a stiver what your opinion of me may be!" I shouted furiously. "But you had better help me quickly — unless you want to murder me."

"Murder you? Oh, no; I assure you I would not lay a hand on you now for any consideration," he laughed. "If you had not chosen this very convenient way of disposing of yourself, very probably I should have murdered you sooner or later. The flesh is weak, and the temptation has been very great. But as it is, I am more than satisfied to have you take the matter out of my hands, and to interfere with your very complete arrangements is the last thing I would think of. Besides, it saves me a great deal of trouble."

"Do you mean to say that you are *not* going to help me?" I exclaimed at last incredulously.

He nodded gravely. "Your perception of the realities of life is vastly quickened by your situation," he observed, waving his pipe oratorically. "But it has taken so much time and trouble to infuse that one fact into your consciousness that I am sincerely thankful I shall never be obliged to force another one on you. You are nearly done with facts now; in less than half an hour more you will cease to be a fact yourself, and will be merely a memory. A memory that all of us will be heartily glad to be rid of," he snarled, with a sudden break in his sneering temper.

"Do you really mean what you say?" I demanded again, unable to believe at first.

"Are you to disappoint me even at the last, most unreasonable creature?" he said, recovering his temper quickly. "I thought you had taken the statement to heart! Know, then, that I mean every word I have said! I have not the slightest intention of assisting you; on the contrary, I would willingly push you deeper, if there was any possibility of your escape, though I am not at all anxious to hasten your exit now. The longer the time you spend at it, the more entertainment you will afford me." I looked down; the sand was about my hips. "Yes, it is creeping up," he proceeded, as he noticed my glance. "Half an hour more, at the most. We will keep this last vigil together; all the rest of my life it will be a pleasure to me to think of it."

He meant all of it; I was forced to believe him. My head drooped, and I gave way to despair — all the greater for my late hope — so sudden, so crushing, that it took away all power of thought: I could not even pray. Yet all the while the voice of my enemy came to my ears, and held my attention, to the exclusion of every other thing. As in a dreadful dream I heard him pursuing his fiendish monologue.

"I have hated you from the first time I saw you. No doubt you knew that. Even your unusual stupidity could not avoid recognizing the fact. I would have hated you before you were born, if I had been aware of such a possibility. Perhaps you do not know what it is to hate any one as I do you? I assure you it is a most enjoyable sensation, especially at a time when one holds the object of it in one's power, or sees him hurried forward, without a chance of resistance, toward a fearful death. It adds spice to one's life, and makes it worth while to live, in spite of life's many troubles. I have longed for your death unceasingly, and I have wasted many valuable hours in planning to bring it about. Once I nearly accomplished it, as you know. I cannot account for my failure that time, nor for your escape afterward; I must have been

abominably clumsy to have allowed it. *This* time
I shall not leave you until I see that the end has
come. However, all's well that ends well, and
your end will be —"

His voice ceased abruptly; I waited in a sort
of lethargy for him to continue. Several minutes
passed in silence, and finally I raised my head to
look toward him. To my intense surprise he was
gone, vanished, disappeared utterly, as though the
quicksand had seized him, too. Yet he had distinctly announced his intention of watching my
body disappear in the clinging sand that clasped
me so lovingly and grasped me so hungrily.

For a moment I was dumfounded at his sudden
disappearance; then remembering his intention of
staying to gloat over my dying struggles, I looked
about to discover the cause of his flight. And
there, just turning the point of the cape, half a
mile above me, I saw a light canoe that I recognized as one in which I had often seen My Lady
paddling about the quiet waters of the sound. I
knew the occupant could be none other than My
Lady herself. I had never before seen her venture out into the open water, but to-day the off-
shore wind had made the ocean almost as still as
the waters of the sound.

My heart stood still while I waited. She was

heading straight out to sea, but I knew she would not venture far in that direction. If she should turn northward, toward the distant mainland, I was surely doomed; if southward, along the coast, as seemed most likely, there was a chance for me, if she could summon help in time. A minute — two minutes — (it was agony to wait thus), then, at length, she turned — southward.

I snatched my cap from my head and waved it wildly, and shouted with all my might; but she neither saw nor heard, though she continued to approach. The wind carried my voice away from her. Halfway — three-quarters — she was hardly more than two hundred yards away now, and nearly opposite the spot where I was fast bound. If she should pass, good-by to the world!

I tore off my coat, and waved that, and shouted wildly. Every motion sank me a little deeper into the horrible sand; but it was as well to risk all. If she passed by, the sooner I was sucked down the better.

"Help!" I shouted. "Help!"

The wind was in my favor now, and she heard. I saw her lift her head and gaze about her. Again I shouted and waved the coat.

She hesitated, and no wonder. She was alone and unprotected; doubtless she feared some trick on the part of a desperate man. But at last she turned the canoe, and approached the shore slowly, frequently letting the boat drift while she regarded me inquiringly. I was sunk nearly to the waist by this time, and must have appeared to be sitting on the sand.

"Help! I am caught in the quicksand!" I called, when she was near enough to catch my voice distinctly.

Ah! She understood now; she had forgotten the very existence of the treacherous spot.

In a moment I saw her paddle dip deep in the water; the canoe fairly leaped forward; it skimmed over the slow swell like the flight of a great gull. She must have known the exact location of the quicksand, for she drove her canoe close to the edge of it. There was but a little surf, and in a moment she was through this, and had leaped out.

"Keep still! Do not struggle!" she cried — a very easy direction to give, but one very hard to obey in such a situation.

I saw her bend over the bow, and work with something, while I waited impatiently. She turned, and I saw she had stopped to untie the long light anchor-line from the boat, and was carrying it and the anchor.

"Call for help, My Lady," I said; "you cannot pull me out alone."

She paid no attention to my words. Rapidly looking about for a good vantage ground, or some assistance in the task, she spied a stout beam sticking out of the sand a dozen paces nearer the dune than where she stood. It had once served as the rib of a good ship that had gone ashore by this bar. My Lady hastily made fast the anchor end of the line to this useful mooring, and proceeded to tie the loose end to a bit of iron she fetched from the canoe. Next she coiled the rope loosely about her elbow. Then her right hand swung back with a grand motion, swung forward, and the iron weight dropped in the sand within easy reach of me, and began to sink immediately. The thing must have weighed ten pounds, yet she tossed it almost as lightly as a pebble, so strong was she by nature's gift, so greatly was that strength increased by excitement. I clutched the line instantly and felt almost safe.

"Fasten the rope around you, beneath your arms," she commanded. "Then throw the weight over to catch and hold it securely."

I obeyed without questioning, though I protested.

"You can never pull me out alone; call for help, I beg!"

"There is no help near," she replied hurriedly; still, she blew her little ivory whistle. I knew that Burton was close by; he would surely answer her call, I thought, and when he came he was bound to assist My Lady, however much against his will.

She drew the end of the line about the beam, until the rope was stretched taut.

"Do not try it alone, My Lady," I begged. "You can never do it, and you will surely hurt yourself. Call for help!"

"What will be, will be," she replied, very quietly. "If I cannot do it, it will never be done." She blew one more blast, and grasped the rope with both hands. "There is no help near, and no time to go for it; even now it may be too late. Lean well forward; fall on your face, if you can. Move gently, and try to keep the sand stirring about you, but do not try to raise yourself just yet. I will stir you first."

She dug her heels deep into the sand of the beach, and pulled, not suddenly, but with a steady pressure of marvellous power for a woman. As she pulled, she threw herself about the beam (which held like a rock), thus taking in the slack of the rope. I leaned forward, as she bade me; indeed, with the strain brought to bear on me,

I could do no less. I wriggled and squirmed like a gigantic worm; I could feel the sand moving about me, but I could feel no lift out of the slough. My face was down close to the sand, and I could see nothing else. When no more could be gained in this way, she rested, securing the rope firmly.

Suddenly My Lady's voice rang out, —

"Take hold of the rope and *pull!*"

I pulled with all my might. Would the clinging stuff never give way? I felt the quicksand flowing about me while I pulled, with closed eyes, my whole mind and strength devoted to the one purpose, my muscles stretched almost to the breaking point. And then, suddenly, without a moment's warning, the world seemed to sink beneath me, and I found myself lying panting, exhausted, on the surface of the quicksand.

"Do not move!" gasped a breathless voice, and then I felt myself dragged slowly across the few yards of soft, quivering surface. But this task was clearly beyond even My Lady's great strength. So, whipping the line about the post until it was again taut, and commanding me to lie quietly stretched out as I was, she ran swiftly to the canoe, and taking thence a large blanket which she had used as a cushion, she ventured into the edge of the quicksands. There was now left between us but a few feet of space, so that the blanket flung out on the damp sand reached nearly to my head. One mighty pull on the line sufficed to place me on the covering, and from that point I crawled swiftly to the hard sand.

For some moments I lay there motionless, waiting for life to flow back to my cramped and strained muscles. The reaction of the nervous strain·increased my weakness, and at first I was absolutely unable to move. Finally I raised my head, and the first thing my eyes encountered was My Lady sitting on the sand, leaning on one hand, while the other was pressed over her heart. The sight helped my recovery marvellously, and I managed to drag myself to her.

"Are you hurt, My Lady?" I asked, with more real anxiety than, two months ago, I would have believed it possible for me to feel for one of her race.

She shook her head, and waved me away impatiently. She seemed to need only time to get her breath. I staggered to the water, and bringing back a capful, set it before her. She dipped her hand into it and cooled her face. There was no drinking water within a mile of us, I knew well. I sank down near her until I saw she was nearly recovered; then it seemed time to speak, though it was difficult to find words meet for the occasion.

"You have saved my life, My Lady," I said, "and I owe you more gratitude than I can either express or repay in a lifetime. I would not have believed any single man, to say nothing of a woman, could have rescued me."

"It is nothing," she said coldly. "I am strong, and you did much when once I had the line firmly about that piece of driftwood. I would have done as much for a stranger, or for one of the slaves."

"Rather, I have no doubt," I returned, somewhat nettled by her ungracious manner, which seemed to me uncalled for just then. "Still, you have my sincere gratitude, and I hope to be able to prove it some day."

"Since you have thrust yourself — and unknown troubles with you — in among us, sir," she replied, turning away, "you can do nothing."

"Thrust myself!" I returned, with heat. "You must know how unjust you are. I have no greater desire than to escape from this place! I came to it involuntarily; I am detained here much against my will; I shall leave it at the first opportunity."

Her face hardened. "You almost make me

regret a mere act of humanity," she said. "I have no wish for further conversation, sir," and she turned as if to go. Once more I had run against the stone wall of reticence that these people had built around them, and, as usual, I had bruised myself to no purpose. They would not even listen to my thanks, I thought despairingly. Heaven knew that hitherto I had had little enough to thank them for!

"You shall not be annoyed further by either my presence or my gratitude, madam," I said, bowing with great ceremony. "I will limit my gratitude to the confines of my thoughts, since I am not to be allowed to express it. However, if you will allow me so much, I will replace your anchor before I go."

"No, no!" she cried eagerly, clutching the rope. "I will do it for myself."

I could not well take it from her by force (though her obstinacy made me feel much like attempting it), so I bowed again, and turned to go. But before going, I cast my eyes seaward, and what I saw caused me to turn and speak to her again, despite her prohibition.

"At least, My Lady, you must allow me the pleasure of recovering your canoe."

She looked, and sprang to her feet with a cry.

Evidently, when she had seized the blanket, she had pushed the canoe slightly enough to set it afloat; the off-shore breeze had caught it, and now it was joyously drifting seaward. Already it was a hundred yards away; if it was to be recovered at all, it must be immediately. I started toward the shore, but she cried out loudly, —

"No, no; I would rather let it go!"

I stopped for just an instant. "What!" I exclaimed savagely. "You would refuse me even that service in return for my life? You are unreasonable, My Lady! I decline to obey you thus far," and I strode down into the water and struck out for the canoe. My Lady cried to me again to come back, but I paid no heed to her call. It was a simple matter to reach the canoe and climb in over the stern. I picked up the paddle, and I turned the little craft shoreward; then I glanced at My Lady, and nearly lost the paddle in my surprise. She knelt on the shore, with her back toward me, and I could see that her hands covered her face. I drove the canoe rapidly toward her, fearing she might be ill. If her late violent exertions had injured her, I felt that I should never forgive myself for being the cause of it.

With a single rapid motion I dragged the canoe

up the beach to where it would be safe. At the scraping sound of it, My Lady looked around, and scrambled to her feet with evident surprise and alarm on her features. I could see traces of tears, also, though at the moment I could not account for them.

"You!" she exclaimed.

"Who else?" I returned. "Did you expect any one else?"

The question staggered her for a moment.

"No; nor you!" she retorted, before she had collected her thoughts. The next moment she bit her lip and turned very red, as though she had said either more than she had intended or something different from what she would have wished.

At first I did not grasp her meaning. I shrugged my shoulders, and turned toward the sea.

"May I be allowed the honor of pushing your canoe clear of the beach?" I asked sarcastically.

She gave me a strange look, but stepped toward the beach without another word, and took her place in the canoe. I waded into the light surf, and pushed it out to where her paddle would have a clean sweep. I was about to give the boat a shove into deep water, when she stayed me with a gesture.

"One moment, sir! I should like to ask why —when you were free and in this canoe, without a chance of being followed successfully—why you did not make your escape in it?"

It was my turn now to be staggered, as the chance that had befallen me presented itself to view for the first time. What a fool I had been! The opportunity I had let slip from my very grasp took my breath away.

"I did not think of it," I answered, with perfect truth. "I only thought of returning your property. Seeing a lady in distress—one, too, who had just saved me from a horrible death—I thought only of your possible loss. No doubt I was a fool. I see it now; it is not the first time! Perhaps I may remember on another occasion, if such a chance should occur again, though I suppose your people will take good care to prevent a repetition of it."

With another salute I turned away, but again she stayed me.

"Mr. Darke, I know it is impossible, yet I wish we could be—friends." Her face took on a softer expression, almost a kindly one, as she spoke. "It is only for my father's sake that you are detained here, and I assure you we both regret the necessity."

"My Lady, if you come to the cause of my detention (of which, I assure you again, I am utterly ignorant), I have nothing to say, except to reassert my entire innocence of hostile intentions. But I do not expect you to believe that."

"No," she responded, as she pushed the canoe further out, while the friendly look faded from her face. "I do not — I *must* not — though I should like to! But still I do not understand why you did not escape when you had the chance," and she shook her head in a puzzled way, as her long strokes carried her swiftly seaward.

And, when I came to think the matter over, neither did I. Everything had been prepared to my hand; long before she could have crossed the island to where the other boats were stored, and have given the alarm, I could have been hopelessly beyond recapture on my way to the mainland. I had been planning for this very thing for months; that very matter had brought me to this spot. Why did I not fly? I did not know; I do not know, unless it was because the influence of her personality so overpowered me that I forgot all else in the desire to serve her.

As I walked slowly and dejectedly back to my bare cabin, I wondered what all this meant, and I resolutely cast aside the only answer that suggested itself. So deeply did I ponder that, until after I reached the cabin, I forgot all about Burton's presence on the scene. And then I wondered how much he had seen and heard, and what he thought of it all? I wondered whether he was as puzzled as I was myself?

COALS OF FIRE

It was not until a week later that I saw My Lady again. I was on my customary stroll to the beach, where I went every day in the vain hope of catching sight of a sail that I might call to my assistance in some way. My Lady had evidently returned from riding very lately, for she carried her whip in one hand, while the other supported the sweeping folds of her skirt. Her face was protected from the sun by a vizard of green velvet, which covered nearly all her features. I should not have looked for such a thing on this island, seemingly so remote from contact with the greater world; but the mere sight of it proved that in some way these people had learned the fashions of the day, and for some reason lived up to them. And yet I had never yet seen so much as a strange sail in the distance, while My Lady, as I felt sure, had not left the island for a single day since I had been there. Nor had the sloop: the condition of the ropes that moored her to the wharf on the western shore, proved that she had not been moved for months. This knowledge only added to the mystery of the place, without bringing me any nearer a solution of it.

Where we met, the path was narrow, running along the top of a long dune. Naturally, I stepped aside to let her pass, pressing close against a clump of myrtle bushes, that she might have plenty of room. There was not a chance of contact, even had she proceeded straight along the path; but she chose to show her contempt for me by stepping out of the path and walking along the edge of the dune — a dangerous proceeding, for on the seaward side it had been eaten away by the spring storms, and was liable to go down with a crash at any moment. However, I offered no protest, knowing how useless it would be; but as she approached closer, I raised my battered cap and stood with it raised until she should be past.

I could have smiled at this childish mode of displaying her feelings, had it not been for the really serious danger she was incurring. I should not have cared to see even my worst enemy walking where, at any moment, the ground might crumble beneath him, and drop him more than thirty feet under a covering of countless tons of sand. And

the death of even one of the slaves, in such a
way, when I was present, would inevitably seal
my fate.   Nothing could persuade the mad inhabitants of this strange island that I was not
responsible for the disaster.

While I was thinking of this, she was approaching, not rapidly, but as though she were casually
strolling along with never a soul in sight. She
held her head high, and her eyes never even
glanced in my direction, though she knew well
that mine were on her; and despite her nearness
to the edge of the dune, she kept her eyes raised
high.   It was this very steadfastness of gaze that
led almost to disaster; for with her eyes so raised
she could not well heed her footing, and failed to
notice a tangled clump of grass that lay directly
in her way.   It caught her foot.   She stumbled,
swayed, and for a moment it seemed to me
that she must pitch headlong over the edge of
the dune.   Instinctively I bounded forward, and
seized her firmly around the waist, and at that
moment I felt the sandy cliff, probably loosened
by the additional weight and shock, giving way
beneath my feet.   For one horrible moment I
thought we were both doomed; the next, with a
supreme effort, I had half jumped, half thrown
myself backward, carrying her with me, while the

whole edge of the bank on which we had stood thundered down to the beach below. I can claim no credit for the act; it was so entirely instinctive and unconscious that when I found myself lying flat across the path, with My Lady by my side, for a moment I wondered where I was, and how I had come there.

I had fallen with considerable force, and the fright and the shock together made me tremble violently as I rose quickly and took My Lady's hand to assist her to rise. If my fingers had been of red-hot iron, she could not have recoiled more suddenly or more violently. With a movement expressing exaggerated aversion, she drew away and sprang to her feet. So suddenly had the whole episode occurred that as she rose she still grasped her whip and skirt, though the mask had fallen from her face to the ground.

"What!" she exclaimed furiously. "You would touch me!"

She drew back her arm with a grand gesture that I could not help admiring, even at such a moment. In another instant the lash would have struck me, but her thoughts were even swifter than her motions. Even as her arm swung forward she checked it, and raised the whistle that hung at her belt.

She said, with vast contempt, after blowing a prolonged blast, "It would be too much honor."

I stood gazing at her passionate face in utmost astonishment. It was true that I had touched her, and with considerable force, too, but only to save her life; and my taking her hand afterward was merely such a measure of common civility as the meanest slave would have offered and she would not have refused. She appeared perfectly sane, and I believed she was so, yet she was swayed by as mad a humor as the other mad inhabitants of this strange island. I had small time for thought, however, for a great negro bounded panting up the dune from the landward side and paused beside her. She extended the whip to him, while with the other hand she pointed at me.

"Theodore, lash that creature's face!"

She spoke in a perfectly calm and even voice, with not a trace of emotion, as though the command were the most ordinary one imaginable. The negro looked at me, I looked back at him; and if my face reflected my feelings, I do not wonder that he recoiled and hesitated.

"But, My Lady, I doan' —"

If she had any scruples about touching me, she had none in his case. She swung the whip with a vicious swish, and a whitish line sprang across the negro's black cheek. He leaped back with a cry of pain.

"Will you argue with me?" she demanded fiercely.

He bowed his head, and extended his hand to take the weapon; she gave it to him, and he approached me slowly. Evidently he had small taste for the deed. For a moment I hesitated. I could not strike her, of course, and the negro was so plainly acting unwillingly and under dire compulsion that it seemed hard to punish him for obeying her command. At the same time, I could not submit tamely to be whipped by any one, least of all by a slave. I had to decide quickly; his arm was already raised when I sprang at him, and with a blow on the chest (for I did not want to hurt him for her fault) toppled him over, so that he rolled down the side of the dune, which sloped gently landward.

My Lady stamped her foot with rage, and blew her whistle again. Half a dozen other negroes, summoned by the first blast, were already on the way; now they redoubled their speed, and climbed the dune pell-mell. Theodore, I noticed, stayed at the bottom.

"Seize that man!" she commanded, as several of them drew near us together.

I had done all that was possible; I knew I could not struggle against such numbers; as there was nothing to be gained by fighting, I submitted quietly. Grasping me on both sides, they drew my arms behind me while one of them produced a piece of cord.

"Stop! You need not tie him; only hold him firmly." She glanced down the slope. "Theodore, come here!"

Helpless though I was, the slave had small mind to come, but he knew there was no escape. I could see the place where she had struck him, still gray, and raised in a high welt. My Lady held out the whip, which she had picked up when he dropped it in falling. "Do what I told you!" she commanded.

From the moment of my striking the negro, she had not looked me in the face, but as she handed the whip to her executioner she turned her head, and our eyes met. After that I was too proud to glance at the negro, whom I could *feel* approaching me. She gazed at me as if spellbound. We stood there like two figures of stone for what seemed to me an interminable time.

Suddenly a line of red-hot iron seemed drawn across my cheek. The pain of it was so sharp and sudden that I gave a convulsive start which almost tore me loose from my captors' grasp. I felt the blood rush to my face, and my cheek puffed up so that the tightly drawn skin was ready to break. Involuntary tears sprang to my eyes; fortunately not enough to betray me except to the woman whose order had caused them. Though I could not help them, and though they were no sign of weakness or fear, I could have killed myself for anger that she had seen them.

While we were still staring thus at one another, I seemed to feel Theodore raise his arm again, and knew that if he struck again in the same place, the blow would draw blood. My Lady must have felt the movement, too, for she sprang forward and grasped his arm.

"Go!" she said. Theodore dropped the whip instantly, and began to move away. "Go!" she said to the others. They moved also, my captors taking me with them, still firmly held.

"Stop!" commanded My Lady. "Release that man! I told *you* to go, not him!" But she did not look at me as she spoke.

The glaring sunshine poured down on us as we stood there alone, neither quite knowing what to do or say. My eyes were fastened on her face, and, in spite of her treatment of me, the majesty and the sweetness of her fascinated me afresh.

I ought to have hated her, and could not; or rather, my head hated her, while my heart — well, it came perilously near to loving her.

At length, when the silence and suspense were becoming unbearable, her hand made a faint gesture of dismissal. For a moment I waited, but her eyes were glued to the ground, and she would not raise them; so, with a profound bow, which I knew she could not help seeing, I turned and walked quickly away toward the end of the dune. When I reached it, my inclination to look back was strong, but I managed to repress it. I walked down to the surf, and bathed my scarred check with cool salt water. It eased the smart greatly, but there was a deeper sting that I thought the whole ocean could not ease. And the worst of the matter was, that I could not decide just what the smart was. Not a feeling of disgrace, certainly; if she had been a man, or if the slaves had been freemen, it might have been different, though I cannot see why a man need feel disgraced by a punishment that he knows is arbitrary and unjust. I was thoroughly enraged, but rage never hurt in that way; and besides, my anger was directed more at the caprices of a fate that put me in such a position, and that would not supply a key to the secret of these incomprehensible people.

Perhaps if I could have understood them, had been able to put myself in their place, I could have sympathized with them. I ought rightly to have felt hatred toward the woman who had used me so, but I knew that I did not. Unless her face and her voice belied her mightily, I was sure she must regret that ill-considered blow even more than I did. Whatever might be the reason these people had for hating me so, she had put herself in the wrong by her action, and I knew she must feel it. She was a lady; in the outer world, one must have called her a great lady, with all a great lady's sensitiveness to rude actions. When I had thought out all this, I ended by being angry at myself because I could not tell the cause or the object of my anger.

For an hour or more I paced the beach, watching the sea from force of habit, though if the water had been covered with sails I believe I should not have noticed them. When I finally realized where I was, I found myself standing by the place where the edge of the dune had fallen beneath us, contemplating the great pile of damp sand, and wondering whether, if I had jumped a second later than I did, any one would have thought of looking for us beneath it. Such falls of sand were common enough; there was nothing peculiar about the aspect of this one. Already the fierce sun had dried the surface of the heap, and except for a slight dampness at the upper edge of the bank there was nothing to show that it had not been in that condition for days or weeks. The thought of being buried alive in that crumbling, clinging mass was not pleasant. I am no more afraid of death than most men ; but when the end does come, there are certain ways that most of us would gladly avoid.

As I turned away a sudden thought came to me, and I walked rapidly to the lower end of the dune, and ascended it as My Lady had done, and followed her steps. It was a silly piece of sentimentality, no doubt, and I did not pretend to account for it or to excuse it ; but if that whip lay where Theodore had dropped it, I intended to get it and keep it. After my escape (which I had no doubt of making eventually) it would serve to remind me of a unique experience. I was neither proud nor glad of the experience, yet I knew I should never want to forget it : who can account for the contradictions of his thoughts ? I was sure My Lady would not care to use the whip again : it would burn her hand if she touched it. The thing would probably be lying near the clump of myrtles, and there I found it and thrust it into my waistcoat — a little thing, no longer than my arm, but to me full of memories, both bitter and sweet.

With a last look at the sea I passed the myrtles to descend the easy landward slope of the dune, and with a low cry of amazement I started back, for there, behind the myrtles, lay My Lady, face downward, with her head resting upon her folded arms. For a moment only I hesitated, and then stepped to her side. The roar of the surf had covered the slight noise of my steps on the soft sand, and when I knelt beside her and addressed her by the only name I knew for her, it must have given her a great shock.

"My Lady," I said, in alarm, "are you ill?"

With a violent effort she rose to her feet, and looked at me wildly for an instant; the next moment she sank to her knees, and her hands covered her burning face.

"Go!" she said, in a smothered whisper. But I could not leave her so, for in that one glance I had seen that her face was stained with tears, and after all that had gone before there could be only one cause for it. It came upon me suddenly that I was no longer angry with her; I only pitied her, for she was in worse case than I — she was ashamed.

" My Lady," I said, in a very uneven voice, " I am not certain of the cause of your distress, but if it is what I think it, I beg you to believe that I am sure you acted in a moment of irresponsible anger. The cause of that anger is unknown to me; but I assure you that if any act of mine offended you, it was done in ignorance and without such intent. And I beg you to believe, also, that I bear no ill will toward any one for what occurred later; and I pray you to try to forget it, as I shall."

I waited to see whether she would reply, but no answer came, nor even a movement of the bowed figure. So, having done what I could, I marched away toward my cabin, wondering whether I had any right to the glow of self-satisfaction that I felt. I had been heaping coals of fire on mine enemy's head; but I was not quite sure that my elation did not arise from the fact that the coals must *hurt her*.

I reasoned upon this all of the day, without reaching a satisfactory conclusion. But I did not forget to place carefully the little green whip with the silver handle in a hollow between two of the logs in my cabin, and conceal it by a layer of moss. When the time came its removal would not cause me the delay of a moment, and I knew that I should not forget to take it with me. Looking at it from this length of time, the act seems inconsistent with my promise to My Lady to forget the whole occurrence; but somehow it did not strike me so then.

VII

TANTALUS

An interminable time elapsed before I met her again. I dreaded yet longed for the meeting, being consumed with a great desire to know how she would act. It seemed as though she dreaded it also, for while formerly I had been accustomed to meet her frequently, now she either kept herself within doors, or else ventured out only when she knew I was safely bestowed at some far point of the island. She must have known that she could not avoid me thus for long; but it is easy to understand how disconcerting the first encounter would be for her, and it was not strange that she endeavored to put off the time as long as possible.

Burton had heard of what had occurred on the dune, and his eyes twinkled maliciously whenever he met me, fixing themselves on the purple mark that clung to my cheek for some days. What he did not know was my second meeting with My

Lady that morning, and the surety of her repentance that I bore with me for my consolation. Hence his malice hurt me little.

The purple mark had a fascination for the slaves, too; whenever they met me their eyes would involuntarily seek my cheek, and linger there. That it was not my own sensitiveness was proved by the evident efforts they made to prevent my noticing their gaze; their eyes would wander and shift and sometimes close, yet always returned to the mark, for they tried to avoid hurting my feelings, having only good will toward me. It was seldom that a blow was necessary among the Master's servants, and probably they had never before seen a white man struck in anger. Perhaps the fact that I was white made the strangeness of the thing to them; Theodore bore a mark also, but they hardly noticed it. Those who had held my hands, and Theodore more than all, avoided me carefully, slinking away when I came in sight, as though fearing that I would seek to revenge myself on them, until one day I stopped Theodore and told him that I did not feel any ill will toward any of them, since they were obliged to obey when My Lady ordered — he, most of all. After that there was no more of the avoidance, and as the scar soon began to fade, the whole matter speedily fell into abeyance and was forgotten by all.

Not so with My Lady, however. There had been no command or compulsion exercised on her, and she was the more ashamed therefor. The longer she brooded over it, the harder the first meeting would be for her; hence the most sensible thing would be to plunge *in medias res*, and have done with it. There were only two courses open to her, as it seemed to me. One was to apologize, either openly or by implication, for her treatment of me; the other, to go on as before, thereby letting me understand that she had no more reason to notice my existence than before. Knowing her pride, I thought the latter must be her course; knowing her truth, and the real tenderness of her heart, it seemed impossible that she could take any but the first. I rejoiced exceedingly that it was not I that had to make the decision. For once, at least, since coming to the island I was master of the situation. I had only to wait. Whatever course she might take could only put me more completely in the right.

But I was sorry for My Lady, both on account of what she had done and on account of what she had to do. No matter which course she followed, it would hurt her sorely.

As usual, it was the unexpected that came to pass; in threading a narrow footpath through the great south woods we were close together before either of us discovered the other's presence. It might be a question which was the more startled or the more discomposed when we found ourselves almost face to face in the dim shade of the forest. But perhaps the very suddenness of it was the best thing that could have happened for both of us, allowing no chance for previous thought or for the nervousness that comes from long anticipation, and so often is infinitely more hard to endure than the reality. As usual, I stepped aside until My Lady should pass, and made her the ceremonious bow that I had never omitted on meeting her, and that she had never returned but once.

Apart from the few times I had met her with her father, we had exchanged words but twice: once when I had returned her canoe, and once when I had saved her from the fall at the edge of the dune. The first time she had seemed almost friendly; the second—well, I have told about that. If there was anything of friendliness about that interview, I had failed to discover it.

Hence, when I stood aside this time, I had little reason for expecting anything but the same ostentatious obliviousness of my existence that I had become accustomed to. It had never ceased to hurt me; but I looked for nothing else, and I was determined not to let her or the Master or Burton know how deeply it wounded me. So I held up my head bravely and waited for the inevitable.

It came, yet with a difference. My Lady passed me without a salutation, it is true. But in place of the open, straightforward gaze, with no acknowledgment that a human being was near, such as I had looked for, My Lady passed me with downcast eyes, and with a flush upon her cheek that testified loudly to her knowledge of my presence. Her tongue did not speak to me, but her face did. I gazed and gazed, as though I could never be satisfied, and, without so much as a glance upward, she felt it.

She passed me, and I turned to pursue my way; regained the narrow track and was striding along it, when a voice arrested me. That voice had been obeyed implicitly for twenty years by every soul on the island; and I, though not one of the servants, was yet held by it. Not because of the command, for there was none, but because of the request implied in the tone, and — because for months it had been shaping itself into the sweetest sound I knew. Yet its unexpectedness gave me a start.

"Mr. Darke!" There was no command in the tone, no scorn this time; instead, it was timid, beseeching. I stopped as though held by a strong arm, hardly able to believe my ears.

"Mr. Darke!" She had not turned, though her ears must have told her that I had.

"Did you speak to me, My Lady?" I could not help an accent of incredulity.

"Yes."

I waited. I would not approach her unless requested; I had had my lesson — a bitter one. The silence grew tense. She would not turn, she would not speak. The light through the trees was dim, and her wide hat shaded her face so that but little of it could be seen. I waited.

Of a sudden she turned, as though compelled. We were not ten yards apart, but she would not look up.

"Mr. Darke, I wish to apologize —"

The remembrance of her self-abasement on the dune hurt me almost as much as it did her. I knew what was coming, and tried to avoid it.

"My Lady, I beg —"

She interrupted me in her turn with a gesture.

"I wish to apologize —"

"If that is all, My Lady, I do not wish to stay."   I turned away, and again she stopped me.

"Mr. Darke!"   Why should she have the power to hold me by a word?   When I looked again her face was raised — flushed and ashamed, but visible.

"Pray hear me, sir," she begged, as though I were lord of the island and she its prisoner.   "It is most necessary.   I must beg your pardon for my conduct — "

I could not listen further.   I knew how hard it must be for her to say it, but it seemed far harder for me to hear it.   The certainty that she wished to make amends was more than enough for me: as effectual as the most abject spoken apology could have been.   From her, the wish meant more than the deed would have meant from so many others.   I wished to spare her as much as possible.

"Only one moment, My Lady," I said.   "After that, if I must — I am sure I know what you were about to say.   You have already said more than enough; pray consider the rest said, also, and the matter concluded.   There are some things that are better forgotten — "

"Ah, I feared you would take it so!" she cried.

"You mistake me, indeed," I said earnestly. "I did not mean it in that way.   I say some things are best forgotten. I hope this one may be so, as much on your account as on my own. I know the thing was unpremeditated, and I regret having been the cause of it. The greatest favor I could ask of you would be that you should put it out of your mind once and forever, as I wish to do myself. You are guiltless and faultless in my eyes."

"Ah, but in my own," she cried, covering her face, "I am abased!"

It seemed impossible to help her in that, at the moment. Then a thought came to me.

"If your own eyes show yourself so unfairly, My Lady, look in mine, and take a message from them."

I was standing close by her now. My appeal had effect, and she did look; at first with doubt, then with returning confidence.

"Do you find resentment there?" I said, very low. Still she looked.

"I find — I find —" She hesitated.

"Nothing that you would not wish to find, I hope?"

"No; but much that I did not expect! Oh, are you deceiving me?" she broke out.

"Not in that, nor in anything else, My Lady," I replied. "I have not tried to deceive you in any way. But now, may I venture an appeal to you in my turn?"

She looked troubled. "If it concerns your freedom —"

"It does not," I interrupted. "I know how little responsibility for that attaches to you. My request is merely that you will listen to my story, the story that I would have told at my first coming if I had not been condemned unheard. I do not ask you to repeat it to your father; I do not ask you even to believe it; only to listen to it. It will not take long, and you can judge of its truth for yourself."

"But why, then, should you wish *me* to hear it? I can do nothing to help your release."

"It has nothing to do with my release. I have abandoned all hope of securing that unless by my own unaided efforts — and they *shall* secure it!" I said, with great determination. "I wish you to hear it only because — oh, because I want to know that you have at least heard my side of the case."

"But why?" she persisted.

"For a woman's reason, perhaps," I replied lightly. "Say there is no reason at all; imagine, if you like, that I ask it as a favor for a mere whim. I have asked few favors, and have received fewer, since I came here." I was taking advantage of her softened mood. Perhaps the thought of the pardon she had just been asking of me moved her.

"I will hear you, sir," she said. "But I cannot promise —"

"To believe me? I do not ask you to, unless you must after you have heard me."

She stood very straight before me, and clasped her hands in front of her, and all the while I was speaking she never shifted her gaze from my face. She seemed to be trying to look into my most secret thoughts, and I cannot imagine how a man could stand before that searching look, and lie, without faltering and contradicting himself.

I told a plain, unvarnished tale : of the summons to join my company, of the storm, and my escape from drowning, and of my meeting with Burton ; assuring her again of my ignorance of the location of the island or the name of its owner.

"And I do not scruple to acknowledge to you that I have tried to entrap the negroes into betraying something about both," I said, "but with little success. You can understand how irksome must be this confinement without reason that I can discover. My company has gone to the war without me ; I have missed a chance of promotion and glory —"

"Or death," she interrupted, speaking for the first time since I began my tale.

"Or death," I repeated. "But that is the chance of war, and to be reckoned with beforehand. And I could hardly have come nearer death than I have done several times since I came here. One escape I owe to you. Whether the sloop that brought me was wrecked or arrived safely, I must have been reported as lost. My uncle and aunt will be in mourning for me, and poor little Dolly will cry her eyes out for grief."

Poor Dolly! How seldom I had thought of her during the last few months! She deserved a better remembrance.

"Who is Dolly?" queried My Lady, showing curiosity for the first time.

"My cousin," I replied. "A sweet little girl, and one of the prettiest I ever knew. We had grown to be such good friends."

"You love her?" queried My Lady, looking downward. "That must be the hardest part of your trouble, to be parted from one you love."

"Yes, I love her very much, though not in the way you mean, I think. We were constantly quarrelling, and the best of friends on account of it, if you can understand such a contradiction. We were perpetually sticking pins into one another, as it were; but there was no poison on the points, and the little wounds did not rankle."

The mention of pins naturally suggested the thought of a pin-cushion, and that in turn brought to my mind the last conversation I had had with Dorothy; and I told My Lady the story of that morning, and how Dolly had behaved with regard to the bur. And My Lady laughed — she actually laughed at the tale, as though we were friends, and stood on common ground. The change was delightful, yet so strange as to be bewildering.

"I wish I could know her," said My Lady, wistfully: a natural enough wish for one who had evidently lived for years without a female companion or even acquaintance of her own station. "We have lived so alone, and there has been so little gayety in our lives! Sometimes I feel a little envy of other girls who have had companions and friends. Not that I would have it changed," she went on quickly. "My father is companion and friend at once, and I would not exchange him for all the rest of the world. But — there is a difference. I wish I could come to know such a maid as your cousin Dolly."

"I wish she could know *you*, even as I do," I said rashly.

My Lady seemed to collect herself with a sudden alarm at finding herself conversing so amicably with an enemy.

"Why, what do you know of me?" she asked coldly.

"More than you think, perhaps," I said. "Probably you do not know how many nights I have stood for hours among the trees in front of your house, watching you and your father, and listening to your singing." I saw a look of suspicion and indignation beginning to cloud her face. "I do not mean that I ever came near enough to hear your conversation," I went on quickly. "Never that; I am no eavesdropper. All I ever heard was your voice in singing, and if you knew how much pleasure it has given to a lonely man, cut off from all his kind, you would not grudge that satisfaction, even to an enemy. But I have seen your tenderness, each for the other, and I know that hearts that are capable of such feeling can harbor no malice or wickedness. What I mean is this: my long captivity had given birth to hard feelings against the authors of it, and I had vowed to bring punishment upon them for it. But what I have seen there has so softened that mood that I tell you that when I make my escape I will let those injuries go, and leave you all in peace. You must be aware that, whatever may have been my supposed crimes, such a detention is most illegal, and might bring a weighty vengeance upon all concerned in it. But I tell you now (and it may serve to ease your mind after I am gone) that in spite of all the injustice I have suffered, I shall not attempt to avenge myself upon the Master."

She began to show some interest.

"You expect to escape, then?" she asked, with a certain curious wonder at my certainty.

"Surely! Even up to this time I had one excellent opportunity that you know of. I let that escape me by my own stupidity, but others will come — they must!"

"I fear — I mean, I hope that no more will present themselves," she said.

"The time will come," I said, and I believed in my heart it would. "Sooner than you think, perhaps. I do not know — I only wait; but it will come."

She stood in deep thought for a while.

"The story of your coming seems a likely one, Mr. Darke," she said. "I believe it, that is, in a certain way that I can hardly explain, even to myself. But my father says otherwise, and I am bound to believe him first. It seems to me that there must be something more behind this matter. I cannot guess what it is, and you may be as ignorant as myself; but my father does not act without good reasons that he knows of. Perhaps he will tell me some day, and then I shall know what to do. It is a strange quandary to be in. I should like to believe you absolutely; I should like to believe that my father had no enemies or persecutors anywhere; yet I know that he has powerful ones, though I do not know who they are. But he ranks you among them, and, for that reason, so must I."

"I thank you for your courtesy and good wishes, My Lady," I returned. "I do not blame you for your attitude in the matter; as a loyal daughter you could not do otherwise. You have listened to my story; that is the most I dared to hope for. Some day you will know the truth of it."

"I hope so, indeed," she said.

She made a motion as though to offer her hand in farewell; the hand was half extended when I stepped back a pace.

"No, My Lady! I recognize the kindness of heart that prompts the offer, and thank you for it; but I will not take your hand until this mistake has been corrected; until I can take it as a friend in the sight of all men. And I think it would not be fair to your father, nor what he would willingly see."

My remarks confused her; she turned red. "You are right," she said hastily. "It was the ill-considered impulse of the moment, though I do not regret it. Good-by, Mr. Darke."

"One more moment before you go, My Lady," I hastened to say. "This meeting has been a great satisfaction to me in many ways, and I shall never forget it. But I shall bury it deep in my memory — so deep that it will lie a forgotten thing among other lost memories — until the day comes when I can return to it honorably. To all practical purposes, we have not met to-day. When next we meet, I shall expect no further recognition than you have accorded me hitherto — which is none at all. Indeed, I do not wish it. If I cannot be known to you as a gentleman and your equal, entitled to all the courtesies that I would have a right to expect as such, I prefer to be overlooked completely."

"Certainly, sir, since you wish it so," she returned haughtily, drawing herself up with much dignity.

"But do not misunderstand me, My Lady," I begged. "Though your father regards me as beneath contempt, I have my pride; your own pride and self-respect should enable you to comprehend the stand I take. Put yourself in my place; think how you would feel in such a case as mine, knowing yourself innocent of all cause of offence."

"I think I do understand it," she said, with more gentleness, after a pause. "I shall respect your wishes, and will not think you discourteous on account of them. I must own that hitherto what discourtesy has been between us has not come from you," growing red again.

I raised my hand in protest. "I only wish to return to our former footing until the day comes when I may meet you on even terms, My Lady; and the wish does not arise from any feeling of anger or any intention of rudeness."

"I understand," she said again. "But — I am sorry."

"So am I," I said. "But the present state of things will not last forever, thank God! There must soon be an end to it."

She shrank as though I had offered to strike her.

"Oh, do *you* think that too?"

"Think what?" I asked, amazed at her shrinking.

"That he is so ill."

"He? Who?"

"My father."

"Good Heavens, no! I had no thought of him. What do you mean, My Lady?"

"I thought you were expecting to be released by his death."

"I had no such thought," I exclaimed, shocked at the idea. "If I had had, I should never have thought of saying such a thing to you, of all others. Why should you think that of me — or that he is ill?"

"He says that your power for harm will end when he dies — and he says that he cannot live long," she answered. There were tears on her cheeks.

"As far as concerns me, he is wrong," I said. "I have no power to harm him, except by prosecuting him for keeping me here. To do that I must first be free; and I have just told you that I should not do so even then. If you do not believe me — and I suppose you do not —"

"I do!" she interposed.

"I thank you for that much confidence, at least. I wish you could believe the rest also. . . . But I think you are too fearful about him. I know he is not strong; but except the weakness that comes with age, he seems in excellent health, and likely to live many years; perhaps more than you or I."

"I pray that he may," she said fervently.

"I, also! I do not think, from what little I have seen of him, that you need fear on that account. Why should you?"

She shook her head. "He says that his months — he does not even say years — will be few; and he knows. I believe him in that, as in other things. He would not say it if he were not sure, for he knows how it grieves me."

"No man can foretell the hour of his death," I said, to comfort her.

"No; but sometimes he can feel it approaching."

"Let us hope that it is merely a temporary despondency," I said. "I wish I could do something to cheer him; but if your efforts fail, all other would be useless, certainly. If my presence has to do with it, you may assure him that neither that nor my absence need trouble him. . . . I do not mean that as a plea for my liberty, though."

"I understand," she said. "But it is not that, or at most, it can be only a small part of the trouble. It began before you came."

"I am glad to know that, at least. That is, I am glad to know that I am not the cause. Could you not bring a doctor to see him?"

"He will not hear of such a thing, and he has

lived apart from the world so long that the presence of a stranger has a bad effect on him. Besides, he says he *knows*, and that a physician could
do nothing for him: how he knows, I cannot tell,
except that he is a very wise and learned man.
He has some knowledge of medicine, among other
things."

"Let us hope that he is mistaken as to the
extent of his knowledge, in that case," I replied.
"It is said that a physician is less than others able
to know or cure his own illness."

She returned no answer, and for a long time we
stood in silence. After the pleasant intimacy,
almost friendship, that had come to us during the
last hour, almost obliterating the gulf that was
supposed to lie between us, neither of us quite
knew how to make a fitting departure. She was
a lady, and there was no demand upon my time,
therefore, it was not for me to make the first
motion toward a separation, even had I wished to
do so. After this it was hard to be obliged to go
back to the old form of outward coldness and suspicion, yet it must be done. My Lady at last
moved restively.

"Good-by, Mr. Darke."

"Good-by, My Lady." There was nothing
else to say, bald as the words sounded.

I stood aside.   She courtesied in answer to my bow, as stately as though we stood on a crowded street.   She gave me one glance that bore no contempt, and made me believe that she would feel no more contempt for me ever.

She passed by me, and was gone.

VIII

JUGGERNAUT

The threshing had been going on for a week, and was now nearly over. The threshing floor was crowded with slaves, just far enough apart to let them swing their flails without danger to one another. I stood in the door for a while, watching them rise and fall through the dust that filled the place. Great numbers of overflowing bags were piled under the shed outside, and from time to time others were brought out and added to the heap. The harvest was ten times in quantity what could be consumed on the plantation.

Justinian was overseeing the piling of the sacks upon his wagon. (It was a curious fancy that led the Master to name his slaves after the old Roman emperors and their consorts.) I wondered what they would do with the immense crop.

"Where do you sell your grain, Justinian?" I asked tentatively.

"At New—" He stopped, and looked frightened.

"At New—what?"

"The Master may tell you. Ask him," said the man, hastily.

"What! Daren't you let me know even that?" I inquired scornfully. "I had no idea of getting you into trouble, Justinian."

"I know," returned the man. "But Marse Burton, he say tell you nothin'."

"Many thanks to Marse Burton," I replied ironically. "Perhaps I had better ask him. I don't see the Master very often."

Justinian looked at me doubtfully, and then laughed. They all knew how Burton hated me.

"Marse Burton's over there at the granary," he waved his hand toward the building, some hundreds of yards away.

"Very well, I'll go over there," I said, and left him.

"Wagon's mos' loaded, Marse Allan," he called to me. "You can ride over on it with me."

It had been a great satisfaction to me that in spite of the detestation and contempt in which the white people of the island held me, the negroes were invariably kind and courteous. If I had been a royal envoy, they could not have been more obsequious.

"Thank you, Justinian," I returned; "I am still able to walk that little distance, and your wagons are too slow and heavy."

It was far cooler and less dusty at the granary. A wagon was standing at the door, nearly empty. The lower floor was piled high with the sacks, and they had begun to hoist the new ones into the second story. I watched the negroes hauling them up through the hatchway in the middle of the building, but I was exceedingly careful to avoid standing close to the hatch, or, indeed, under any place whence a sack might fall accidentally. Since one day when Burton had "accidentally" thrown down a sack of last year's grain at me, which actually grazed me as it fell, I had been very cautious as to where I stood in his neighborhood.

I was not certain that Burton was there, for I could neither see nor hear him; but I knew it was his business to be about when the sacks were being stored, and I knew, also, his reputation for attending to the business that belonged to him, so I felt sure that he was somewhere near. At the same time I had not the slightest desire to encounter him: his company was too dangerous. It was mere curiosity and idleness that had brought me there, and I felt safe enough from his dastardly attempts at assassination as long as there were plenty of witnesses present. His attempts on my life had all been made when we were alone together.

K

I stood outside the great double doors where the cool breeze could strike me, and watched the panting horses approach, on the run, the slight incline that led to the door, so hard was it for them to pull the heavy wagons up that little slope. The sacks were hoisted faster than the wagons could bring them over from the threshing-floor, and during the intervals of waiting the negroes came out and stood about the door, where they could get the benefit of the breeze, for the day was a scorching one. They stood beside and behind me, but said little, even to one another, saving their breath for the effort of hoisting.

"Where is Burton, Romulus?" I asked.

He pointed toward the upper floor, without speaking.

"Doesn't he come down when there is nothing to do up there?"

"Not this mo'nin'. He stays there till the sacks is all up, mos'ly."

I looked down the road at the wagon that was approaching. "That's an unusually heavy load they have there," I remarked.

"Yes, sir," he answered, after a careful survey. "Make us sweat, Marse Allan," he grinned.

"So it will, Romulus. But it won't be for long, and you will soon have a chance of rest again. I don't believe any of you will hurt yourselves by working too hard."

He laughed. "Des no need," he said. "Ole Marse, he don' care see us wu'k too ha'd."

"And you don't want to disobey such an order as that, eh?"

He laughed again. "Yuh she comes!"

The wagon was close at hand, the horses panting and straining, and the wheels sinking deep into the sandy road, already cut by earlier trips. Justinian, the driver, cracked his whip; the horses strained, for they knew that incline only too well, and they knew that they must give the wagon a good impetus, else it would roll back, dragging them with it, and making double work necessary. Creaking loudly, with wailing cries from wheels insufficiently greased, the wagon gathered speed as it came rolling on to the plane, until it was dragging upward at an unusually fast walk, almost a trot. I stood almost within arm's length of the horses as they were about to pass through the door.

Suddenly, without a moment's warning, I heard a quick cry, and at the same instant some one fell violently against me, striking me squarely between the shoulders. Standing loosely, unprepared as I was to resist any shock, a touch might have thrown me off my balance, and this weight against me did infinitely more. Helpless to assist or catch myself in any way, I pitched forward between the wheels of the rapidly moving wagon, and fell flat upon the ground.

There are times in imminent danger when the body seems to act by a sort of instinct before the mind has actually grasped the situation, and yet does exactly the best thing that could be done under the circumstances. I hardly knew that I was in danger, but as I fell I must have turned, so that instead of landing upon my face my back struck the ground. As I touched the hard soil I looked upward, to see above me the rapidly moving body of the wagon; without any reflection I knew that my legs were lying between the wheels, and in a flash they were drawn close to my body. At the same instant I reached upward and grasped the low axle as it came above me, lifting myself clear of the ground, and holding myself thus until the horses stopped upon the level floor of the granary.

I let myself drop upon the floor and looked about me, hardly realizing what had happened, so quickly had it all occurred, during the time it had taken the wagon to travel little more than its own length. It seemed to me that while the wagon yet moved I had heard a man's voice cry out in agony, and now, as I looked about me, I heard another voice — a woman's, this time; a voice that cried out in horror — that brought me out from beneath the wagon and to my feet in a second.

A man lay in the dust of the incline where the wagon had just passed, moaning loudly and holding his wrist in the other hand. I ran toward him, and at the same moment My Lady reached the spot and bent over the prostrate figure.

"What is it, Theodore? Are you hurt? Speak!"

The man gathered himself up, groaning, and held out his wrist, still clasping it. His face was a livid gray.

My Lady shrank and cried out again, and I had much ado to keep myself from doing the same. The hand hung down in a way to show clearly that the wrist was broken, if not worse, and I could see blood flowing freely from it between the fingers that clasped it.

The man turned his face, distorted with pain, from one to the other of us, mutely imploring assistance. I could not pass by such an appeal. My Lady stood helpless, and I went to his side.

"Let me see it, Theodore. I will do what I can."

He held the wrist firmly, but suffered me to lift the hand. As I did so, the hideousness of the thing turned me sick. It was worse than broken: the heavily weighted iron tire, cut almost square on the edge, had crushed and cut through bone and tendon and muscle. They were severed as cleanly as though with an axe; only some slight shreds of flesh and skin held the hand to the wrist.

"Quick, fetch me water, and stuff for bandages, and rum, some of you!" I cried.

For once, no one thought of questioning my right to give orders. Some of them started off pell-mell; the rest crowded about us.

"Stand back!" I commanded. "Give him room and air. One of you fetch a sack of grain." It was the nearest thing at hand to form a seat that I could see. I made him sit down on the sack and lean against a post.

"Now, which of you will hold his wrist, tight and firm, while I dress it?"

"I," said a quiet voice behind me. I looked around; I had almost forgotten her presence.

"You, My Lady! It is no sight for you!"

"I will do it," she said. "He is our servant." As though that fact were reason enough for her doing and daring anything. It might have been for a man, but for her —

"You cannot!" I said. "You will faint. The hand must be amputated."

She stepped forward and took hold of the wrist.

"The man suffers: be quick, if you can help him," she commanded, in a tone of reproof. She was very pale, but determined. There was nothing for it but to accept the situation; after all, if she did faint, there were plenty to take her place. She knelt beside him, and held the arm firmly across her knee, while the blood ran down her dainty gown in long streaks of crimson.

"Press your fingers *here*, your thumb *there!*" I said, quickly. "Hold them so for a moment."

The blood flowed less and less freely as she pressed the arteries. I threw off my coat, and tore some strips from it to make a tourniquet, winding them about a couple of pebbles to produce the necessary compression at the right spots. The blood merely trickled now; there was no danger of his bleeding to death at least, and again I tried to get My Lady to leave us, but she would not.

"Proceed, sir, if you feel yourself competent," she protested. "If you do not, I will summon my father, though I would spare him the sight — and the knowledge — of it, if it might be."

"I believe I am competent for this, since the

sharp tire made such a clean cut," I said. "It will require little surgical knowledge, as the thing stands; a more complicated case I would not have undertaken. But I wish you would let some of these men take your place. There are plenty of them, and there is no necessity for harrowing your feelings."

She shook her head obstinately, and I was compelled to go on. I beckoned the negroes to one side, within the granary. I did not want Theodore to hear me: he was already suffering enough from pain and fright.

"Which of you has a sharp knife?" I asked, in a low tone. Almost every man of them put his hand in his pocket and produced a knife of some kind. I held out my hand.

"Give me a sharp one," I said, and was about to lay hold of the nearest when it was suddenly withdrawn from my reach and returned to the owner's pocket.

"What is the matter?" I exclaimed, in astonishment. "Are you afraid I will spoil it? I will not, but if I should the Master would give you a better one."

"'Tain't that, Marse Allan," said one of them. They all appeared much embarrassed.

"Well, what is it? Be quick!"

They hesitated for a moment, but they knew that time was precious.

"Marse Burton, he say not to let you have a knife, suh, fo' fea' yo' hu't some one," said one of them, at last, hanging down his head.

My heart swelled with rage. I strode out to where my patient sat, with My Lady holding his wrist.

"My Lady!" She started at the harshness of my angry tone. "My Lady, I have asked these men for a knife to use in this business, and not one of them will let me have one. They say they have orders not to let me have any weapon, for fear I will hurt some one," and the sneering tone that I could not keep out of my voice must have cut her sorely, for she flushed deeply, and looked first very much ashamed, and then very angry.

"It is not my doing, sir, nor even with my knowledge. I am sorry," she said. "Come here, quickly!" to the negroes, who had been watching us apprehensively, doubtful as to whether they had done rightly or wrongly in refusing me. They slunk toward us.

"How many of you have knives?"

They were produced as before.

"Give me them, every one, instantly!" She held out her hand, and one by one the knives were laid in it, to the number of a dozen or more. My Lady held them out to me. "Take your choice, Mr. Darke."

I selected one, and laid the others beside me while I tested the blade, finding it quite sharp enough for my purpose. Theodore leaned back heavily against the post, almost insensible. Close by I saw the messengers returning from the house with the things I had sent them for.

"Turn your face away, My Lady, but hold fast. It will take but a moment."

I knew the bruised flesh could feel no pain for a while. I held the drooping hand in mine, and with a few quick strokes finished severing it, and cast it to one side where neither she nor Theodore could see it. The slaves had brought in the meantime bandages and water which they placed at my side.

"Give him a drink of rum," I ordered. "A big one. And, My Lady, I beg you to take some, also."

It was good for both of them, and My Lady looked less pale while I cleansed the wound and bandaged it, drawing the edges of the skin as close together as possible. Under the circumstances I thought it was rather neatly dressed. I knew I had seen much worse wounds more carelessly attended to that had healed perfectly ; and there was no reason why a strong, healthy man, such as I knew Theodore to be, should have any great trouble with it.

By my directions, again, the sacks were hastily tossed from the wagon and Theodore laid on the floor of it, and then we took our way toward the slaves' quarters. As the wagon passed through the door, I turned to My Lady, and pointed to the little heap of knives that lay beside the place where Theodore had sat.

" I have left them all there, My Lady," I said, with meaning that she understood perfectly. She gave me a look of reproach that hurt me more than anything she could have said. Perhaps she guessed it, for she contented herself with that, and did not reply otherwise.

" Let him rest quietly," I bade Justinian, as the wagon moved away. "The wound will need no dressing for a day or two, and then I will see to it."

" And tell Burton — where *is* Burton ? " said My Lady. Somehow we had all forgotten that he was supposed to be in the barn; now his absence seemed strange.

" I don' know, My Lady," said Justinian. " He was heah this mo'nin'."

"He was heah jus' a little while back," said Romulus. "'Twas him 'at frew The'dore under the wagon."

My Lady looked as though a bomb had burst at her feet. I laughed aloud.

"Ah, I thought so!" I exclaimed.

"Thought what?" asked My Lady, quickly.

"Thought he must have had a hand in it."

"And why?"

"It is very plain," I explained, with an assumption of carelessness. "He did not mean to hurt Theodore: he meant me to be the victim."

"Mr. Darke!"

"You think I am too suspicious?" I laughed again. "Oh, no; it is not the first time he has plotted against me!"

"Mr. Darke, your unfounded suspicions of us pain me greatly," said My Lady.

"I have no suspicions as to you or your father," I returned. "For the matter of that, I do not suspect Burton: I know!"

"It is impossible you can believe such a thing!"

"Is it? Well, perhaps it is, or perhaps a miracle has happened. As I said, it is not the first time. Perhaps you are not aware that I myself was standing *in front* of Theodore, and was thrown entirely under the wagon? If those wheels had caught me there—" I left the consequences to her imagination. "Romulus says it was Burton that fell against Theodore; he 'fell' hard enough to throw me so far, and even to hurt poor Theodore, against whom he could have no enmity. As I understand it, his place was in the loft. Why was he on the ground, and why did he disappear after causing the maiming of a slave who was working under his direction?"

"You make out a terrible case against him," said My Lady, thoughtfully. "But I know you are wrong; your prejudices blind you."

"Prejudices—*my* prejudices!" I exclaimed bitterly. "That comes well from one of those who condemned a stranger to imprisonment without allowing him to speak in his own behalf! But there; I must not go into that question, or I may forget courtesy."

"At least you will allow me, in my father's name and my own, to thank you for your kindness to Theodore," she said.

"It is entirely unnecessary," I replied coldly. "When I wished to thank you for saving me from the quicksand, you told me you 'would do as much for any of the slaves.' May I not also be allowed the privilege of assisting one of the slaves on occasion?"

My Lady looked downcast, almost sorrowful.

"Doubtless I have said many things that were far from courteous," she murmured, looking down at the ground. "Some of them were so intended at the time, some not so. But I regret them all, and it is painful to me to think that you should have them always in mind, as you seem to do."

"I have had few pleasant things to think of since coming here," I answered gently. "What few there were, I owe to you. But I did not mean to be rude or quarrelsome; and when I break out in that way, I beg you to believe that it arises from a certain overwrought feeling of irritation begotten of my imprisonment. It is but lately that you talked with me in all kindness and courtesy, and the memory of that one time is very pleasant to me. Only our ideas as to facts and causes are so radically opposed that we have no common ground upon which we could meet to talk of this question, or hold even a short conversation without a clashing of them; and this cannot be amended until one or the other of us shall come to view these things from a different standpoint."

"I know; yet may we not both be sincere in our beliefs?"

"Undoubtedly. I am sure we are both sincere.

Yet I beg you to observe this : my views of this matter are grounded on absolute knowledge of my own identity and actions; yet you and the Master will not believe one iota of them, and so believe that I and my story alike are false. Your belief and his cannot have any such certainty, since it concerns another person, and it is founded on what I know to be a mistaken assumption that I am some man of whose existence, even, I know nothing. Yet observe that while I absolutely deny the correctness of your assumptions, I do feel sure that you and he believe in their truth. If there is any discourtesy here, it surely is not on my part."

"No, Mr. Darke," she replied. "I have not accused you of anything of the sort. It seems rather that I and my father are on trial before you in that matter. For myself, I have heard your account of yourself and the manner of your coming; otherwise I have no knowledge of the matter. My father has told me nothing of his reasons. But, right or wrong, I must stand by my father and his word."

"I would not have it otherwise, My Lady," I replied eagerly. "But you may remember that this present discussion did not arise from any mention of yourself or the Master. I doubted neither of you. I spoke of Burton only, and you accused me of prejudice against him. I know what I know, and it is in my mind to speak to your father concerning it. Meanwhile, I will not distress you further by more mention of it."

We had been walking side by side down the road, and were now near the slaves' quarters. I knew she would wish to see Theodore made as comfortable as possible. We parted with befitting ceremony.

That afternoon Romulus sought me at my cabin. On his arm he bore a coat of dark blue broadcloth, such as I had not seen for many a day.

"With the compliments of the Master, to replace the coat destroyed in the Master's service," he said, with a ludicrous attempt at stateliness that made me laugh, as he presented it. He laughed as well, when his little speech was made.

"Mr. Darke's compliments to the sender, and reply that he is profoundly indebted to her," I returned; and Romulus grinned again more broadly, knowing that I had seen through the little ruse. For I was sure that the coat had been sent by My Lady, and equally sure that the Master had not yet heard so much as a whisper of the event that had caused me to tear my old coat.

IX

It seemed to me quite time to make some kind of a protest. Here were five different attempts on my life — all made by the same man, and all made by insidious, underhand means. I did not want to stay on the island: nothing would have pleased me better than to discover some means of escaping from it. But, if I must stay, there would be a certain amount of satisfaction in knowing just what was to come, even though it were the worst. The Master evidently held the whole island and its inhabitants in the hollow of his hand. If he had intended that I should be done away with, it would be the easiest thing possible to have it done quietly and quickly, since there was no one within reach to know of it, or to question his action even if it were known. But he had spared me, and had given orders for my sustenance and safe-keeping; hence it must be intended that I should live. Any wanton attempts against my life must be contrary to his wishes.

Thus I reasoned, and put the result into practice promptly. There was no time to be lost; any day might see me laid out in state, a victim to Burton's malevolence. I waylaid the Master that very evening, while he and My Lady were on one of their short strolls about the grounds. I walked straight up to them and removed my cap, making such a bow as I had been taught in my boyhood to use in a ballroom or on occasions of great ceremony.

When she saw me approaching, My Lady turned her eyes away, as though unwilling to have me address her. The action struck me as almost childish, and made me smile involuntarily. It hurt me, too, after our late conversations, though perhaps it was only loyalty to her father that made her do so. She need not have feared, however; my business was with the Master, though I was rather glad that she should hear it.

The Master saw that I had matters of importance in my mind, and waited for me to broach them. I plunged straightway into the midst of things.

"Sir, when I was first brought to your notice, I understood you to say that if I had any complaint to make of my treatment by your servants, it would be heard, and the matter amended."

"It is so," he returned gravely.

"I also understood you to say that I should not be harmed unless I offered to use violence myself."

"I gave orders to that effect," he answered. "You heard me do so."

"I did hear it," I said, "and I believed at the time that the order was given in good faith. I have since had reason to doubt it."

If I had deliberately intended to rouse him to anger, I could not have taken a more effective way. The remark was a rash one, spoken on the spur of the moment and without reflection. It was not likely to help my cause, and I heartily regretted it the moment the words had issued; and, in truth, I had not meant them in the way they sounded. The Master flushed with indignation, and My Lady shot a glance of reproof and anger at me. The old man took a step toward me; I believe he was ready to strike me, and I could not have blamed him had he done so. But the girl's hand restrained him, and the girl's voice forestalled his speech.

"Mr. Darke, did you come here to insult an old man?"

She was both angry and disdainful.

"Indeed, madam," I protested, "I had no such

thought.   If my words seemed to convey an insult (and I see now how they might be so construed), I beg you both to believe that it was unintended, and I apologize most humbly for my fault.   Sir" (I turned to the Master), "my words were ill chosen.   I did not mean so much to doubt the good faith of the command as the good faith of the obedience to it.   Possibly your servants may have supposed that your order was not intended to be obeyed literally; possibly some of them are afflicted with an excess of zeal in your cause, and took it upon themselves to serve you in their own way by disobeying you."

There was a long silence, while the eyes of those two bore upon me fixedly.   If I had been guilty of any meanness or crime, I believe that steady, questioning regard would have broken me down.   As it was, I managed to sustain it without flinching; and it seemed to me that the Master was somewhat surprised and a little disappointed that I did so, and My Lady a little relieved.

"State your complaint, sir," said the Master, at length.   He spoke coldly, but I fancied his manner was not as hostile as it had been at first.

"I am here on your island by no will of my own," I began.   "I ask nothing better than to leave it.   But since you have both the will and the power to keep me here, it seems only just that you should look to my safety, since you have put it out of my power to guard myself. It is true I heard you give orders that I was not to be harmed, and I believe you fully intended it to be so; but what confidence can I feel in such a command when it is deliberately disobeyed — and not once only — by your servants? The sword of Damocles was a mere plaything compared with what hangs over me! He, at least, had no promise of safety, and he knew the manner of the death that threatened him; I cannot even guess that. I have no wish to harm any one; but cannot you see that such a state of things is likely to drive even the most peaceably disposed man to desperation? If I must die, I hope I shall be able to meet my fate as a man should; but if I am to be kept on such a continual strain of expectation of I know not what, you need not be surprised if it should unhinge my mind. And if harm should come of it, you alone will be responsible for what may happen. I have warned you!"

I had warmed as I went on, and at the last my tones must have carried to both of them a conviction of my truth and earnestness. Both father and daughter stared at me in genuine astonishment, but neither of them attempted to interrupt me.

"But I do not understand you, Mr. Darke," said the Master, at length. "Do you complain of the conduct of any of my servants? If so, state your accusation, and I promise you I will have it investigated directly, and corrected. I am compelled to keep you a prisoner, much against my will; but I have no wish to make your captivity more irksome than is necessary."

"My detention, by itself, is a sufficient cause of complaint," I answered; "but I pass over that for the present, since I know that you will not listen to reason on that subject. What galls me most, now, is the later and deeper treachery."

"Treachery!" exclaimed the Master, straightening his bent form suddenly.

"Yes, treachery!" I retorted hotly. "There is no other word for it in my vocabulary. If you and your people seek my life, take it openly and quickly; but this suspense is unbearable."

"No one seeks your life, Mr. Darke," replied the Master, soothingly, as though trying to reason with a frightened child. It was plain that he thought me the victim of some wild hallucination, and it did not make me the cooler for knowing it.

"So?" I said with a sneer, half turning away.

"I see, then, that your promise of safety was a lie. I shall know what to expect hereafter."

The Master's face flushed again, and his hands clinched, but he restrained himself with a great effort.

"Wait, Mr. Darke! A prisoner must be allowed certain privileges of speech, I suppose," he said coldly. "As I said before, if you have a complaint to make, state it, as concisely as possible."

"I will, then!" I returned. "Despite your order that I should not be molested, my life has been attempted three times within a month, and other times before that. Is that definite enough?"

"Almost too definite," he replied, with an incredulous shrug of his shoulders. "And who were your assailants?"

"There was only one," I said. "Burton."

"Burton!" they exclaimed simultaneously.

"Yes, Burton! Why not?"

The Master turned to My Lady. "Call him," he commanded, with a smile.

My Lady raised the little ivory whistle that swung always from her belt, and blew two shrill blasts. Whether Burton had been watching us I do not know; probably he was, for he appeared with suspicious promptness, coming from the house.

"Burton, Mr. Darke has an accusation to make. State it, Mr. Darke, if you please."

"About a month ago I stood in the west granary beneath the hatchway, which was open. A great sack of wheat was thrown down at me, and missed me by a bare hair's-breadth."

The Master looked at Burton inquiringly.

"What has that to do with me?" said the man, quietly.

"You were the only man on that floor of the granary. Immediately after the sack fell, you peered over the edge of the hatchway to see whether it had accomplished your purpose."

He turned to the Master, and the Master nodded to him. "Answer!" he commanded.

"When I heard the sack fall, of course I ran to the hatch to see what had happened. That is all I know about the matter."

"You were on the spot when it fell," I retorted; "for I had barely time to take two steps before I looked up, and I saw you there then."

He shook his head contemptuously, but said nothing.

"Answer!" said the Master, again.

He spoke to the Master, not to me.

"The man was probably frightened, and was not capable of estimating how much time had passed before he saw me. It was as I said," he returned sullenly.

"I did not see him throw it down, of course," I said in my turn, being willing to give even the devil his due. "But it is very curious that it should have fallen just when I was beneath the hatch."

"Stranger things than that have happened, and will again," he rejoined carelessly.

"Also, none of the slaves had left any bags near the hatch," I went on, watching him narrowly.

Burton gave a slight start. I did not know whether the others noticed it; but I was looking for signs of guilt, and saw this one plainly.

"How do you know that?" he demanded hastily.

"I have asked every man, woman, and child, among the slaves on the plantation, and they all denied leaving the bag there. They say, too, that the bags are always stowed carefully at the ends of the granary, away from the hatch, *and that you always see that it is done.*"

I thought I had him securely, this time, for he had admitted the fall of the bag; but he did not take the trouble to meet the obvious inference. Perhaps he was too confident of the Master's implicit faith in his fidelity to orders.

"I deny this also!" he said, with calm insolence.

"It seems to be that my word is put against theirs, and the Master can judge which is the most trustworthy." He glanced toward the Master and laughed, as one sure of his victory. The latter looked slightly troubled, but he made no remark on the matter in hand.

"Is that all, Mr. Darke?" he inquired.

"No," I said, "that is only the beginning! Within less than a week afterward I found a copperhead snake snugly hidden between the blankets of my bed."

I saw My Lady shudder, but Burton only laughed again.

"Really, this is absurd," he laughed lightly. "Do you mean to make me responsible for the movements of all living things on the island? I am no snake-charmer. When I see a snake, I kill it, if I can!" His eyes told me plainly that he included me among the reptiles named.

"The blankets had been moved since the morning," I returned.

"Are you perfectly sure of that?" demanded the Master, whose brow was wrinkled by a frown of perplexity.

"I am sure," I returned positively. "I have always turned the edges of my blankets in a certain way; this time they were laid flat, and I noticed the change even before I discovered the snake. The creature was put there by human hands. Who did it, and why, is for you to discover or infer." I turned to the Master, but he only shook his head.

"Your accusations are very vague, Mr. Darke," he said. "The fall of a sack of wheat, the creeping of a snake into a warm place — these things are common cnough. You yourself admit that you have seen nothing to connect Burton directly with these accidents."

"Very good," I retorted. "I will be more definite with the next. Two months ago I attempted to escape from this island by swimming. A canoe was driven at me with all the speed that one man could give it. The stem struck my shoulder; if it had struck my head, I should have gone down like a stone. This man was the occupant of the canoe."

Again he laughed. "Pursuing an escaped prisoner on a dark night is no joking matter. If you had not tried to escape, you would have been in no danger."

"You never mentioned this to me, Burton," said the Master, reproachfully.

"You have had enough troubles," replied Burton. "As he did not escape, I thought it folly to disturb you by the story. When I gave up the search in the water, I thought he was drowned, for he gave no sign of his presence; indeed, I do not know, even now, how he found his way back to the island from such a distance."

"I can tell you something about it, you scoundrel," I cried, in a sudden access of rage. "You yourself helped me without knowing it!"

"How?" he demanded eagerly.

"I am not going to tell you all I know; the trick may be of use to me another time! But I assure you that you were the instrument of my salvation, as you were that of my danger."

I knew by his eyes that he would have given anything to clutch my throat with his powerful hands. But he had his own game to play, and he watched the moves warily.

"You should not have attempted to escape," he rejoined. "You were warned. You risked the consequences, you know, and you just missed suffering from some of them. If you saw my canoe coming, you should have had no trouble in avoiding it; if you could not see it, how could you expect me to see you?"

"You could see me well enough to follow me," I retorted.

"I followed the faint line of starlight reflected in your wake," he returned calmly.

"Yet you drove over that line at full speed," I said.

"It was quite time to try to recapture you," he laughed. "You were nearly two miles from shore."

I was silent for a while, during which he regarded me with a malicious glance. He had plainly worsted me at every point, by giving a perfectly natural and probable explanation of every move of his. I could see the Master and My Lady watching both of us closely, but I could not tell from their manner what impression I had made upon them. To myself I was obliged to own that from their point of view my grounds for accusing Burton must seem singularly weak.

"Is there anything more, Mr. Darke?" queried the Master.

I collected my thoughts with a struggle.

"Yes. During the first month of my detention here, while I was wandering about the island, I fell into a quicksand near the north end of the island — probably you know the place?" The Master nodded, and My Lady flushed a little.

"You should have been warned to avoid that spot." He glanced reproachfully at Burton.

"I forgot it," said the latter, apologetically. "I am not used to having strangers about, and every one on the plantation is so familiar with the danger that I never thought of warning Mr. Darke."

"It was a grave oversight," remarked the Master. "Perhaps I am equally culpable, for I did not think of it, either. But, since you escaped the danger, that is hardly a reason for distrusting either of us, Mr. Darke."

"Oh, I did not mean to accuse any one merely on that account," I returned quickly. "My point is this: when I approached the quicksand, Burton was following me; he saw my danger, and failed to warn me, though he could not have helped knowing what must happen. And after I was fairly in the trap, he came to the edge of the dunes and mocked my helplessness. If my life had depended on him, I should have disappeared utterly in that horrible place. It was only the sudden appearance — almost miraculous, as it seemed to me then, when I had given up all hope — of one whose good and kindly nature I have had no reason — *no reason* — " I repeated, with a profound obeisance to My Lady, "to doubt, that I escaped."

My Lady blushed a deep crimson and hung her head. She knew perfectly well that I alluded to that memorable day when the edge of the dune had crumbled beneath us; and the thought of the blow given that day humbled her now as it did then.

The Master turned to her proudly.

"It was what I should have expected from you." He spoke with great pride and tenderness. She shook her head, but did not speak.

"You say that Burton was there, and refused to help you?" asked the Master, after taking thought.

"I do say so, and more than that! He sat on the slope of the dune and mocked my plight. He said he had not expected to get rid of me so soon, but that if I had not done for myself effectually, he would have put me out of the way before many days."

He looked intently at Burton. "What have you to say to this?"

"I know nothing about this," he replied sullenly. "The man must have been mad with terror, and imagined all sorts of things. He hates me, you know. See how many other imaginary grievances he has just recounted! I was not there. I did not even know of his danger or his escape until afterward."

"Did *you* see Burton there?" questioned the Master of My Lady.

"No. After I had caught sight of a man in the quicksand, I had no eyes for anything else.

The whole plantation might have been close by without my knowing it." She looked at him as she spoke, and then, for the first time, addressed me directly.

"If you knew Burton was there, why did you not mention it to me?"

"Because I knew that he was not likely to stay close by," I answered. "He fled when he saw your canoe coming round the point. If he had appeared, he would have had some very awkward questions to answer to you; and when he did not respond to your first whistle, I knew he intended to keep himself out of sight. Besides, if I had spoken of it, you would not have believed my story."

The Master shook his head doubtfully.

"It is strange," he mused. "Are you positive that you could not be mistaken in this matter? Might you not have taken some tuft of grass or seaweed, or perhaps a piece of driftwood, for a man's head? Such mistakes have been known."

"Do grass and seaweed and driftwood have tongues?" I rejoined. "I tell you I heard the man, as well as saw him. Of course I do not expect you to believe me, when he denies it; it is many weeks since I ceased to hope for justice or humanity in this place." I spoke bitterly, for

I felt bitterly. "Why did you tell me that my complaints would be heard, if you had no intention of doing justice after they were made? Why did you give orders for my safety, and then allow this man to waylay me? If you intend to assassinate me, it is easy to do it, without all this hypocritical pretence of carefulness."

He started, and bent his brows sternly on me.

"Assassinate?" he queried, with great dignity.

"What else would you call it, if any one of these attempts had succeeded?"

It was no more than natural that he should be angry. Yet he restrained himself admirably; how admirably I did not appreciate until afterward, when I learned how my words must have affected him.

"You forget, sir," he said quietly. "You have no witness of these things except your own word. You know how little reason I have to rely on that, and it is directly contradicted by the man you accuse. Of the two, I should naturally trust to the man who has served me faithfully all his life, rather than to one whom I never saw until a few months ago, and who has given me the strongest reason for distrusting him. Indeed, in all but the last case, your whole theory rests merely upon suppositions. I acknowledge that, admitting your ac-

M

count to be perfectly exact, the coincidences are
certainly strange, perhaps suspicious — to you; yet
your own sense of justice must tell you that I cannot condemn a tried and faithful servant on such
vague suspicions.   I have never known him to lie
to me, and have the very best of reasons for believing that he would never do so; nor to disobey
my orders.   Could I begin to suspect him now, on
the strength of the wild and unsupported accusation of a stranger and an enemy?   You see I am
willing to argue the case with you, though there
is no necessity for so doing.   I have not refused
to hear you; indeed, it seems to me that I have
listened to your statements and your accusations
with more patience than most men would have
done.   I make allowance for the peculiar position
you are in, as well as for your original beliefs regarding me.   They are wrong; but, knowing what
I do, I can hardly blame you for that.   In your
place, I should doubtless look at the matter in the
same light.   However, all that is beside the issue.
I have not refused to hear you; on the contrary,
I am ready to listen to any further statements you
may have to make; only, I pray you to remember
that, in laying your accusations before me, you
voluntarily constitute me the judge of their suffi-
ciency."

It was galling. I had a good case. I knew, absolutely, that Burton was guilty on every occasion I had mentioned; and it had seemed to me, before I began to state my case, that any one else *must* see it as I did. Yet both defendant and judge put me hopelessly in the wrong by a few words; as the Master had said, even to myself I had to acknowledge how weak my theories must seem. But, since the thing was begun, I resolved to play it out; and I had one more point to make.

"I am past hoping that my words may have any effect," I said. "Still, there is one other 'coincidence' that I wish to bring to your attention. To-day I stood close to where the grain wagons were passing; several negroes stood around me. Just as a heavily loaded wagon passed, Burton gave the fellow who stood back of me a violent shove; the negro fell against me, and flung me between the wheels of the moving wagon. Only unusual quickness and a violent exercise of strength saved me from being crushed beneath the wheels. I do not expect you to take notice of my own peril, but probably you do not care to have your own property injured. The slave who was pushed against me was less fortunate than I; his wrist was caught beneath the wheel, and — he lost the hand."

"Who was it?" he demanded, quickly.

"The slave? Theodore."

"Theodore? Oh, that is terrible! Did you know of this?" turning to My Lady.

"Yes; I helped dress the arm," she answered, in a low tone.

"Could not the arm be saved?" asked the Master, eagerly. "Why did you not tell me of the accident immediately?"

My Lady hesitated a moment.

"The hand was almost completely cut off," she replied, without looking up. "And as this — gentleman — kindly attended to it as well as you could have done, I did not think it necessary to trouble you. Theodore has had all the attention and care that is possible. You are not strong enough to risk any unnecessary shocks."

The Master looked from her to me, and back again, several times.

"I thank Mr. Darke for his kindness to one of my people; more especially since I know he has small reason for good feeling toward any one of us. I wish," he said wistfully, "I wish it might be possible for us to be friends." It was the same wish that My Lady had made weeks before, and in the same words.

"It is through no fault of mine that we are not."

I spoke warmly, with a rising hope that at last the misunderstanding might be cleared up. His manner had softened me, so that for the moment I forgot my anger at his callousness in regard to the charges I had made against Burton. I saw My Lady raise her head, and her eyes shone brightly, hopefully, I thought. But I was to be disappointed again.

"I wish we might have been friendly, I say. But I know that until the whole truth is known there can be no friendship between me and your father's son."

Had I at last come upon a clew? It seemed so.

"My father!" I cried eagerly. "Did you know my father?"

The Master frowned, and seemed disturbed.

"I have said more than enough, and much more than I intended to," he said coldly, and with a certain air of contempt. "For a moment I was almost tempted to believe that you — Well, it shall not happen again, I assure you." I saw My Lady's head droop again. Why could I not put her out of my mind? I seemed compelled to watch her, and to gauge everything by what I could read from her face. "You have my thanks for your kindness to Theodore; I shall not forget it. There remains the matter that led you to seek me to-night. I must acknowledge that there have been a series of curious coincidences in regard to it, but I cannot bring myself to believe that they are anything more than coincidences. I am compelled to think that the prejudice you brought with you has blinded you, or perverted your views of things. At the same time —"

"Good God, sir," I broke out, "did I not tell you that on one occasion the man openly proclaimed his enmity and his intentions?"

"I do not credit the statement, sir," he returned, with dignity. "I am more inclined to believe that for reasons of your own (which I can easily surmise), you wish to turn my mind against a servant who has been more faithful and more obedient than you could ever have dreamed. I know him; I have known him well for more than thirty years; and in all that time he has never caused me a single anxiety, though he has saved me many, never given me a single reason for distrusting his perfect truth. Therefore it is only to be expected that I shall not believe him a villain on the mere unsupported statement of one whom I well know to be an enemy of myself — and therefore of every one connected with me."

I caught a swift glance of My Lady's eye. Did she, too, think that? I could not believe it.

"It is not so, sir," I answered sadly. "I have told you before this that I am no enemy of yours. How should I hate a man whom I never saw before — of whom I never even heard?" He made a gesture of impatience, but I went on. "You do not believe my assertion, and until you tell me upon what ground your conviction of my enmity rests, I am powerless to right myself. I have told you frankly who and what I am; if you would only speak as plainly, this thing could be made right at once."

I paused for him to speak. I saw My Lady lay her hand softly on his arm, as though in appeal, and my heart went out to her for the act. He threw it off with an angry gesture, the only one I ever saw him make toward her; and from the astonishment and pain depicted on My Lady's face, I felt sure it was the only one she had ever known. I felt for her, and hastened to put an end to the awkward situation.

"In any case, sir," I went on hurriedly, "whatever may be the supposed cause of my enmity toward you, there is no reason why it should include the members of your family, much less the rest of your household. There is but one person on this island toward whom I have unfriendly feelings; and it is due, in his case, entirely to his uncalled-for and unprovoked attempts on my life. I see that your prejudices in his favor and against me are too deeply rooted to be moved, so I will take my leave of you, with apologies for the intrusion. After all, it is only the matter of a man's life, and apparently that is a very trifling matter in your estimation." The Master started violently, and his eyes blazed fiercely, but I went on undaunted. "Whatever may occur, I shall not trouble you again. But I believe you have a conscience, and for its welfare I tell you this: when my life shall have been taken in some secret and underhand way, the crime will be on your head quite as much as on that of the actual assassin. I only hope that you may discover the truth before any other man — or woman — shall suffer for the error."

I bowed, and was turning away, when the Master stopped me.

"Wait, sir; this matter is not yet settled. No other man has ever accused me to my face of being unjust, nor shall you, with any good cause. While I do not believe in the truth of your accusations, I wish to convince you that I am not careless of your safety, though a cruel fate compels me to deprive you of your liberty for a short time. Burton!"

The man had been standing a little behind me during the late dispute, and I could fancy the grin of triumph that would have spread over his face if he had been as other men. Now he stepped forward, and touched his cap, without speaking.

"You have heard Mr. Darke's accusations and my answer to them. I repeat my order that no harm is to come to him that can possibly be prevented. I make you responsible for his safety, and if anything should happen to him that cannot be attributed to perfectly natural and inevitable causes, I shall hold you to account. If the act itself is not chargeable directly to you, I shall hold you indirectly guilty for not preventing the occurrence. If necessary, you will devote your whole time and attention to this, and use the services of as many of the slaves as you may consider necessary to make it absolutely sure. Do you understand?"

"Yes, sir; I understand perfectly," said the man, as he stepped back.

"Are you satisfied, sir?" demanded the Master, turning to me.

"Perfectly satisfied as to *your* intentions," I replied. "As I told you before, I had no doubt of them from the first moment of this interview. Not so as to his, however."

"But have you no further suggestion to make?" rejoined the Master, with a gesture of weariness. "I am more than willing to do anything in my power to disabuse your mind of this apprehension."

"None whatever," I answered. "There is only one solution of the difficulty, and that lies in the death of either him or me. You can guess which is most likely to happen; I am entirely unarmed, as you know well. I thank you for the patience and courtesy with which you have heard me — I know that I have tried them sorely — and for the good intentions you express."

I bowed low to both of them again, and walked away. Before I had taken twenty steps, some feeling got the better of me, and I turned and glanced in their direction. I seemed to see only the woman, upon whom my mind dwelt so constantly, and if there was not a look of sympathy for me on her face, my reading was greatly at fault. Yet I knew that her love and trust were given absolutely to the Master. However much sympathy she might feel for my hard case, she would never demur to the correctness or justice of his measures.

I had said to the Master that I knew no cause for enmity between him and me. I was wrong;

for in keeping her mind and mine apart, he was the worst enemy I could have, not even excepting Burton. Unceasing vigilance might serve to protect me from the latter, for he sought only to take my life. Not so with the Master, for he was (however unwittingly) destroying my peace of mind, and against his influence with My Lady I had no defence.

X

OUT OF SORROW COMETH JOY

I WAS roused from sleep by a heavy hand that shook me roughly by the shoulder. A bright glare dazzled my eyes for one moment; the next, I had shaken off the hand that held me and sprung to my feet, prepared to resist to the uttermost, for I recognized Burton standing beside me, holding the torch. I looked about the room to see the number of my assailants, and at my evident alarm Burton's face almost showed an expression of amusement as he said grimly, —

"You need not fear — this time!"

"What do you want?" I demanded.

"The Master wishes to see you, and quickly."

"The Master — at this time of the night? What for?"

"What is that to you? I say he wants you; who are you, to question his will?"

"I do not believe you," I said stubbornly. "This is only another of your cowardly attempts on my life. I will not go!"

"Fool!" he exclaimed impatiently. "If I had intended harm, I could have killed you easily enough while you slept. Am *I* likely to give you any chances when your time comes?"

That was true enough; and I was forced to believe him.

"What does he want?"

"How do I know? He will tell you what he pleases. Hurry; there is no time to lose!"

His manner impressed me strangely, in spite of my previous knowledge of him and his devious ways. I dressed myself hurriedly, and followed him to the house, wondering not a little about the meaning of this hasty summons. It could hardly be that the Master was going to give me my freedom at this time of the day — or rather, of the night; he would not have had me called until the morning, in that case. Burton strode along quickly, not vouchsafing me a word, and I kept by his side.

As we entered the inclosure that surrounded the mansion, I noticed that several of the upper windows were brightly illuminated; a sure evidence of some occurrence of importance, for every one on the island — except possibly myself, who had many things to keep me awake — was wont to be asleep soon after dark. My heart began to beat quickly, with a vague expectation of some event that should work a change in my circumstances.

Burton led me into the hall, which I had entered only once before, though I had seen every minutest portion of it during the long evenings when I kept my solitary vigil in the park. But this time he did not stop there. Grasping a candle that stood ready, he led the way toward the stairs. Naturally, I had stopped in the middle of the hall; and he, seeing that I did not follow him, waved his candle impatiently toward the stairs, and said, "Come!"

I followed to the upper floor. Burton tapped gently at a partly closed door, through which the light gleamed brightly, and a voice that I knew well called to us to enter.

I had watched the Master growing weaker day by day, yet it gave me a shock to see him propped up in bed, with a look on his face that enlightened me as to the cause of my being roused at such an hour. He was a dying man, and he knew it well. And My Lady, who sat beside the bed, holding his hand, knew it also; and Burton, who turned his face away quickly, knew it; and the negro house-servants, several of whom stood at the farther end of the room, knew it too. And, in spite of the treatment I had undergone, I believe there was not one of them — except, of course, My Lady — who was more heartily grieved than I was that it should be so.

I felt — I had recognized all along — that their treatment of me arose from some great mistake, and I believed that they felt themselves fully justified in the course they had pursued. Perhaps I should have taken the same measures under similar circumstances; I do not know. Certainly my whole feeling of resentment arose from the fact that they assumed they knew all about me (which claim I knew to be founded on a monstrous blunder), and that, in consequence of it, they refused even to listen to my story, and deprived me of the chance to clear myself of the unknown charges.

I had but a moment in which to note the scene so suddenly offered to my sight, and then My Lady turned her head and spoke to me.

"Sir, we owe you an apology for disturbing you at this hour; but my father would have speech with you, and the time — " her voice trembled, and she pressed his hand closer — "the time is short." She dropped her head for a moment upon the hand she held, and clung to it despairingly.

I bowed to both of them, but I looked at My Lady only. My heart shone through my eyes, though she could not see it, for she did not look up. If she had — But one other saw it, and he made no sign at that time.

"I am at his service and at yours, both now and hereafter," I said.

She turned red and then pale, but said never a word. She did not even turn her head, but left the Master to speak.

"It is hard to believe that you can have any feeling but that of enmity toward us, sir, yet I am compelled to ask a favor of you, and would speak with you alone before — " He glanced at My Lady's bowed head, and failed to finish his sentence. There was no need, however, to complete it. There was only one more event before him, and we all knew what it was.

"Leave us alone, dear," he said to My Lady; and she rose obediently, though with evident reluctance, and moved toward the door. The others followed, except Burton, who remained standing with his back to us, near one of the windows, apparently absorbed in staring out into the blackness of the night.

"Burton!" He turned quickly. The Master motioned toward the door, but he made no offer to move.

"Leave us alone!"

He took a step toward the bed. "Alone with *him?*"

" Certainly."

" I am afraid; he may do you harm," he muttered.

" Harm a dying man? He could not if he would. Go, I say ! "

Slowly and sullenly the man moved, casting a glance of inextinguishable hatred at me as he passed.

"Close the door after you," commanded the Master; and we were alone together. Since I had first spoken, I had not moved from where I stood; but now he beckoned me to him, and I took my station beside the bed. For a few moments he hesitated, not knowing how to introduce his subject.

" Mr. Darke," he began finally, " you see my condition. In a few hours at the most I shall be out of reach of your enmity. You see that I can have no object in speaking falsely, and for my daughter's sake I wish to make a statement, on the oath of a dying man, that I could never prove legally. By that oath, I swear that you were mistaken when you pursued me here. I swear that I was innocent, though my flight justified the belief in my guilt. But I was taken by surprise, and had no time to reflect on the consequences of what I did; I fled by instinct. When I came

N

to my senses, it was too late; the whole country was aroused, and searching for me, and in the state of public opinion at that time, I knew that I should receive scant justice — slight belief in my improbable story. I do not know the guilty man; but I do know that it was not I. For the sake of my child I ask you to believe this. Even if you still disbelieve, spare her! She, at least, has never harmed a living soul. Let my death, after all these years of exile, serve to expiate the crime that I never committed, but do not visit it on her innocent head. She knows not the name I bore at that time; let her live in ignorance of the disgrace that blackened it; let her believe her father a persecuted man, not a guilty one!"

I would not have believed that a man's countenance and voice could express such pitiful beseeching. He was in deadly earnest; his whole soul was moved by the one idea of convincing me, that My Lady might be spared all knowledge of the thing he spoke of. And I could not hazard even a guess as to his meaning, except that it concerned some crime done in long-forgotten years.

I took time to think, though his appealing eyes disturbed my reflections, and then spoke deliberately, striving to impress him in my turn with the truth of my words.

"Sir, when your servants first brought me before you, I told you that I came here through mischance, and knew absolutely nothing as to where I was, or who you were. Now, speaking as to a dying man, whom I could have no object in deceiving, I repeat the assertion ; I was not seeking you or any one. To this very moment I do not know where I am; to this very moment I do not know even your name or your daughter's. I have never heard of you, save as ' the Master ' of an unknown island where I have been detained through misapprehension on your part. If you were ever accused of a crime, I know nothing of it ; nor, since I have known you, would I have believed the accusation, had I heard it. I am not pleased with my inhospitable treatment here, and the attempts your servant has made upon my life ; but otherwise I have no cause of enmity toward you, and would gladly have been your friend months ago, if you would have let me. And, even before you ask it, I will give you one other assurance ; if I am permitted, I will guard your daughter with my life from all sorrow or trouble that I can ward off. Apart from your wish, I would rejoice to do this, from the affection I have felt for her this long time."

As I spoke, I saw doubt and incredulity expressed on his face changing to wonder, and then to belief — a belief that he hardly dared to entertain.

"You are Allan Darke, of Chilton?"

"Yes."

"Son of Allan Darke of the same place?"

"Yes."

"And you were not in search of me?"

"As I told you, I was on my way to Virginia in haste, and was in search of no one."

He suddenly sat up, and grasped my wrist with more strength than I would have believed he could possess.

"Swear it!" he cried. "You could not so deceive a dying man. Swear that that is the whole truth!"

"I swear it," I said solemnly.

"Thank God!" he cried, joyfully, falling back on the pillows in exhaustion. "Call them in — call *her!*"

I seized the bell-rope, and tugged it sharply, at the same time calling aloud. They rushed in, My Lady first; she sank on her knees, white and breathless, beside him, crying out to know what was the matter. Close after her came Burton, ever ready to believe the worst, and, seizing me, he attempted to drag me away from the Master, who still retained his grasp on my wrist. The old man felt the pull, and opened his eyes; in a moment his old spirit flared up.

"Hands off!" he cried. Burton sprang back, abjectly obedient to the last.

The Master looked at My Lady, and took her hand in his.

"It was all a mistake, dearest," he said faintly. "He is no enemy, after all. You were wiser than I. Make amends; pay my debt to him." And then, to me, "I am sorry. . . . Burton will explain. . . ." He put My Lady's hand in mine, and a great wave of delight swept over me as I touched it for the first time with her consent. There was no answering pressure when I grasped it; it lay in mine passively, not quite by her own volition, but at least not unwillingly. Curious thrills of emotion shook me from head to foot. "You will be good to Marjorie . . . you will take care of her."

Marjorie! It was thus I learned My Lady's name.

Her hand lay passively in mine, and I bent and kissed it. "All my life, if she will let me," I said reverently.

She may have heard my words, but she gave no sign.

He gave me one glance of gratitude, almost of affection, and turned his face to her, so that his last glance might be on her and for her; and so, without further sign or struggle, he fell asleep.

A DREAM

FOR many minutes not one of us made a sound or a motion. My Lady knelt by the bed, with one hand clasped in mine, and the other in the Master's, as though turned to stone; and I dared not move, for I feared to provoke some wild outbreak on her part, that might do her harm. I think she had forgotten who I was, but I believe the mere fact of a living hand helped her, through the strength of sympathy, and the knowledge that there was one close by who felt for her, and on whom she could depend.

At last the painful tension was broken by one of the negro women, her own maid, who stepped forward and gently tried to raise her. In this I assisted, and we led My Lady from the room. At another door, nearer the head of the stairs, the maid stopped, and looked at me significantly, and I knew this must be My Lady's own room. Before releasing her hand, which I had held ever since the Master had put it in mine,

I raised the hand and kissed it with great respect and affection. She looked at me dully, as though wondering how I came there; but the familiar look of doubt and distrust was gone — forever, I hoped — and I even found that her fingers showed a disposition to retain their clasp. She and Claudia stepped within, and the door closed.

Just at the instant I was at a loss to know what should be my next move. The Master's last words proved that I was no longer to be regarded as a prisoner or an enemy, at least not after I could have a full explanation with the mistress of the island; but how or when this could take place was left uncomfortably vague. Should I attempt to stay in the house, on the chance of being of some use to My Lady, I might have trouble with the servants, who did not know of the sudden change in the Master's mind regarding me. If I returned to my cabin, I voluntarily replaced myself in the position of a prisoner.

I was spared the necessity of deciding. A touch on my arm made me turn to face the man who had brought me fresh misfortune every time he had crossed my path. And though his face was as impassive as ever, the light that shone in his eyes was ominous of further trouble.

Whatever might have been his original reason for hating me, he had heard the Master's words of regret for what was past, and his request that I should "be good to Marjorie." He must have known that I was no enemy; yet he seemed to hate me more than ever.

"Go back to your hut," he commanded curtly, but in a low tone, so that My Lady should not hear.

"Why? You know now that you were mistaken about me."

"*He* may have been mistaken; I was not!"

"What do you mean?" I demanded, still in a whisper.

"He had one reason for fearing you; I had two!"

"And what was the second?" I asked with much curiosity.

He seemed to think he had said too much, for he hesitated.

"You will know in good time," he replied finally. "I am not obliged to enlighten you until I choose."

"So?" I asked incredulously, "and will My Lady's commands count for nothing?"

The mention of her made his wrath blaze up fiercely. He grasped my arm, and pushed me toward the head of the stairs.

"Do not dare to speak of her!" he exclaimed. "Go quickly, before I do you harm!"

It was the last place in the world that I would have chosen for an altercation, and the time and circumstances aggravated the unfitness of it. He was angry enough to forget these things, if provoked but a little more; and I went unresistingly, though every muscle of my body seemed overstrung, and aching for a struggle with him. His manner had always been insolent and irritating to the last degree, and had rolled up a mighty list of grievances against him in my mind, even without his cowardly attempts at assassination. Against the strict orders of the Master he had attempted my life again and again in ways that none but a perfectly diabolical imagination could have conceived, and that left no trace of his agency — not even a possibility of proving such a charge, though I knew perfectly well, and he knew that I knew, the truth of it.

Therefore, now that I was reinstated in the good opinion of the Master who lay dead within a few yards of us, and in that of My Lady, who would accept unhesitatingly any dictum that came from her father; and since I knew just as positively that Burton was thoroughly acquainted with all the facts of the case — even better than the Master, if the statements of both of them carried any weight — my rage boiled up in me so that I longed for a life-and-death struggle with mine adversary. I thought that a certain fear of My Lady's opinion restrained him from commencing such a struggle himself, though I was sure that nothing would have pleased him better than to provoke me to begin it — thus putting me in the wrong and enabling him to claim that he acted only in self-defence. So, for the sake of My Lady, and out of respect for the majesty of death, I curbed my growing irritation, and submitted to be led like a cowed prisoner out into the grounds and out of hearing of the house. Once there, he released his hold.

"Go to your kennel, you dog, and stay there!" he commanded, as though I had been one of the slaves; and as obediently as a slave I left him, only cursing inwardly the necessity that constrained me, and adding one more to the black marks that I had scored mentally against his account.

For three days, neither sign nor sound came to me from the house. The field negroes came and went as usual, though the great bell was never rung; I kept myself aloof from them, and asked no questions.   Every moment I expected to receive a summons from My Lady to come to the house and receive with her the promised explanation from Burton.   I knew that she was as ignorant of the true facts in the case as I was myself, and it never occurred to me that she might interrogate him without sending for me to hear the story.   I believed myself practically a free man; I knew that the Master, realizing and repenting his mistake, had acknowledged it, and commended My Lady to my care.   There was no longer any reason why My Lady should hate or despise me; and — and this brightened the whole horizon as I sat in front of my poor cabin that first night waiting for the dawn, for I could not sleep for thinking of these things — there was no longer any reason why we should not meet as equals; there was no reason — and here my heart leaped — why I should not woo and win her, despite her former prejudice against me.   So far as I knew I had no rival; my conduct had been such as must give her a good opinion of me, if she reviewed it calmly in the light of the later revelations.   And now the possibility of winning her first came actually within reach; now for the first time I dared to acknowledge to myself that I loved her.   And when I did finally own the fact to myself, I seemed to have known it for many weeks. With some surprise I recognized that it was already an old story.

For three days I waited for a sign from her, but no sign came. It was no time to intrude upon her grief while her father lay unburied. I spent most of my time as near to the house as I thought it possible without seeming to thrust myself upon her notice. I knew where the Master would be laid, in a pleasant grove a few hundred yards to the right of the great house. There had been laid the body of the Master's wife, with that of their son, who had died young. To that grove I had often seen the Master take his way, sometimes alone and sometimes in company with My Lady. These visits usually took place just after sunset; and thither, just after sunset of the third day, he made his last and final journey.

I had seen the grave dug, and knew when the Master was to be buried. I waited near the entrance of the grove until the coffin, borne by six of the slaves (for Burton and I were now the only white men on the island), had passed, and then stepped quietly into what seemed my proper place, just behind My Lady, who walked with Burton. If My Lady saw me she made no sign.

Burton read the beautiful service for the " Burial

of the Dead," and though the absence of expression in his voice detracted somewhat from the great solemnity of which it is capable, yet I am bound to say that he did it as well and as reverently as though he had been a regularly ordained minister. His voice was oppressively monotonous, yet at times it faltered, as if to prove that the man had affections, and that they were deeply stirred, although nature had denied him the ability to evince them as other men did. It was natural enough that he should be moved, for he was parting with a good friend and a good master, to whom he was blindly devoted; and he had other affections, too, as I was to learn in due course.

When the last words were said, we stood in silence for some minutes, each with his own thoughts of the Master, until My Lady moved and turned. I stepped aside; the servants opened their ranks to let her pass, and she took several steps away from the grave. I fully intended to do nothing to attract her attention to me in any way; but when I saw her stop and sway as though she were going to fall, I sprang forward instinctively to catch her if she should faint. I was quick, for love made me so; but hate, for this time at least, was quicker. Before I could reach My Lady I was seized from behind and thrown aside with great violence, so that I brought up against a tree with a shock that left me breathless, while my head rang with the force of the concussion.

It dazed me for a moment; but, when I realized what had happened, and looked up, I saw Burton standing between me and My Lady, with his fists clinched as though he would attack me again, and his eyes, the sole features of his countenance that could demonstrate his feelings, glaring defiance and hatred. Nay, more; they expressed the desire to *murder*, if ever eyes spoke.

The force of my blow against the tree had taken all the strength out of me. I was helpless as a child, and if Burton had attacked me further, I should have been powerless to resist. He seemed to have forgotten the place and the sacred service in which he had just taken part; he had become a hungry panther whose prey lies within his grasp. If he had forgotten even My Lady's presence, so also he had forgotten his pretended indifference to me, in his overwhelming passionate desire to kill; and he let the full force of his intense hatred be seen by all, though to My Lady it appeared but a sudden access of fury. She could not guess how long he had been nursing it in secret.

The occurrence had one good effect, for the excitement it caused her made My Lady forget her grief for the moment, and there was no further sign of weakness on her part. She straightened herself, and grasped Burton by the arm. I knew she was no weakling, but I should never have looked at this time for the strength with which she forced him to face her. He was an unusually powerful man, too, as I had the best of reasons for knowing. For a few moments their glances met and contended, until the uncanny fire in his waned and fell before the concentrated scorn and command in hers. She was the daughter of the Master — the Mistress now — and her look proved it. He closed his eyelids, as though blinded by her gaze. I was very glad that I was not the object of it.

"Are you mad?" said My Lady, in a low tone of intense displeasure.

His mouth opened, and the muscles of his throat moved as though he would have replied, but he answered never a word. For two or three minutes they stood thus, My Lady still grasping his arm. Upon my honor I pitied the man. If he had dared to meet her eyes, I believe he would have fallen to the ground; but he did not dare.

At last she dropped his arm.

"Go to the house," she said, "*and stay there !*"

The last words had a significance that touched him hard, and he showed it in his bearing as he moved slowly away. My Lady watched him, until he had passed out of the grove and was well on the way to the house, and then turned to me and spoke with lowered eyes.

" Mr. Darke, it seems to be the fate of our family to be always in the wrong where you are concerned. Though I do not yet know how it has come about, it seems that we have done you many wrongs; many things for which we have " — she spoke as though there were others, forgetting that she was the last of the family — "we have to crave your pardon; and not the least of them is this last unwarranted assault upon you by our servant. Perhaps our offences may be past forgiveness. I do not know. I cannot tell until I hear the whole of the story that now Burton alone can relate. When I find out the facts, it will be time to see what reparation may be possible; and I assure you that we will do all that is in our power to make amends for whatever mistake has been made. But this last attack is so unwarranted by any thought of ours, so utterly against our wishes, that I beg your forgiveness for our servant's conduct, and hope you will believe it is

entirely unlike anything we would have approved
—least of all at such a time and place as this!"
She remembered suddenly where she was, and
why she was there; she cast a sorrowful look
toward the open grave so close at hand.

Perhaps the recollection of the events of all the
past few months, and the realization of how they
must have appeared from my point of view, came
upon her in one great rush; for when she finished, and held out her hand timidly, as though
doubtful whether I would accept it, she raised
her eyes. And what I saw there almost made
me forget myself, and declare then and there my
feeling toward her. For her eyes were bright
with the sheen of tears that yet did not fall, and
they were dark with shame for her own part in
the treatment I had received the last few months.
And, still more, they showed as much fear as any
eyes could do. My Lady was afraid of me — of
me — who never, even at my darkest moment,
had harbored any feeling of resentment against
her, for I was aware that she did not know even
the cause of my captivity. As she had said, she
trusted blindly to the word of the Master, and he
had not informed her of his reasons for his arbitrary act. Doubtless he had intended she should
know at some time in the future; but when I

came to discover what those reasons were, I understood fully what a painful subject it must be to him, and how reluctant he must be to tell her a story of such shame, as long as it could be postponed. While he lived, he hoped; and the end came upon him so suddenly that there was no time for explanations.

I felt a mighty longing to tell her the truth about myself, yet I saw it would be neither fitting nor prudent just then; and it was much better that I did not since I was far from having an inkling of the real state of affairs. My story would have been true enough, as far as I knew it, but of the things that had been leading up to this matter for a quarter of a century I knew as little as she did herself. All along we had played at cross-purposes, though none of us were aware of it. But we both knew there would be ample time and opportunity to set matters right later on; and, just at present, if I spoke at all I could not stop until I had told her all I felt. So I took the timidly extended hand in both of mine, and held it for a moment so firmly and withal so tenderly that I think something of my heart must have passed to her through the pressure of our hands; for, when our eyes met again, it seemed that much of the shame and fear were gone from hers. If my wish could take effect, I knew it must be so.

Then, seeing that she was now entirely alone, I silently proffered her my arm, and, after a momentary hesitation, she laid her hand lightly within it, and we paced slowly back to the house. The negroes fell into line behind us, and I knew that they would never again look on me as a spy or an enemy. That touch of My Lady's hand had set me right in their eyes; how or why the change had come might be a mystery to them, but the fact was accomplished. From henceforward I was to be regarded as a gentleman and a friend, and I knew that I could count on their services and assistance in anything that did not seem directly to threaten My Lady's welfare.

It was only a few hundred yards to the house, and on our way there was not a sound save the noise of trampling feet; and even that seemed to be muffled, out of respect to the dead Master and the living Lady. From my previous experience I would not have believed that a crowd of negroes could march for even such a short distance without an outbreak of that garrulity — the universal passion for noise, of whatever sort — that possesses their class. Their conduct that evening raised my estimate of the human possibilities of the race, and at the same time magnified my already high opinion of the personal force of the Master. The man who could exert such influence three days after his death must have been a creature of unusual endowments.

As we approached the house, the negroes dropped out of line, one by one, and went to their own quarters. My senses that evening were attuned to an abnormal degree of perception; and, though I hardly noticed it at the time, my whole thought being devoted to My Lady, there was not the sound of a breaking twig, or the sight of a belated blackbird, that I could not recollect years afterward with a distinctness that was astounding. Yet, at the time, the only thought in my mind was of My Lady. The whole world, for me, contained but two figures — hers and mine; and if all the slaves had been swallowed up like Korah and his followers, I should not have noted it — should not have missed them. Those who have been fortunate enough to experience such supreme moments will understand; those who have not will have something to live for. And one is never too old, — Love does not count the years of those to whom he comes.

At the open door of the house, we paused, and the sweet dream in which I had been moving came to an end. My Lady removed her hand, and performed a sweeping courtesy, which I returned properly. It made me almost laugh aloud, to think of such civilities between a man in the soiled and tattered habiliments which covered me, and a woman sumptuously dressed like My Lady. For she made no pretence of a parade of mourning; there was no world of society surrounding her, to gauge the depth of her grief by the sombreness of the garb she wore. The thought of a mourning garment never entered her head. Instead of mourning she wore her richest garments; if she had been bidden to a feast of kings, she could not have done more to honor the occasion and the cause. He had loved to see her beautifully adorned; this last occasion demanded the most absolute submission to his lightest wishes. And I, who stood by her side, ragged, dirty, burnt by the semi-tropical sun, honored her for what to my mind was the highest mark of respect she could have shown.

My Lady moved to enter the house.

"I thank you, sir, for your kindness," she said, with a humbleness that was mightily becoming, but that irked me as coming from her, and somehow lowered my opinion of myself (which was fast becoming complacent).

"My Lady," I murmured, with a humility that was quite as heartfelt as her own (even if she did not know it then), "I beg you to believe that I am ever your true servant."

She blushed, and seemed slightly confused.

"You have my thanks again, sir," she said. "I will not disparage your generosity. To-night I feel hardly able to undergo any more painful scenes, and must therefore beg your patience until to-morrow. There is an explanation due to me, as well as to you, and we will have it then, if such is your pleasure. There is but one man who can furnish the clew to this coil, and he shall give it." Her lips closed firmly, and her brow contracted. I knew what was in her mind; that Burton might be reluctant to publish the facts in his possession, especially when they must necessarily work toward my rehabilitation in My Lady's good graces. By this time, I knew that she had already placed me in my proper sphere. That the Master had declared his approval of me was quite enough to work this change in her, without any knowledge of his reasons. She accepted his second judgment as blindly as she had done the first. But Burton's evident hatred of me might possibly prevent him from believing this, and he might think it possible to injure me in her sight by withholding the truth, or by telling a false tale.

However, I had great faith in My Lady's powers of persuasion and command; and I had no doubt that if these failed, she would use her utmost endeavors at compulsion. Either way I foresaw a bad quarter of an hour in store for Burton.

Looking back on it at this late day, it seems strange that it never struck either of us, until long afterward, that the altered relation between us would have more than justified her ordering accommodation to be prepared for me in the house. Instead, we parted at the door with much formality, and, while she entered the house, I took my way unconsciously, and as a matter of course, to my rough cabin in the grove half a mile away. In truth, I had other and more important matters to think of than a temporary lodging-place; and, in the now altered state of things, my cabin was endeared to me. Since I had been free to go when and where I would, the place was a home.

It was fast growing dark when I reached the cabin, but there was a glow of happiness in my mind that kept me from noticing the gloom without; and for hours I sat in the door, thinking over the past, and dreaming dreams too grand and too holy to be recorded even here. Almost unconsciously I had sought the little riding-whip, and disinterred it from its place of concealment, and sat with it in my hand, drawing it often through my fingers as though exchanging caresses with it. The little thing seemed to me to intensify the contrast between my present standing with My Lady and that at the time I had first made acquaintance with the whip. How long ago that was!

At last I roused myself and felt my way to my hard couch, and threw myself upon it without undressing. Even then I tossed restlessly for a long while, unable to free my mind of the thoughts that would come surging up like the breakers off Henlopen. But at length I fell into sleep; and then I dreamed strange dreams, that passed in a confused kaleidoscopic train, until finally they crystallized into one which I knew, even while asleep, would last long in my memory.

I dreamed that I was once more battling with the storm in the darkness, until I was cast violently ashore. As I crawled up the beach, the sun rose with a bound, and flooded the sand and the dunes with light; yet the place was cursed with an appalling loneliness. I was fearful of I knew not what, and sat there for an interminable time, not daring to stir, until the night fell once more, and I welcomed the darkness as a friendly shelter from the fear that devoured me. Then I rose and walked the beach for miles, until my knees bent for very weariness, and the soles of my boots were worn through by the grinding sand. At first I felt confident and hopeful in the shelter of the darkness ; but, as the time passed, and weary mile after mile was traversed, my earlier terror began to return, growing ever stronger and stronger, until I could hear, as well as feel, my heart beating swiftly and heavily under the excitement. I dragged foot after foot, wishing to stop, to turn, yet utterly powerless to resist the force that drove me forward to some unknown dreadful fate, until at length I entered a sort of tunnel formed of shining threads, that grew narrower at every step. Far ahead I could see a Thing — massive, powerful, horrible, though I could not discern its outline. I knew that it lay in wait for me — and I could not avoid it. Nearer and nearer I drew, until I could make out a part of it, and it grew into the form of a monstrous spider. And as I came nearer still, it threw out a coil that caught me round the chest and bound my arms to my sides. I struggled helplessly, but silently — for I seemed to know the uselessness of any outcry — while thread after thread was wound about me, until I lay bound hand and foot. The creature's eyes grew brighter, glittered more hatefully, as it approached me, until the glare of them became maddening ; and, as it neared me, the spider's head took on the likeness of a face that I knew. Even in my impotent writhings, it seemed of greater moment to recollect the owner of that face than to break the entangling cords. The glare of the eyes grew and grew, until I could feel the rays of heat issuing from them and scorching my face. I ceased the hopeless struggle, but gave one great cry of utter despair, and awoke.

AN AWAKENING

Struggling back to consciousness, I still felt the heat striking on my face, and, as I awoke, the glare from the eyes of the spider ceased abruptly, to be replaced by another quite as intolerable, which I finally made out to come from a torch held close to my face. Behind the torch I could make out a face staring into mine, and it was the face of the spider of my dreams. In sleep, I had not been able to recollect it; but waking, I saw the face of my enemy — the face of Burton.

Instinctively I knew that his presence there boded no good to me, and instantly I attempted to spring to my feet; for, though I knew his strength to be immensely greater than my own, there is an instinct deep in the nature of every man that compels even the weakest to fight for his life — or for his death — against whatever hopeless odds. But my endeavor ended quickly, when I found myself bound hand and foot to the couch with coils of rope that wound around me and it. They had not been drawn tightly enough to wake me, yet they were close enough and numerous enough to prevent my moving even a joint, except my head and neck, which were free. At once I realized the situation, and wondered why he had not gagged me as well.

I let my head fall back, and for some moments we gazed at one another without speaking. He gloated over the condition of his captive, and I glared back at him in a rage that left me no mind to think of the probable outcome of the business. Finally, seeing that I was not likely to speak first, he burst into one of his ghastly, expressionless laughs.

"What a come down from our late heroics!" he remarked tauntingly. "Knowing me as you did, did you really expect that you were going to depart in honor and favor? Fool! I did not underrate *your* ability, as you found when you attempted to escape; you should not have despised mine. You have had enough experience of me and my ways! Why, if I had been in your place, I should have barricaded my doors and windows, and sat watching all night; you would never have caught *me* asleep and helpless. You knew it was either your life or mine, and that the matter must be settled before to-morrow night — and yet you did not take the pains to guard yourself at this last moment, but let me bind you at my leisure. Such carelessness is astounding; it is hardly credible. But you will never have a chance to profit by the lesson!"

He chuckled fiendishly, and my heart stopped beating as I realized his meaning. He was right; knowing his hatred, I had been a stupendous fool. He meant to murder me, quietly and leisurely, and in some way that would leave no ground for suspecting him. And here I lay as helpless as I had been in the spider's net of my dream. There seemed to be something prophetic about that dream — or perhaps it was merely a sleep-distorted perception of what was actually occurring at that time.

I tried to keep my voice steady, as I asked, "You mean to murder me, then?"

He nodded affirmatively, although his answer was a negative — a mocking one.

"Oh, no; we won't use such an ugly word. I have a well-founded notion that you are going to disappear; that is all. An accident will happen at an opportune moment."

"Not the first of the kind, perhaps," I said slowly.

" No, not the first," he returned, as quietly as though he were speaking of the most ordinary event imaginable. " You know something about that. The occasion calls for a fresh sacrifice, and the call is going to be answered quickly."

" Why ? "

" Why ? " he shouted. " Because it is your life or mine ; because I hate you ! Because you love My Lady ; because My Lady—" He choked, and I saw a chance, slight though it was.

" And what will My Lady say to you when she learns this last deed of yours ? "

He glared fiercely at the mention of her.

" Do you think I do not know that she is out of my reach already ? " he cried. " Whether she suspects me or not, she will be no farther from me. I never had any hope ; I knew my own position too well."

A light was breaking on me ; his wild words told a story that I had never imagined before — a story of hopeless passion for a being infinitely above him in mind and station. Now I thought I held the secret of his hatred toward me ; he would have hated any white man who landed on the island, through fear that My Lady might come to care for the stranger. But to have been jealous of me, the despised spy, the distrusted enemy! Despite my situation, I laughed aloud at the idea.

"So you loved My Lady, and were jealous of my presence?" I remarked, still laughing. "You called me a fool, just now, but you have shown yourself a greater one! Could you not see that My Lady ranked me lower than the negroes? Even you stood higher in her opinion than I did. She took me for a criminal — a spy, an enemy of some sort — Heaven only knows what! You had no cause to be jealous of me, of all men."

"So *you* do not love her, then?" he queried, with a sneer.

"What has that to do with it?" I returned. "Yes, I do love her; I do not see how any man, high or low, could help doing the same. So I can understand your feeling, and have a sort of sympathy for a fellow-sufferer. But certainly she has never dreamed of such a thing; and, if she had, it could have made no difference to her. I have had as little hope as you yourself, my friend, as you must have known very well."

It was true, yet not the whole truth. As I said, I *had had* as little hope as himself; but the events attending the Master's death had altered all that, and now the whole situation was vastly different. No insuperable obstacle blocked my path any longer.

Burton saw the distinction as clearly as I did myself. However mad he might be, he was no dullard.

"But now?" he asked cunningly. "Would you have no hope *now* if I should let you go?"

I was silent for a moment while he scanned my face, and, doubtless, read its expression easily.

"Yes, I should hope," I answered slowly, "but I have no reason to believe that my chance would be any better than any other man's." Of course I meant a man of her station and mine; I put him out of the question, and he knew it.

"So!" he said very quietly. "Well, whatever you may have hoped, you may as well give up the thought. You and she will never meet again — on earth, at least. I know I cannot have her myself, but no other man shall! You are the first that has come, and I intend to remove you. Perhaps it may comfort you to know that as long as I live no other man shall fare better than you."

"You surely don't expect to murder every man who looks at My Lady with admiration?" I asked, amazed.

"Why not?" he returned coolly. "Not many

P

are likely to come here; those that do shall 'disappear' in one way or another. Nor shall she leave the island, if my ingenuity can prevent it. You can guess whether my cunning will be sufficient for the purpose. You have encountered it several times."

"Yet in one way or another I escaped at least five times when you counted me as surely dead," I said. "You may be as unsuccessful another time."

"But the last time will not fail," he returned, with assurance.

I took time to think. If I should cry out for help he could easily strangle me, or beat out my brains before I could utter a second sound, and long before help could arrive, even though my cry should be heard, of which there was hardly a bare chance. The negro quarters were nearly half a mile distant; even in the stillness of the night it was hardly possible for any cry to reach them, much less to awaken any of the sleepers. If one of them should come, it was almost certain that Burton would order him back again, and that he would obey. They were friendly enough to me, but he was their overseer. My Lady might hear of it afterward, but it would be too late to be of help to me.

"What are you going to do with me?" I asked, seeking to gain time.

"Put you out of the way, as I said."

"How?"

He laughed cunningly. "I'll tell you that after a while. There is no hurry. It is barely midnight, and a single hour will give me plenty of time to do my work."

His reticence did not tend to lessen the feeling of panic that I felt creeping over me. I was so helpless, and so far from help, lying there corded from head to foot! But I forced the feeling away for the time; if I lost my head I was as good as dead, for he might take it into his head at any moment to make an end of me without delay, and every moment of time gained gave an additional chance, though the hope was but a forlorn one. I could not imagine from what quarter help could possibly come, and, indeed, expected none; but still I hoped. If I could keep him talking for a while, something — anything — might occur. I had everything to gain and nothing to lose by delay.

"Why did you not kill me as I lay asleep?" I asked.

"Oh, I am no common murderer," he answered, as demurely as an innocent girl. "If such work is forced on me, I like to get all the pleasure I can out of it. I have thought of this moment for hours at a time, and have changed one scheme for another over and over again, until I have every detail planned, and a resource prepared for every possible contingency. Floods and earthquakes could not interfere with my intention this night! Merely to put you out of the way would have afforded me only a moment's gratification; as it is, I expect to get several hours' entertainment out of you before the final performance. I have a story to tell that may interest you; it ought to interest you intensely. I think the telling of it will be as dramatic to both of us as the best play that ever was written. You see, I can talk frankly to you, for you are as good as dead, as far as repeating it is concerned; so I can tell all the truth of it for once. I have carried the thing with me for nearly thirty years, and I have often longed for a confidant on whom I could rely. If I could have told it before, I believe I could have forgotten the thing long ago. But I have had to conceal it, and that has made me uncomfortable. There — "

"But, if you murder me, what will become of you then? You will have to conceal that secret, too," I interrupted.

"Not at all," he returned. "I shall merely tell it to the next one who finds himself in your situation. I am very sure there will be others, for not even my skill can keep an occasional visitor from stumbling on this place. But, as I was going to say : there is no better confidant than a dying man," he chuckled, gloating over his victim. "There is no danger that *you* will tell any tales, even by accident."

His cool bearing and his intense glare made me suspect that his story, whatever it was, had crazed him, and that I had to do with a maniac, or a man who was on the verge of becoming one. If I could but wile him to give me respite. I could not realize death. The blood coursed strongly through my veins; I was as well and strong as I had ever been in my life, and a new vision of possible happiness had burst upon my view but a few hours before. To give up that at his bidding, to regard myself as one who was already done with the things of this world, was impossible, and I simply *could not* resign myself to my apparent fate.

Burton lit a fresh torch, of which he had a number, and stuck it in a cleft among the logs and lay back in his seat, while he picked up from the floor a heavy club of oak (such as no doubt he had used times out of mind to cow rebellious slaves) and shook it over me.

"I feel like talking to-night," he said, as coolly as though a human life was not concerned. "If you are disposed to listen to me quietly, very good; you will have so many minutes more to live, though I warn you it will not make the least difference in your ultimate fate. Of course you know there is no chance of any hearer being about; but, if you commence to make a noise, I shall quietly hammer in your head with this, and finish my work at my leisure."

He shook the club menacingly, and I could not help shrinking from the motion, whereat he laughed again.

"If you like the prospect, very good," he went on. "If you choose, you can listen to my story — or my confession, if you prefer to call it so — and thus prolong your life until I have finished."

Life is sweet, even for a brief respite. There was small choice, and I told him so. More and more, he convinced me of his madness. I must humor his fancy.

Perhaps you are brave in the ordinary acceptation of the term; perhaps you are a coward. I thought I had as little fear of death as the average man; in fact, I knew it, for I had found it necessary to face it more than once, and had not found my courage wanting. But it is one thing to face death in fighting, where the excitement of the struggle keeps one from realizing the possibilities, or at least makes him sure that if he does fall, he falls gloriously, and with a chance of revenging himself. Even to die a captive, in the face of the enemy, has its compensations, for there are others present whose presence may fortify him, and who will testify to the victim's courage. I believe, now, that more than half the courage in this world is born of fear — of the fear that others may cast an imputation of cowardice, of which every man is horribly afraid. I wonder how many men have gone into battle and acquitted themselves gloriously, who were upheld only by the thought of what somebody might say if they shirked? I think that such courage — the courage that is afraid to shirk — is far greater than that of the man who " has never known fear." *He* is brave through ignorance; the other, through knowledge, which is always superior to ignorance; through moral courage or moral fear — whichever you please, only he is the greater and the braver.

For myself, I must own that at this moment I was an abject coward; and if you wonder at my state of mind, you have only to wait until you are helpless, with some one else ready at the word to beat out your brains, and then compare your feelings with mine.

"I shall be glad to hear your story," I answered as easily as I might. "Perhaps it will clear up, this thick cloud of mystery that has surrounded me ever since I was cast up on your island."

"*A la bonne heure*," he responded less fiercely; and I stared to hear a man of his station, and at such a time and place, using a French expression as though brought up to it.

<h1 style="text-align:center">XIII</h1>

THE story which Burton told that fearful night became graved upon my memory to the least incident. I may have failed in the lapse of years to remember his exact words, but not one fact of the strange tale has escaped my memory. Engrossed in the story, I was able for the most part to forget my dreary situation — to think only of what he was setting forth so carefully. He seemed to relish the narrative, too, and to dwell lovingly on all the details of his early life, as if he were painting for my benefit the picture of a familiar scene, which for thirty years had burnt itself into his imagination. From time to time he interrupted himself to light a fresh torch, or to gloat over me. But for the most part, his tale ran on steadily, swiftly, to its strange end.

"I was born in Sussex County, Virginia [he began]. No doubt you know that Sussex is not a rich or a very fertile country, and my parents were of the poorest among the few people who lived there by choice or necessity. Consequently, when my mother died — I was hardly more than ten years old at the time — it was decided by the parish that I should be bound to service for a term of years to whoever should make the best offer for me. Unfortunately for me, unlike the man you know, I was so small and so weak in appearance that most of those who saw me declined to have anything to do with me, probably thinking it would be many a day before my labor would pay for even my food and clothing. Only one man offered to take me; and though my guardians quickly took the offer, when I saw my new master I would have escaped even into the wilderness, if it had been possible. If ever a man's face was that of a brute, his was. His tight-shut lips, and his square heavy jaw, over which his cheeks hung down in great folds, spoke of avarice and cruelty. Those who had me in charge must have known the fellow's character, but they were anxious to get me off their hands, and cared little whether I should have my brains beaten out, or be starved, in my new home.

"He took me with him when he returned to his plantation on the northern edge of the county. I had thought myself miserable enough in our poor home, but that man showed me worse things. Constantly half-starved, I was kept at work that was too heavy for even a strong boy — and I was far from being strong, *then*. When he had a mind to he beat me unmercifully. If it had not been that I was knowing for my age and could live on the plants and roots that grew in the woods, I should have been dead the first month.

"I spent two awful years in this way. Weak as I appeared, — I was only a bag of bones, — there must have been tough fibre in my puny body, otherwise I should never have got the strength you have felt. I owe that to my deliverer, and I have never forgotten the debt — except once.

"One day my weakness made me fail in some task that my owner had set me. As usual, I expected a fearful punishment, and it came; he beat me, not like a dog, but worse than a dog. My screams and his efforts prevented his hearing the approach of a horseman, who had heard my outcry as he passed by on the main road, a quarter of a mile away. He gave a great shout as he approached.

"'Stop, you brute!' he cried.

"My owner, as he considered himself, stopped, though more from surprise than anything else.

He was burly and powerful, and the newcomer, though well-built and no weakling, was slighter than himself.   He stopped for a moment, and then, without appearing to notice the stranger further, struck me again.   The stranger leaped from his horse, and faced my brute.

"'I said stop!' he cried.   'Do you want to kill the boy?'

"'What is that to you?' snarled my owner. 'Go about your business, or I may serve you the same, little man!'

"'Me?'   The young man (he was not over twenty) laughed at him, and then frowned.   'Let that boy go! You have beaten him more than enough, no matter what his fault was.'

"'Go away, I tell you,' growled my owner. And they had it back and forth until, the next I knew, the stranger sprang forward, and struck a beautiful blow.   The brute went down, with a discolored spot on his cheek that began to drip blood.

"For a moment he lay on the ground, glaring at his assailant, who stood with clinched fists waiting for him to rise.   But, as he fell, it chanced that his hand touched a slim stick of cord-wood, and, when he scrambled to his feet, the club was in his hand.   He turned to me, lying where I had fallen when he released me.

"'You first!' he howled, savagely aiming a stout blow at me.

"If he had struck me as he intended, you would have had nothing to fear from me. His stick struck me a glancing blow on the side of the head, that was not enough to stun me completely, yet left me unable to move, though perfectly able to see and understand what followed. I may as well mention here that that blow paralyzed nearly all the muscles of my face and certain of the vocal muscles (I am not learned enough to know which ones), so that since that time I have been utterly unable to express feeling of any kind by my face or voice.

"When I opened my eyes, the stranger still faced his opponent, but his hand held a pistol thrust into the face of the other.

"'Drop that club!' he commanded sharply. 'Drop it,' instantly, or I will kill you where you stand, murderer!'

"The man started at the word, and glanced toward where I lay.

"'Move back five paces!'

"He obeyed mechanically. The pistol was a powerful argument.

"'Stand there!' the young man shouted. 'If you take a step forward or backward, I shall shoot you like a rabbit. And I warn you that I can hit a button on your coat at five times the distance.'

"'I understand,' my master grunted in surly fashion. 'The boy's not hurt much, anyhow.'

"The victor then turned to me, while he still was watchful of his prisoner. As he came close to me, I managed to move. He raised my head.

"'How do you feel?' he asked, in the first kindly tone I had heard for months. He felt my head. The blow had not broken the skin, but it had raised an enormous lump, and I winced and cried out when he touched it.

"He pushed and prodded vigorously but kindly, and though I could not help squirming, I managed to keep quiet except for an occasional gasp, and a final sigh of relief when he had got through with me.

"'Bone not broken, I think,' he remarked, 'though we will see further about that. Now, my lad, sit there, and you will see something to do your heart good.' He propped me up against a neighboring post, and, after putting his pistol back in his pocket, approached my owner.

"'Is the boy yours?' he asked.

"'Yes.'

"'Your son?'

"'No.'

"'What then?'

"'Bound boy,' growled the fellow.

"'Ah! What will you take for him?'

"The man's eyes gleamed covetously, but he shook his head. 'I don't want to sell him — he's too useful,' he answered.

"My protector wheeled around and looked at my puny frame, and then laughed, though with a dark frown on his face. 'Yes, he surely looks very useful, and if I had not interfered your course of treatment was likely to make him invaluable! You need make no pretence to me. How much will you take for him?'

"My owner shook his head obstinately, and my hopes, which had been exalted to the highest pitch by the preceding conversation, began to fall, for I knew the man's strength (and physical strength was the only thing that he had taught me to appreciate), while that of the stranger was unknown to me. At best he appeared too slight to win in case of a struggle.

"Well, they had more words on the matter, but at last my owner gave way.

"'Ten guineas,' he said, evidently thinking the price higher than the other would be willing to pay; but the stranger did not hesitate. He drew a handful of gold from his pocket, at the sight of which my owner's eyes grew greedy enough. The other continued to search in his pockets for something. 'Can you write?' he asked briskly, drawing out an old letter. After scribbling a few words on the back, he handed it to the owner, with the gold pieces demanded.

"'Sign the receipt!' he ordered. My owner hesitated for a moment, but perhaps the pistol influenced him — perhaps the clink of the gold pieces. He signed, and the stranger put the paper into his pocket.

"'Much good may the good-for-nothing young hound do you!' the old villain exclaimed.

"'That settles my own account with you,' the young man answered. Then I remember how a twinkle of amusement seemed to come into his eyes, as he said: 'Well, now, I must pay the boy's debts, I suppose. And he evidently owes you for a sound thrashing you were giving him as I came up.'"

Burton laughed with quiet enjoyment, as if the scene had taken place only yesterday. Then he resumed: "The bully took another step backward. 'I don't want to fight,' he growled. 'You've bought the boy; take him away!'

"'What, without paying his debt to you?' my new master asked. 'Oh, no; we don't do things that way; we rob no one. The debt must be paid, and if you are not satisfied when I am done with you, you shall have a little more for interest. You didn't quite kill him, so I will not quite kill you; but I will try to balance the account as nearly as I can.'

"'I won't fight,' repeated the man, turning to move away. Two steps, and then —

"'If you move another step farther, I shall fire,' said the stranger, sternly. 'I intend to give you a thorough trouncing as a quittance; but I give you an advantage that was denied to the boy. You may defend yourself, and I promise you that I will not use a weapon as long as you fight fairly.'

"He was approaching the other man as he spoke, and, as he came within reach, his arm went out, and he struck the farmer a resounding smack on the cheek with his open palm.

"'There is something to warm your coward blood!' he said.

"The coward was roused at last, since there was no escape.

"'Damn you, you insolent puppy!' he cried, as he sprang at his assailant. 'I'll kill you and the brat both!'

"You can imagine with how much interest I watched the fight. I had suffered so much and so long from the brutality of my late master, and had seen so many evidences of his strength, that I could hardly believe it possible for any one to overcome him. I felt sure that if my new owner should be conquered, the stronger man would drive him away and keep me, and in that case I knew how much more I should suffer for the stranger's attempt at interference. I might have taken heart from the knowledge that my cham-pion was armed, only I had heard his promise not to use his weapon, and the ring of truth in his voice convinced me that he would keep his word, no matter at what cost to himself or me. There have not been many men whom I have met, whose word I would have taken in such a matter, when the issue was going against them.

"But even to me, cowed as I was, the issue, after the first few moments, was not in the least doubtful. The elder man had the advantage of his heavier weight and a longer reach, but the younger was wonderfully quick in his movements, and used his hands in a way that proved he had had good training. The long struggle showed me that even a bully and a coward may fight to the death when it comes to the final contest. The man must have seen how little chance he had, yet he fought desperately; time and again he was down, and time and again he arose, half-blinded and half-stunned. Nor did my purchaser come off free; despite his activity and skill, he suffered more than one hard knock that left its mark for many a day afterward. But at last a harder or a better planted blow than usual stretched the bigger man on the ground, insensible.

"The stranger gazed at him for a moment, waiting for him to rise, and then came to where I sat, and leaned against the post, breathing heavily, while he pulled a handkerchief from his pocket and began wiping the blood from his face wherever he could feel it running. 'Can you get me some water, boy?' he panted.

"Throughout the struggle I had sat motionless, in a passionate desire to see my new friend victorious. Now I scrambled weakly and clumsily to my feet, and hurried to the well, staggering back with a bucket half full of water. He drank, and then dipped his handkerchief in the water and approached his helpless enemy. Raising his head, he cleaned the face of the insensible man, who soon began to show signs of consciousness. The man was not dangerously hurt, and that was all he cared to know. After he had cleaned his own face, he remarked,—

"'Well, lad, are you willing to go with me, or would you rather stay here?'

"It was a useless question, and he knew it. I seized his hand and clung to it in a way that must have convinced him without words.

"'All right! We must be in a hurry; come.'

"His horse had stood like a statue during all this time; now he took me up behind him, and, after a farewell glance at the still prostrate man, we rode rapidly away. I have never seen either the place or the man since that day. If I had ever met the man, after I was grown, I should have killed him; after what he had done to me, no one would have blamed me for it.

"At the first available place my new master had my bruises and his own wounds patched up, and provided me with clothes of fair quality, suitable to the station in life that he expected me to take. He also bought a horse on which I could ride beside him. My new peculiarities of face and voice did not strike him as strange, at first, since he had never known me before. When he found that they dated from the day of my rescue, he had me examined by the most skilful physicians and surgeons; but not one of them could assist me, or even offer any hope of cure. They could not even account for such an effect following a blow on the head, though there was no doubt that the blow had caused it. They said that any blow hard enough to have paralyzed me in that way ought to have killed me on the spot.

" My rescuer was on his way to his home, a hundred miles distant. In the course of the journey he explained his intentions regarding me. Young as I was, my past hardships had aged me mentally much more than one would have supposed; my companion perceived this, and flattered me by talking to me as though I had been nearly his equal in age and intelligence. The overwhelming gratitude and admiration I felt toward him developed during those few days into a perfect adoration that never but once failed to prompt me to work for his advantage.

" It was his intention, he said, to make me a sort of confidential body-servant, if I was willing to accept the place. When I came to legal age, I could feel at liberty to remain with him or to seek my fortune in the world at large, as I should elect. Would I accept? I should not have objected if he had chosen to make me a field-hand among the negro slaves! He had bought my life with both money and blood, and it was at his disposal."

"What was his name?" I asked curiously.

"It is too soon to mention names," Burton replied, with a cunning smile. "You will see the reason for this later on."

He rose to light a fresh torch to replace the one that had burnt low. Then he paced back and forth near my couch, his hands nervously twisted behind his back. Evidently these early scenes when he first met the Master (as I could not doubt the gallant rescuer would prove to be) moved him deeply. No wonder he had had a doglike fidelity toward the Master.

A DARK DEED

" The plantation was owned by a gentleman whom I will call Colonel X. He had a nephew (my new master) named Edward, who was the son of his only sister, dead many years before, and two sons, Harold and Allan."

" Allan! " I interrupted hastily.

" Yes, Allan," returned Burton, quietly. " Why not ? — Oh, I see ; you are thinking of your own name. But you are not the only man in the world, or even in Virginia, who bears that name."

" No, I know that well enough, only the name struck me," I replied. " Go on ; your story grows in interest."

" It will be more so presently," responded Burton, grimly. " But the story will come to an end soon enough, and when it does, you will end too. I am in no hurry, however, even if you are. I am enjoying myself more delightfully than I have done for years."

" I had almost forgotten my state," I answered

ruefully. "Why need you have reminded me of it?"

He favored me with a critical but approving glance. "It seems almost a pity to kill a man with so much appreciation," he remarked. "But I am not to be flattered into changing my mind.

"They had all grown up together, and though Harold, as elder son, was expected to inherit the lion's share of the estate, and even at that time was practically master, still it had always been understood that Allan and his cousin were to share equally in the remainder. Even this remainder was quite large enough to give each of them a fair estate, if managed rightly; and I must do Allan the justice to say that he never showed the slightest jealousy of his cousin. He and Mr. Edward were like brothers, though not very affectionate or congenial; whereas Harold stood aloof from both of them. He had a disagreeable, overbearing way about his every movement that made him a host of enemies on all sides. Allan had a trace of the same disposition, which prevented his being the general favorite that his cousin was; still he managed to make and keep a goodly number of friends. Harold was envious of both of them, — of their manners, and of their popularity, but especially of Mr. Edward; and he lost no chance of making him feel that he considered him an interloper in the family. If it had not been for Mr. Edward's pleasant disposition, and his desire to avoid giving or taking offence, there might have been grave trouble between them long before the final break came. Doubtless Harold would have been glad to have a quarrel, especially if he could have managed to make his cousin appear the aggressor, as he plainly tried to do. His quarrelsomeness was evident to all, except to Colonel X, from whom all the younger men endeavored successfully to keep all knowledge that there was any trouble among them. Many a time my blood boiled at Harold's treatment of my kind protector, until I was ready, child as I was, to fly at his throat and tear him like a beast. Neither my patience nor my temper is very long-suffering, as you know, and the only thing that kept me back was the certainty that the least sign of rebellion on my part would make trouble for him.

"I had my own causes of complaint, too; for, being blindly attached to Mr. Edward, and constantly about him, I came in for a full share of Harold's hatred. He never addressed me except with a frowning face and harsh words that made my blood flow fast, and even blows were not lacking when Mr. Edward was not present. These I endured in silence for the sake of my patron, knowing that he would have taken my part, regardless of the consequences, if I had mentioned the matter to him. So I said nothing; but I treasured every word and every blow in my heart, until in the course of years they grew to a goodly grievance, and Harold had his reward.

"If it had not been for the affliction that makes me incapable of showing my feelings in the usual way, he could not have failed to read my thoughts on my face; and yet this very affliction made him jeer at me. Allan, too, who had some of the jeering manner of his brother, often tormented me in the same way, though his words never carried the sting of Harold's. Looking back now, I do not think he really meant to be cruel, or realized how terribly he hurt me. But, naturally, I was sensitive on the subject, and though Allan never raised his hand against me, and in all other respects treated me well, his frequent irritation of my sore point soon made me hate him almost as much as I did his brother.

"One great boon that I enjoyed was that of education. Mr. Edward had me instructed by the same masters that taught the country youth; he even went farther, and had me given special lessons by some of the tutors who were engaged to teach the sons of the neighboring gentry. He sometimes condescended also to teach me himself, though more through general conversation than in any set course of study. It seemed as if he could not do enough to make up to me for the advantages I had lacked in my earlier childhood, though that lack was in no way connected with him or his. I was by nature quick at learning and made rapid progress, so that Mr. Edward came to take pride in my accomplishments, and was always ready to give them a fresh spur. If my manner of speech surprises you, as being above the general style of a man of my class, this is the cause of the difference. I have been well educated and have associated with gentle folk. My infirmity cut me off, to a certain extent, from free companionship with other people, and caused me to prefer solitude and the companionship of books during my leisure time. They, at least, never cast my weakness in my face. Of all the people I met while living on that plantation, there was only one who always spoke to me in terms of sympathy. You can guess who that one was; and, sensitive as I was to any mention of my affliction, his few words were so chosen that they drew my heart closer to him.

"Some six years passed in this way. To the end,

I was treated no better and no worse than at the beginning.

"But I learned in those years more lessons than books could teach: I learned to know men and to hate those that had made me suffer. That lesson I have never forgotten.

"At the end of six years Colonel X died. As I said, it had been understood that Mr. Edward and Allan were to share alike, and Allan never said or did anything to show that he objected to the arrangement, nor did Harold. It was to the amazement of all that, when Colonel X's will was read, it was found to leave everything to Harold, 'trusting,' so it ran, with what seemed a sort of grim sarcasm, 'that his generosity will lead him to do even more substantial justice to his brother Allan and his cousin Edward, than I have felt at liberty to do. Hitherto they have lived in brotherly affection, and as a united family; let them continue so to live.' Little the old man knew of the real feelings that existed in place of the 'brotherly affection' he depended on!

"Harold soon showed openly the disposition that had been evident to every one except his father. He called the others to him and announced that for the present things must stand as they were. Allan should have the use of the old home as heretofore, and a moderate allowance for his personal expenses; the rest should depend on the future. As to what that future might be Harold was vague enough in his words. As for Mr. Edward, he, too, should have the use of the house, but without an allowance; and Harold pointedly remarked that Edward had better seek some kind of employment as soon as possible. There was no chance to mistake the meaning of his words or his manner.

"A few days later, Harold met me coming from the house one afternoon. Perhaps he had forgotten my presence in the household before; perhaps he was merely waiting for a suitable opportunity and excuse for what he had in mind. At any rate, when he met me, he drew his horse across the path in such a manner that I could not pass him.

"'What the devil are you doing here?' he demanded roughly.

"'Why, Mr. Harold, I am Mr. Edward's body-servant,' I answered, in surprise.

"'Mr. Edward's body-servant!' he echoed. 'Mr. Edward is little better than a servant himself, now, and he can keep no hangers-on about my place.'

"'I have been his servant for years, sir,' I answered.

"'There are no servants here except mine,' he retorted, frowning; 'and you are not one of them. Be off!'

"'I don't understand you, sir,' I replied, bewildered. 'Where should I go?'

"'I don't care a brass farthing where you go,' he returned. 'To the devil, if you choose; that is not my business. But it is my business to see that the plantation is kept clear of useless trash like you. Understand, I will not have you about here.'

"'But I am Mr. Edward's servant,' I repeated obstinately, 'and I must see him first.'

"'You will go now!' he said savagely. 'Go at once, or I shall set the dogs on you!'

"'I must see Mr. Edward first, sir,' I said firmly.

"He uttered an oath, as he spurred his horse toward me, and slashed at me savagely with the whip he carried. It was a heavy one, fit only for such a brute as he; the sharp thong caught me on the cheek, and cut deeply — you can see the scar even now, for it never properly closed up. The pain and the shock made me throw up my hands; as I did so he clubbed the whip and struck me with the butt. As I reeled, dazed, though not quite stunned, by the blow, he leaped

from his horse and seized me by the collar.
And then he beat me savagely, as he would never
have thought of punishing a slave; in my dazed
condition, I could struggle but little against him,
and he whipped me to his heart's content. Then,
when I was exhausted, he pulled me toward
where the horse stood, and mounted the animal,
still holding my collar. Writhing and half-choked,
I was dragged down the long lane to the entrance
gate of the plantation, and cast out into the middle
of the highroad.

"'There!' the brute bellowed, 'if I ever find
you on my land again, I will set the dogs on you!'
and he turned and rode back to the house.

"Set the dogs on *me!* If he had attempted
that, it would have been strange if I could not
have turned them against *him.* They knew and
loved me: him they knew only through blows.
I had no fear of the dogs.

"Mr. Edward was somewhere about the country, I knew; I waited for him there, at the gates,
nursing my bruises and my wrath, and it would
be hard to tell which tortured me the worst. I
know that, the longer I waited, the deeper grew
my anger and indignation at my treatment. If
I had committed a fault, or if Mr. Edward (whom
I felt to be my master, body and soul) had beaten

me, even without cause, I should not have complained. But such treatment, without cause, from a man who had neither lawful nor moral authority over me, was the last injury in a long story of petty persecution. I nursed my wrath, and so gradually a desire for vengeance shaped itself into a settled and determined plan.

"Mr. Edward came at last. I stopped him, and told my tale; to prove to him that I did not exaggerate I pulled off my shirt and showed him the marks that stood out, blue and purple, all over my body. As he listened and looked, his face grew dark and stern.

"'Wait for me here,' he ordered, as he swung himself on his horse and rode rapidly up the avenue to the house.

"In almost an hour, as the twilight was coming on, he returned, his face stern and set as before. Attached to his saddle were a pair of well-filled bags, and he carried another pair in his hands and also two guns. A second horse, ready saddled, was led by a line tied to his arm. Such horsemen as we were brought up to be in that part of the country needed no reins to control their mounts. You should know something about that, eh?

"'It is all over, Burton,' he remarked quietly,

as he stopped beside me. 'I have had a last row with my cousin, and he has turned me out of the house on half an hour's notice. I suppose he is within his *legal* rights, but it seems hard! For a wonder, he did not claim my horses, nor my clothes, nor arms; I ought to thank him for his forbearance, I suppose,' and he laughed bitterly. 'Allan was good enough to offer to lend me money to carry me along for a little while; enough, with what little I had on hand, to last for a couple of months. Who knows what may happen before then? I suppose you don't care to stay here any longer?'

"'Here, sir?' I cried. 'I could not, even if I were willing to leave you. Mr. Harold would kill me, I believe.'

"He nodded. 'I shouldn't wonder — unless you killed him first; we just escaped having a struggle as it was. He was ready to fly like a madman at me, and I was angry enough to make me welcome an attack. Only Allan prevented it. No doubt it is better as it is,' he went on, thoughtfully. 'We are fairly well matched, and probably one of us would have met his death. . . . Well, you and I are both out in the cold, boy; will you go with me? I cannot promise you wages, at present; I have barely enough to get us

food. I am going out into the world to wrestle
·with Fortune,' he laughed. 'If she throws me,
you can feel quite at liberty to leave me and
struggle with her on your own account; if I
succeed, you shall share the benefit. Or, if you
like, you may take part of what I have, and go
where you please.'

"I took his hand and kissed it. 'Mr. Edward,'
I said brokenly, 'all this has come to you through
me! If I had thought of such a thing, I would
have gone away into the woods and died there,
rather than bring trouble to you.'

"'Tut, tut, my boy,' he answered, smiling.
'You know very well that the trouble was bound
to come sooner or later, in any case. I have seen
it brewing this long time. Your affair with my
cousin Harold has only brought it to a head a
little sooner, that is all. Put that other idea out
of your mind. The only question before us now
is whether you prefer to follow my fortunes or
seek your own. I should not be surprised if your
chances were very much better by yourself, for I
have not the slightest idea what is going to become of me, or which way I ought to turn.' He
continued in this strain some time, trying to make
me choose what would be best for myself.

"'You bought me and my life six years ago;

both are still yours,' I exclaimed, interrupting him. And, after a few more words on his part, in which he made light of the claim he had on my devotion, I settled the question thus, —

"'Up or down, I go with you,' I reiterated.

"'Very good; that settles it!' And, giving me a horse and one of the guns which was loaded, he mounted and took the Williamsburg road.

"I followed him. As we rode away, I could not help casting a backward glance at the house we were leaving. In spite of the persecution and ill treatment I had received, it had been my home for six years, — the happiest years of my life up to that time, and perhaps in all my life, — and I could not help regretting the cruel necessity that drove us from it. My master must have had even more of the same feeling, but he concealed it by chatting gayly as we rode, pretending not to notice my silence and gloom. It was nearly dark, and as I looked back I saw lights appear in various rooms, and the cheerfulness of the aspect was not calculated to raise the spirits of the two people who were being driven away from it. One light in particular I recognized with mixed feelings, for it burned in the library, a great room at the end of one wing of the house, practically isolated from the other rooms; and I knew that

Harold was sitting there, and would probably sit there for the rest of the evening. That room had been in my mind for some time; but now my half-formed plan was shattered by this expulsion of Mr. Edward, and his invitation to me to accompany him. The two things were incompatible. Either I must leave him, or else abandon my scheme for revenge. For me there could be no choice. I went with Mr. Edward as a matter of course, yet it was hard to give up the thought of the vengeance that had been the only thing to ease the smart of my bruises. When we lost sight of the house the bruises began to smart anew, and I felt that, long after they were healed, the recollection of them would be quite as painful as the things themselves had been. Did you ever have to give up a satisfactory plan of revenge that lay absolutely within your grasp? Then you know what I went through — for a time.

"Some miles from the plantation Mr. Edward drew rein.

"'I want to see a friend and bid him good-by, before I leave,' he said. 'Wait for me here in this clump of trees. I shall be gone for more than an hour; perhaps two hours. Here is something that may help to comfort your loneliness,' and, laughing, he handed me a flask of Hollands. 'Don't let yourself or the horses be seen, if you can avoid it. While neither of us has anything to be ashamed of in this matter, I don't care to have to explain the circumstances to all the world — especially to-night! I should have to apologize for my present position, — or lack of position, — though my conscience acquits me of any wrong.'

"'I think I understand you, sir,' I said. 'I will keep out of sight, and you need not hurry on my account.'

"He strode away, while I tethered the horses back in the grove, well out of sight and hearing of any passers-by. Not that there was very much likelihood of their being discovered. The plantations in that neighborhood were large, the houses far apart ; at that particular time of night people were usually within doors — either their own or their neighbors' — and chance travellers were few. Still, I neglected no precaution for secrecy ; and, as I did so, a sudden idea shot through my brain rapidly enough to stun me. It left me weak and trembling. I pulled out the flask, and took a great drink of the Hollands. In a few minutes the fiery stuff set my heart beating like a hammer, and my spirits rose, until my will was set upon one idea. I was a boy of eighteen, but I felt myself

a man in experience, and able to do a man's deeds.
I was excited, yet I was cool enough to make a
rapid calculation, and then I acted with a coolness
and promptness that would have done credit to a
man thrice my age.

"The horse Mr. Edward had given me was
almost as good as his own. We were less than
half an hour's rapid ride from our old plantation.
I could ride there, do my work, and return long
before Mr. Edward could need me or miss me.
This thought completely filled my mind, to the
exclusion of all others. To the possible consequences of what I proposed, I gave not the slightest consideration. If I had, probably I should
have postponed my design until a more convenient
time, though that time would surely have come,
sooner or later.

"I mounted and rode rapidly back to the plantation. At the entrance of the avenue I tied my
horse in a clump of trees. My gun was in my
hand, and I took a pistol from the holster hanging at my saddle, for I did not intend to fail. As
I neared the house, some of the dogs barked. I
whistled to them softly, and they came around
me, leaping with joy. I quieted them with a word,
and ordered them back to their kennels. As they
obeyed me, I laughed silently : these were the

dogs that Mr. Harold had threatened to set loose on me if I ever approached the place again ! After what he had done to me, it would have been well to take greater precautions, and rely on something more faithful than the dogs."

Here Burton broke off abruptly. His hands clinched stealthily on the club he carried, and I shivered lest the memory of the old crime might incite him to do violence to me before the time he had set. His eyes glared with a sudden ferocity that made me feel how fierce were the passions that swayed him, how perverted and diseased his mind had been. Yet I could not altogether blame, so strongly had he made me sympathize with the misery and wrong of his life. Suddenly he resumed :—

"When I crept softly up to the open window of the library and looked in, I saw Mr. Harold sitting there alone, with just such a savage frown on his face as he had worn when he assaulted me a few hours before. Perhaps he was thinking of that — or perhaps of his quarrel with Mr. Edward. But I wasted little time in such speculations. What I had come there to do must be done quickly.

"I tapped softly on the wooden window-sill. He looked around, but did not move. I kept myself well hidden from his sight, and tapped again, for I wished him to come nearer. With a muttered oath he arose and approached me, and my heart did not quicken its beat, nor did a single muscle tremble. When he was close to the window, I took a single step, so that the light from the candles could fall full upon me. The frown disappeared, and gave way to a look of terror when his eyes fell upon the barrel of the gun that was thrust almost against his face. I think —I am sure—he knew me just for an instant. The next, I pulled the trigger. When I saw the thing that fell and lay where he had stood, I knew that he, at least, would never betray my secret.

"One glance was enough. It was an ugly thing that I gazed upon, and one that I would not care to see repeated, even in your case. There are other and *cleaner* ways, though none quicker or more certain.

"I crept away noiselessly, and as quickly as possible. Some of the dogs, attracted by the report of the gun, ran up to me again, but I dismissed them with a low word. Once out of hearing of the house, I broke into a run down the avenue until I reached my horse. I glanced back to look for moving lights or other signs of excitement in the house, but there were none, as yet. Still, I knew my act must be discovered soon, even if the shot did not attract attention.

" I turned my horse the way we had travelled before, and flew back to the grove. The other horse was there, but no sign of Mr. Edward. I had done my work within the expected time, and had met no one on the road, either going or coming; whatever suspicion might fall on me, no witness could testify against me. Yet, while I waited for Mr. Edward's return, I took the precaution to clean the barrel and pan of my gun and reload it. I stood forth ready to face the world with a clean, loaded gun, and nothing more than the vaguest suspicion possible against me.

" And I had had a glorious revenge.

" After cleaning my gun, I walked to a corner of the wood, where I could see any one approaching from the lane, or along the highroad, and waited. For nearly an hour I stayed there, drunk with delight at the success of my plan. Do not imagine that I was drunk in any other sense. The one draught of Hollands (though a deep one) that I took when Mr. Edward left me was all that I had had, and I could have swallowed twice the quantity without feeling any ill effect from it. A savage joy fired my brain as no spirits could have done.

"But as the end of the hour approached, something occurred that sobered me completely, and caused me to realize, as I had not realized before, that, despite the lack of witnesses, there was still danger connected with the affair. Before God, I swear that never, even to the last moment, did it enter my head that the matter could cause danger, or even trouble, to Mr. Edward. What I had done was my own deed, which I was ready to stand responsible for, if necessary; and I was not old enough or wise enough to see how it was likely to affect him. If I had supposed such a case, I would have foregone my revenge and blown my own brains out rather than draw a breath of suspicion against him. I did not know what I had done to ruin him until it was too late to remedy it, except in the one way that I was resolved not to take unless in the last extremity.

"The event that I speak of was the thud of horses' hoofs on the road. I heard them coming from afar, and, as they drew nearer, I could distinguish the tread of four horses. I drew back into the deeper shadow, and as they passed I heard one of the riders say, 'He has not more than an hour's start of us!'

"I could not hear the reply as they tore past me. But I knew, instantly, that they were in pursuit of the murderer, and I laughed to myself to think how easily he had fooled them. I knew they would go on at breakneck speed until they reached the river and the ferry. Doubtless another party had set out in the other direction, for there was no escape from our narrow peninsula except by water, unless one travelled inland. That would be to ride straight into the more populous part of the country, where a greater number of pursuers could be aroused; no doubt there were others already in that direction also. Naturally, they would expect the murderer to make for one of the ferries and escape into a part of the country where he was less known.

"I let them go by, and laughed. I drew back into the grove and waited again; it was quite another hour before Mr. Edward called for me. Everything was ready; in fact, I had been leading the horses up and down the lane for half an hour before. When we mounted and rode away, you may be sure I did not speak of the furious riders who had passed so lately, though our course lay right in their track. I knew we must meet them, sooner or later, either at the ferry or on their way back, but I was sure they must be ignorant of my connection with the affair, and was prepared to face them boldly.

"We had been riding along leisurely for some five hours; the road now led into a thick wood. As we drew near it, four dim figures stepped out of its shadow, and blocked the way. There was enough light from the stars to glance and reflect from the muskets that two of them displayed; how the others were armed we could not tell.

"'Halt!' commanded a voice.

"We halted, not ten yards from them.

"'Dismount and surrender!' continued the voice.

"Mr. Edward turned to me. I had already drawn a pistol, and was prepared to fight. 'Highwaymen! Take the man on your right!' he whispered, as he drew his pistol and started his horse at a walk toward our assailants.

"'Halt where you are, I say, or we fire!' challenged the menacing voice, not five yards away now.

"He did not obey. The flash of his pistol was his only answer, followed an instant later by mine. I know he hurt his man, for I heard him cry out; what became of mine, I could not see. But I saw Mr. Edward, the moment after he fired, put spurs to his horse and ride over the second man who opposed him. I followed as I could, though, not wearing spurs, I was slower. But his swift movement had cleared the way for me, and I followed safely. There was a flash of firearms as we passed, but, wherever the bullets lodged, it was not in their intended marks.

" Now, I cannot imagine what object those men could have had in dismounting. On their horses, they could have effectually blocked the way, for the road was narrow, and we could not have ridden over them easily. We should have been forced into a hand-to-hand fight, with the odds two to one against us. We realized — and so did they — the clumsiness of their arrangements, when we came across their horses tethered several hundred yards beyond. Mr. Edward had noticed them, but was about to ride by, when I cried, ' Wait ! '

" I saw the immense advantage we might gain. I slipped quickly to the ground and loosed the animals. Two I held myself, and the bridles of the other two I handed to Mr. Edward. The shouts of our pursuers rang in our ears, for they could hear that we had stopped, and must have guessed the reason. They were less than fifty yards away when I remounted. Several pistols were discharged in our direction, but at such a distance, and in the darkness of the night, rendered deeper by the shadow of the trees, it would have been a miracle if we had been hit. As we moved away, Mr. Edward broke into a laugh, and shouted back to them, 'Good-night to you, gentlemen, and better luck and more foresight next time!

"'You seconded me well, Burton,' he said, as we left our pursuers in the distance; 'better than most boys of your age would have done. Those highwaymen must have been new to the profession, else they would never have left their horses so far away, and without a guard.'

"'Belike they expected little resistance,' I answered.

"'Perhaps. At any rate, we seem to have the advantage in arms as well as in strategy.'

"'They were foolish,' I remarked. 'What shall we do with the horses?'

"'Turn them loose and start them away at the first cross-road we come to. We don't want to steal them, even from thieves.'

"'And we might be taken for thieves ourselves, if any one should meet us.'

"'Yes, it is an unusual thing at this time of night to be leading so many horses with saddles.'

"We turned them loose at the first cross-road. A cut on the flank started them off, one after another, and we were reasonably sure that they would travel a goodly distance before being captured by any one."

THE TALE OF A HUNTING

My interest in Burton's story was such that I had forgotten my peculiar predicament. As he stopped to wet his dry lips with the water that stood on my table, I exclaimed : —

"Go on!"

Burton responded to my eagerness with a cunning glance from his eyes. "So anxious?" he seemed to say. But he resumed : —

"It was broad daylight when we reached the river.

"'Have they caught him yet?' asked the ferryman when he had been brought from his cabin.

"'Caught whom?' asked Mr. Edward.

"'The murderer.'

"'The murderer? I have heard of no murder.'

"'And you come from up the country? That is strange!' He looked at us suspiciously. 'Why, the whole peninsula is alive with it already, and it only happened last night. Surely you must have met some of those who were hunting him?'

"I trembled lest Mr. Edward should connect this tale with the men who had attempted to stop us last night, but he was so sure they were highwaymen that the idea never came to him.

"'Nobody has said a word to me about it,' he said. 'But I have not spoken to a stranger since I set out last evening. What is the story?'

"'One of the great planters near Charlestown was murdered last night by his cousin. It seems the fellow owed everything to his relatives. I forget his name, though some men who were here searching for him told me last night. He will get short shrift if he is caught; they will kill him at sight. I would like to get a chance to shoot him down where he stood. It was a cold-blooded killing. Shooting is too good for him; he ought to be burned alive!'

"'Who is he?' asked Mr. Edward. 'I may know him, or at least of him, for I know most people about there.'

"'I cannot remember his name,' said the ferryman. 'But if you know of a family of two brothers and a cousin who were brought up together, you may guess.'

"Mr. Edward looked troubled, as well he might. 'I do know of one such family,' he said. 'But I know they are all still alive.'

" I was afraid of what might be said next, and took the liberty of thrusting myself into the conversation unbidden.

" ' Has the news been sent across the river ? ' I asked.

" ' Not yet. It is not likely the man could have crossed anywhere about here without my knowing it, and he may have taken some other road ; they could not tell which way he had gone. I am going to spread the story when I cross. The whole country on this side of the river is up and searching, and the scoundrel can hardly miss falling into the hands of some of them. And when he does—' he stopped to laugh. 'When he does, there won't be much time for prayers !'

" ' They will have to give him a trial at least,' exclaimed Mr. Edward.

" ' He has had all the trial he will ever get,' said the ferryman, sullenly. 'You seem to have a good deal of sympathy for a cowardly murderer ! I heard the story, though I don't remember the names. The two men had a quarrel, and the dead man turned the other out of the house, as he had a right to do, since it was his. Then the other waited until nightfall, stole back secretly, and blew his cousin's brains out.'

" I saw Mr. Edward turn very pale and tremble

slightly. I knew he was beginning to realize how exactly the circumstances fitted his own case, as I did also; and it was also coming home to me that he, and not I, was the one likely to be suspected. *His* quarrel had been well known; the whole household knew of it, and knew that he had been turned out of the house in consequence of it. My own cause of hatred was known only to Mr. Edward and the dead man; there was nothing to connect me with the affair, and everything combined to point him out as the doer of the deed. The circumstances, the testimony of the household, must all count against him, — against the man to whom I owed my life and all the happiness and comfort that I had ever known. Mr. Edward's trembling could have been nothing to mine, for I was afraid for *him*. I felt incapable of keeping a quaver out of my voice, yet I knew that I must speak. But for once I had reason to bless the infirmity that has been the curse of my life, for, when I found my voice, it was as even and expressionless as ever.

"'How do they know the cousin did it?' I asked; and both of us hung breathless on the answer.

"'They know it because the dogs made no noise. If a stranger had approached, they would have run out and barked. The fact that they were quiet proves that it was some one they knew, and there was only one man whom they knew who had cause of enmity against the dead man.'

"I trembled still more. If Mr. Edward should suspect *me!* I cared little what the rest of the world might think of me, but to lose *his* confidence and regard would have made my life worthless. I saw that the story, knowing what he knew, must point more to me than to him. Yet, strangely enough, to the last day of his life, such a supposition never entered his mind. He saw only the way the circumstances bore against himself; he believed me as incapable of such a thing as he knew himself to be.

" 'What are the names of the people you know?' asked the ferryman, curiously. 'I am sure I should know the name if I heard it again.'

" Mr. Edward hesitated. The ferryman looked at him with growing suspicion in his face.

" 'Well, what were the names?'

" 'The family name was X,' answered Mr. Edward, at length. 'The name of the cousin was Edward C.'

" The ferryman leaped up from the stump where he sat. 'That's the name!' he cried joyfully.

"'*What* is the name?' demanded Mr. Edward, sternly.

"'Edward C.! That's the murderer's name!'

"'A lie!' cried Mr. Edward, furiously, flushing a deep red. 'Edward C. is no murderer! You have made a mistake in the name. Don't ever dare to repeat such a lie again, or you will have to answer to me for it!'

"'To you? What business is it of yours, anyway?'

"'It is my business, because —' I held up my hand for him to keep silence, but he never heeded it, and went on unhesitatingly — 'because *I* am Edward C.!'

"The ferryman's eyes opened wide in astonishment, but he looked Mr. Edward over from head to foot, while an expression of recognition grew on his face.

"'Like the description!' he muttered. 'What a fool I was!' He sprang up, holding his heavy push-pole in his hand, and raised it over his head. 'Here's for you, murderer!'

"It would have fallen in another moment. But, before his blow could fall, I had drawn my pistol and struck him heavily on the side of the head with it. I could have shot him quite as easily, but I had enough blood on my hands. The man dropped senseless.

"'Good God, you have killed him!' cried Mr. Edward, springing to the man's side.

"'He is only stunned,' I said. 'I did not want to kill him, though he would have killed you in another minute, if I had not struck. Let us secure him before he comes to.'

"'What for?' he asked, in surprise.

"'So that he cannot give the alarm until we are well out of reach,' I answered.

"'What alarm?' demanded Mr. Edward, curiously.

"'Did you not understand what he said?' I cried. 'You are accused of murder!'

"'I believe the man was mistaken,' he said quietly. 'But, even if it were so, why should I fly? You and I both know it is false. I shall return and meet the charge, if there really is one.'

"'You shall not!' I shouted. 'Did you not hear him say that they would shoot you on sight? You would never live to be tried, and your name would be branded with the crime forever!'

"He hesitated. 'But I cannot fly from such a charge without disgracing myself.'

"'It is no disgrace to fly from a gang of murderers,' I replied. 'If you escape now, you can easily return after the first excitement is worn off, and stand a trial, if you then need one to vindicate you. Probably the real murderer will be discovered before then; but now a return means certain death.'

"He sat down and pondered, paying no heed to the ferryman, whom I was securing.

"'There is sense in what you say,' he said. 'If this thing is true, and I am accused of it, they would shoot me as that man said. I can quite sympathize with their state of mind,' with a melancholy smile, 'even though their anger is directed against myself. I can return (that is, provided I succeed in concealing myself) in a few weeks or months, when the wrath of the people has cooled a little. But where could I hide, and what would become of you?—Since we were together, you may be implicated too,' he said, with a sudden afterthought. It was perilously near the real case, if only he had reversed our positions; so near that it startled me.

"So I persuaded him to help me carry the ferryman's body to a little ravine, where we laid him on a bed of dead leaves. We did not gag him, and the first traveller that passed would answer to the shout that he would be certain to give.

"Then I occupied myself in getting Mr. Edward away from the scene, knowing that, if I could once commit him to the course I had resolved upon, it would be impossible for him to retreat later.

"I had noticed a canoe tied to a tree a few yards above the ferry-boat, and it had given me an idea. I brought this down, and fastened it to the scow, and then led our horses aboard.

"'We must be our own ferryman, Mr. Edward,' I said. He gave an apathetic smile, and took up a pole. The river was only a few hundred yards wide, and neither deep nor rapid, so that we had no difficulty in crossing.

"'I am sorry, Mr. Edward, but we must part with our horses,' I said, when we had crossed.

"'Why so?' he demanded.

"'Because our best plan is to escape by water. On land we could easily be tracked; the river leaves no mark. Besides, they will look for us first on the road, knowing that we had horses; and, while they are searching there, we shall be travelling farther away in another direction.'

"'I see your plan,' he replied, with a little brighter expression. 'Your head is more capable than mine, just now. Take your own way; it can matter little if it fails!'

"His words lifted a weight from my mind. Despondent as he was, he was willing to go. If we could once get a fair start, I felt confident of throwing our pursuers off the trail; and, once started, he must soon see that a return would be worse than immediate surrender would have been. He could not reason all this out for himself; the news he had just heard seemed to have stunned him so that he could not get his thoughts in order; but my brain seemed to work more rapidly and accurately than usual under this excitement. The danger from our pursuers, the chance that Mr. Edward might suddenly seize the main point of the situation and upset all my plans, were a wonderful stimulus to my invention.

"Everything worked for my main plan, which was to prevent a separation between us; I did not see then that *my* companionship was a far different thing for him from what his was for me. At the time, my one object was to keep him from suspecting me, and to keep myself with him. I thought that surely anything that was good for one of us must be good for both. Perhaps, if I had realized all that our flight meant, and would mean to him in the days to come, I should have hesitated about dragging him away, and should even have sacrificed myself so far as to take the responsibility of my deeds on myself. But, being young, I did not see it all then.

"We reached the other side. From the horses I

removed the saddles and bridles and placed them in the canoe. A sharp cut of the whip started the animals off at full speed.

"I shoved the ferry-boat from the shore, and pushed the canoe out into the current; then I cast the scow loose. I intended to let it drift; the loss of it would help to delay our pursuers, and they might well suppose that we had cast it loose for that very purpose, and not suspect that we had gone down the river. The plan was a good enough one; but I had forgotten that, finding it gone, the ferryman would immediately seek for his canoe, and its loss would arouse suspicion at once. Well, I was young and foolish, and had not yet learned to calculate as far ahead as I have been obliged to do since. Still, for a boy, it was not so bad. Eh?

"I picked up a paddle; Mr. Edward did the same, and in five minutes more we were out of sight of the ferry landing, and I began to breathe more freely. No one had appeared; my only fear had been that some chance traveller might arrive while we were still in sight. Once clear of the landing, we were safe for some days, I thought.

"As soon as the regular motion of the paddles had calmed his excitement, Mr. Edward began to brood on the situation and to reproach himself for having involved me in his troubles! Fortunately my face did not betray the emotion his kind words aroused in me. I protested truly enough that I was his for life or death, that nothing could separate me from him.

"He laid down his paddle, and turned himself around to face me.

"'You are more than a servant, Burton,' he said warmly. 'You are the sort of friend one hopes for, but seldom finds. And I know I shall never have another; one such friend in a lifetime is as much as any man has a right to expect.' He stretched out his hand to me; for the first time, I felt a thrill of repentance and shame run through me. I had not thought, at first, of the chance of involving him in my crime. With a man's reasoning, I had seen that there could not be more than a bare suspicion against me, at the most; but, like a boy, I had not worked out my calculation to the farthest possible results: I had not foreseen how the consequences of my act might affect him. I did not want to take the hand so offered, yet I dared not refuse it. Indeed, my momentary hesitation caused him some surprise.

"'Why do you hesitate?' he asked.

"'You do me too great an honor,' I replied,

hardly able to meet his eyes. But he only gave my hand a warmer pressure before releasing it.

"We paddled swiftly nearly the whole day, only stopping once to gather some berries, for we had but a small supply of food with us, and we dared not, as yet, stop at any of the plantations to buy anything. In fact, in approaching a plantation, we were careful to cross to the opposite side of the river, and kept as much as possible in the shadow of the overhanging trees. We saw nothing to indicate that we had been watched, or even seen; and when, about the middle of the afternoon, our arms began to grow weary, we pushed the canoe into a little, well-sheltered nook, and lay down on the mossy bank to rest. We had had no rest the night before, and it was not surprising that before long we were both sound asleep.

"We slept for hours, until long after nightfall, and I was the first to wake. Some suspicious noise had roused me — far away I heard the baying of hounds.

"It was not the season for hunting. For a few moments the sound died away, and then it came again; and clear above the sharper cries of the foxhounds my ears distinguished a deeper bay, like the tolling of a great bell afar off. I knew the sound well. It was the bay of the blood-hound, and I knew what the hunters sought. Their game was man!

"I could hear them, now, coming down on both sides of the river. Our pursuers were shrewder than I had expected. They must have returned to the ferry, and the ferryman had made his presence known to them. In my heart I cursed the foolish feeling of humanity that had caused me to leave him there ungagged. Doubtless, while some of them crossed the river and followed the road, others had noted the chance of our escape by water, and had roused the country on both banks of the river. Perhaps the dogs had caught our scent where we had hugged the shore and were following it down the stream.

"I knew how far a noise would travel in the stillness of the night, and especially over water, but I felt sure they must be within a mile of us. The dogs must be leashed, I knew, and their rate of travel must be limited by the ability of the men to follow them through the bushes and the swamp that lined a great part of the river bank. But even then, another half-hour or so must bring them to the spot where we lay, and I shuddered to think of what would have come to us if I had not wakened when I did.

" I grasped Mr. Edward, who still slept soundly, and shook him roughly.

" ' Wake ! ' I cried. ' We must leave here quickly.'

" ' What is the matter ? ' he demanded hurriedly.

" ' Listen ! '

" In a moment the sounds came again, travelling down the stream with startling clearness. They were approaching fast.

" ' They are hunting us ! ' I whispered. ' And they are on both sides of the river.'

" I could not see his face, but I heard him draw his breath in a sort of sob. I knew how he must feel, conscious of his own innocence, and yet being hunted with dogs, like a savage Indian raider.

" We crept into the canoe, and pushed off into the darkness. Refreshed and strengthened by our sleep, we made the canoe travel fast. On the face of the water the darkness was intense, but the faint light of a few stars, showing the dim outlines of the tree-tops on either side, enabled us to keep in the middle of the stream.

" ' They will lose our scent where we slept,' I said, to comfort him.

" ' For my own part, I should care little if they found us,' he replied sullenly. ' If I am to be

hunted like this all my life, I do not care how soon
the chase is ended.'

"'Indeed, sir, you know it can be but for a little
while,' I answered eagerly, though deep in my
heart there lay the certainty that he would never
go back to the old place.

"'A little while is too long,' he returned impatiently. 'What can those people be thinking of?
They should know me better than to believe me
capable of such a dastard act. What have I ever
done to make them think it possible? Was there
no one but me who had cause of quarrel with
Harold? In all his life he never had a friend,
that I know of, and he has made enemies innu-
merable. Why, even *you* had more cause to murder him than I had; in fact, after the way he
treated you, it would not have been so very
strange if you had taken some sort of revenge.
I almost believe I should have done it myself, had
I been in your place.'

"I shook as though with an ague. For a moment I was on the point of confessing all; then
more sober reflection came to my aid. In spite
of his hasty words, I knew he could never have
revenged himself in such a way; his words did
not agree with his character, and, if I spoke, I
knew he would turn from me with loathing, though

I felt sure he would not betray me. I could endure danger and suffering and death if need be, but I could not bear to think of being separated from him. All gratitude for what I owed him was overwhelmed by the fear of this.

" ' I hope, sir,' I began to stammer, ' I hope you — do not — do not — think — ' For my life I could not keep a quaver out of my voice.

" ' No, of course I do not think you did it,' he interrupted. ' I did not mean to imply that. Indeed, I know you could not possibly have done it, even had you wished, for he was alive when I left him, and we have been together ever since.' (He forgot the hours he had left me alone in the grove with the horses, nor did he ever remember them.) ' No, I did not mean that, only that you had more cause than I to harm him, and yet you are not suspected. If you are not, why should I be, only that I quarrelled with him at the last? But we have quarrelled many times before, and so have other men ; and nothing ever came of it, and no one ever thought of such an outcome. He was always quarrelling and making enemies. Why must *I* have been the one to be singled out for suspicion — and at just such a time, too, when I was on the point of leaving the house forever? How many others there must have been ! Though he

was my cousin, almost my brother, I have many
a time been ashamed to own the relationship, on
account of the way he treated other people. Yet
interference or remonstrance only made matters
worse. You know as well as I do — none better,
since you have suffered from it so often! Oh,
I knew how he treated you, and the only thing
that kept me from interfering was the certainty
that such action would only make it worse for
you in the end, even while my uncle lived. You
know what hold Harold had on his mind, and
what implicit confidence the old man placed in
him. He was terribly mistaken, of course; but
was it for me — a mere dependent — to try to set
his mind against his own eldest son? At the very
worst, I owed it to him to let him die in peace,
thinking that we all lived in friendship, regardless
of what might come afterward. Allan made it
plain that he felt the same way, though we never
exchanged a word on the subject. But there was
no doing anything with Harold. I believe he was
tyrannical and bad by nature. *He* was the master; the old man confided in him, and he knew it
— no one better. He was so much older than I
that he was well justified in treating me as a child
for many years; though he continued to do so
long after I had reached man's estate, and was

able and willing to do a man's work in the world. We shall have a chance, now, to see how nearly such a boast can be fulfilled, eh?' He broke in with a laugh that had little of amusement or enjoyment. 'But what is the use of telling you such things? You must have known them quite as well as I did—they were patent enough! While I was still very young, I learned the uselessness of interference; it only turned him more strongly to his tyranny, and did his victims more harm than good; and every such act of his made him a new enemy. The whole country knows it well; and yet they must needs pick *me* out as the only man who could have killed him.'

" He had been running on in a sort of hysterical attack, and I dared not interrupt him. He wound up with a little laugh; the course of circumstances had turned his whole nature sour, and indeed I could not wonder at it. Everything about the plantation had worked against him from the first, and only his own innate sense and good nature, his sweet and patient disposition, could have prevented his breaking away long before. And now, to think that I, who loved him so, and owed him so much, should be the one to drive him away at last! It made me writhe in my seat.

T

"Not a sound now broke the silence of the night; the river was crooked, and well wooded along its banks, and the cry of the hounds, if there was any, was taken up by the leafage and lost among the trees. They must be far behind us, for we had paddled fast, and stopped for nothing; while the hunters had had to overcome all kinds of delays and obstructions in the woods.

"'We *have* shaken them off,' I gasped, relieved. 'Until we land again, they cannot regain our trail; and when we are once safely out of this part of the country, we need only change our names and live quietly for a while, to be lost sight of completely. This thing will make a great cry for a few weeks, and then it will die out, and no man will ever so much as remember it once in a month. At the worst, it means only making a new name and a new career for yourself; the career was a necessity in any case, since your uncle's death, and you will soon become used to the new name.'

"My argument seemed convincing enough to me, but it did not strike him with the same force.

"'I want no career of any kind under any name but my own,' he replied gloomily, stirring uneasily in his seat. 'You forget that *I* am the one accused; that it is an honored name that is disgraced by this thing. I am not ashamed of my name; if I am compelled to conceal it for a time, I will do nothing to grace any other. I will live and die in obscurity, if I must; but if I seek honor or fame, it must be under the name that belongs to me. I will try for no good fortune until this matter has been cleared up and my reputation has been vindicated. That is settled. But I do not wish to hold *you* down to the obscurity I must court. I know of no other friend who would have done as much for me as you have already done, and you have my deepest gratitude for it.'

"'Oh, sir,' I broke out; 'gratitude from you to me!'

"'Surely,' he replied. 'It is due, and it is given with all my heart. But it would be worse than selfishness to keep you from the chance of fortune that every man looks and hopes for. You must leave me at the first opportunity; I would say even now, but for knowing that my pursuers must be still on our track. It would not do for you to incur the risk of meeting them; but as soon as we are surely clear of them we will divide what money I have, and separate.'

"I felt as though he had struck me in the face. Was it for *this* I had brought him into peril and disgrace, only to be dismissed after a week or two? I had not shrunk from involving him, merely that I might continue with him, and I was not going to let my sacrifice of him be rendered useless so soon.

"'Mr. Edward, you may as well make up your mind to this, first as last. I will not touch a penny of your money, except in your company; I swear I would rather throw it into the river! And I swear that, through good or evil, whichever may chance, I will not leave you. I owe you a life, and many years of comfort and happiness, and I have an ambition to repay them to the best of my ability, and to make up in some little degree, as far as my efforts can go, for the greater things you have lost. My brightest hope has never gone beyond that; and heaven and earth — and hell, if it opposes — shall not keep me from following that object!' I spoke as passionately as I felt.

"He made no answer, but he stopped paddling, and after a little while I heard sounds that proved to me he was weeping silently."

Burton sat quiet for some moments; he seemed to be mentally reliving that part of his life. He had told his story in such a quiet impersonal way, that it was hard for me to realize that he was speaking of himself, or that he was a man with a terrible criminal past behind him, a deadly hatred toward me at the moment, and a fixed purpose to commit a fresh murder before another day dawned. The whole thing sounded like a dream from which I must wake presently. It appeared so utterly impossible that I could be lying there bound and helpless, listening to a confession whose length measured the hours I had to live. I knew that after he had told such a tale to any man, he must for his own safety put the hearer beyond the power of repeating it; that each succeeding sentence only rendered more inevitable the grim fate that he had prophesied for me.

And yet, in spite of this, I was so wrapped in interest in the words that fell steadily from his lips in his curious expressionless monotone, that I was constantly forgetting my condition, and talked with him as though we were almost comrades. Heretofore I had thought him almost incapable of any human feeling except hatred; but his story, and especially the manner of its telling, proved to me that he was endowed with as much sensibility as other men. Only it had been warped and distorted into grotesque proportions, until his mental parts resembled the deformed body of a gnome. All the parts were there, but the malignant inclinations were over-developed, except where they came in contact with his Master — and his Master's daughter.

"You are a strange compound," I said wonderingly. "You are capable of deeper affection and devotion than most men, yet they seem to be directed in only one direction. If you had tried to exert a little more charity and kindliness toward the rest of the world, you might have been a happier man. You have great capacity for affection; a little more extended use of it might have brought you great returns."

He laughed somewhat bitterly. " I have given my affection where it seemed good to me," he said. "I have poured the whole of it at the feet of three people, and two of them are gone. As for receiving a return, Mr. Edward gave me more than I deserved after the trouble I had brought on him, though infinitely less than I desired. He would have sacrificed his life to save me as easily as I would have given mine for him; but he would have done it from a sense of duty, and as readily for another's sake as for mine; and he would never have felt the same joy in the sacrifice that would have animated me. I knew that I had no right to expect it; I never did expect it."

"And My Lady?" I asked.

He sprang up with an oath; I had unthinkingly touched upon the one subject that unbalanced his mind.

"Do not speak of her!" he cried furiously; and I thought he was going to make an end of me on the instant. He stood for a moment breathing hard, and glaring at me like some great wild beast. "You have done mischief enough on this island," he went on, more quietly, as he slowly resumed his seat. "You will do still more if you drive me insane before you die!"

"*I* don't want to drive you insane," I answered, as quietly as I could, though I had little to gain by conciliating him. "I believe you have travelled more than halfway on the road to madness already. No man in his senses would have felt such unreasoning hatred as you have shown toward a stranger."

"Unreasoning, eh?" he snarled. "I think we won't discuss that matter now; each of us knows too much about the other! Do you want to hear the rest of my story, or shall I make an end of the business now?"

"Oh, since you have gone so far, you might as well finish your tale," I replied. "Every hour counts." Yet I could not believe he really intended to murder me.

"Still in love with life?" he laughed. "You had better prepare for the end, for there is not much more to tell.

"We travelled down the river all night, and by daylight we had reached the flats that fringe the mouth of it. Our pursuers had lost the track, and we heard no more of them, but we had no means then of learning that, and hid in desolate places by day, and resumed our way only at night. We suffered from the hot sun; sometimes we were half-starved, and often we were parched with thirst, so that we had to dig with our hands in the sand of the flats, and drink the brackish water that collected in the holes. But always some event happened to relieve our immediate necessities, and we never quite died, though we often seemed near it. In the course of a week, during which we shunned every human being, we reached the lower part of the Chesapeake; and there, one quiet evening, when there was nothing worse than a long, low swell anywhere on the water, we crossed to the Eastern Shore without mishap. Once there, we felt comparatively safe, and ventured to show ourselves, and purchase a few supplies that we needed badly. People sometimes looked suspiciously at the gold that we offered in payment; but in spite of torn and soiled clothing and evident marks of hardship and exposure, there was that about Mr. Edward that proclaimed him a gentleman, and they believed the story I told them, that we were hunters on our way northward. We rounded Cape Charles, and made our way leisurely up the coast, keeping within the shelter of the islands where we could, until we reached this spot; and here we rested.

"Even now it is the only island within twenty miles that is cultivated; the mainland is so much better soil that no one has cared to take up land near the sea, unless he loved the neighborhood of the sea, and did not fear solitude. Mr. Kingsley, the owner of the island, was such a man, though he had another motive also, — the belief that the place would some day be the site of a town, on account of the situation, and the safe and excellent harborage on the western side. But the town did not develop in his day, and we have not been anxious to encourage neighbors.

"I say we stopped here to rest. Mr. Kingsley recognized a kindred spirit in Mr. Edward, despite the difference in their ages, and his son, who was nearly Mr. Edward's age, conceived a great liking for him. The result was that we were both offered employment by Mr. Kingsley, and as Mr. Edward gladly accepted, though the payment was not great, of course I stayed with him. We were not yet ready to seek a fortune; a safe and comfortable shelter for the time was all that either of us hoped or desired.

"But one thing disarranged our plans. Mr. Kingsley had another child, a daughter. Before long, I saw what was coming; and when Mr. Edward told me that he was going to marry Miss Margaret, I was neither surprised nor disappointed. But, in spite of my utmost persuasions, he insisted on one thing. He told the whole story of our flight and escape (as far as he knew it) to father, son, and daughter, and I am bound to say that the result was as satisfactory as even I could have wished. They believed the story, and scouted at the idea of his guilt; and it was agreed among them that the whole subject should be dropped entirely, unless a time should come when he could appear before the world and redeem his name. He was married under his own name, but the surname was never used afterward. Until Mr. Kingsley died, they were always known as Mr. Edward and Mistress Margaret.

"Before Mr. Kingsley died, his son was dead also, and Miss Margaret and her husband inherited the land and the slaves. No new slaves were ever bought; all that are here are the descendants of those Mr. Kingsley brought at his first coming. I loved Miss Margaret for her own sake, as well as for the sake of Mr. Edward, though I would have tried to love a rattlesnake if he had shown affection for it. When My Lady was born I gave her a double portion of love as the child of her father and her mother; and as she grew older that love increased on her own account. I knew she was not for me, but I swore to myself that while I lived no other man should claim her." He glanced significantly at me.

"Miss Margaret died while My Lady was yet a child, and after that Mr. Edward began to age fast; partly through grief for her loss, and partly through regret that he had never been able to clear his name of the charge of murder that had clouded it so many years. For, after we had been here some two years, and after Mr. Kingsley had been told our story, the old man set on foot some cautious inquiries. And the message brought back was that a coroner's jury had judged that 'Harold Darke, of Chilton, had come to his death at the hands of Edward Cunningham;' and that Allan Darke, the heir of his brother, was most bitter and relentless in his search for his brother's murderer."

XVI

ORDEAL BY FIRE

I HAD been half expecting some such ending, and yet, when it came, it gave me a shock. The murder of my uncle, whereby my father had come into possession of the estate, was an old story, so old as to have become practically forgotten. For my own part, I had not even thought of it half a score of times in my life, for it had happened before I was born; in fact, it was not until my father had become the heir unexpectedly that he had felt justified in seeking my mother's hand. The occurrence had not been mentioned in my hearing until after I was well grown, and then only as a matter of remote family history. No one ever expected to find Edward Cunningham; he had disappeared so completely that it was generally believed that he and his servant had perished from exposure or starvation while hiding from the hue and cry that had roused the whole colony.

Now a great light broke on me, and, in a rapid review of the events that had taken place since my coming to the island, I easily understood all that had been so incomprehensible before.

"So *he* was Edward Cunningham!" I said wonderingly. "What a strange chance! Then that was why my name seemed to startle you?"

"Of course. I knew you had discovered us, though I don't see, even now, how you did it; nor do I understand why you were so foolish as to give us your real name. If you had used a false one, I should never have suspected you."

"I had no reason for concealing my name," I returned, with some impatience. "I told you at the first that I did not know where I was, and that all I wished was to get away again."

"Naturally — to get away and bring the law to bear on us as soon as you had made quite certain of our identity!"

"I tell you I had no idea of anything of the sort," I reiterated. "You were both supposed to be dead many years ago; why should I be hunting for dead men? I tell you, until to-night I had no thought of your story; I should have known nothing about it if you had kept silence."

"You keep up the game still?" he sneered. "You must think me a fool!"

"So I do!" I retorted. "You *are* a fool to refuse to see a fact that is thrust in your face. A

little reflection should convince you that I am telling the truth. If your story is true, you have
committed one murder already, and I know it
cannot have contributed to your peace of mind;
indeed, you have owned as much. You may have
been justified, to a certain extent, in revenging
yourself on my uncle — I don't know. At any
rate, you had strong provocation. But you have
no provocation and no reason for committing a
fresh crime. I will give you any assurance for
your safety that you can demand. I will strike
a bargain with you; I am in very comfortable circumstances, and can afford to make a tempting
offer. If you will release me, I will take an oath
not to move in this matter for a full year, which
will give you plenty of time for escape to Europe
or concealment. I will give you a bond for one
thousand pounds, which will enable you to make
a good start in the world; you can easily turn it
into money anywhere in Virginia, and I will promise to stay on the island for any time that you may
require to negotiate it. I will not set in motion any
pursuit of you. At the worst, the most I will do will
be to clear the Master's name of the charge of murder that has stained it so long; and that only on
account of My Lady, who would wish it fervently.
I have no personal feeling in the matter; I never

knew my uncle, and after all these years, there is little use in raking up the affair again. I offer you a chance to escape, with a clear conscience and ample means, and the assurance that there will be no pursuit through my action."

He listened to me with more patience than I had expected, but he seemed utterly unmoved.

"And My Lady?" he asked, in his turn.

"My Lady—" I hesitated. "My Lady is her own mistress, and my cousin, if you have been telling me the truth. I should try to persuade her to leave this plantation, since she could hardly continue to live here alone."

"To leave it for yours, eh?" he inquired.

Again I hesitated. I wished to avoid irritating him, for I believed I saw a chance of bribing him to let me go, if I could offer sufficient inducement; but not even for that could I deny myself where My Lady was concerned.

"Yes, if she would! I have no reason to believe that she would,—at least not now; but if I could persuade her to confide herself to my love, I should be the proudest and happiest man alive."

His eyes lighted up. "Ah, I thought we should come to it at last!" he cried. "Poor fool, do you suppose such childish bribes could tempt me? Do you not know that, after what I have confessed, not

all the gold ever coined could buy your life? And
even without that, your designs as to My Lady
are enough to decide your fate. I tell you
again, no man shall have her while I live; you
will be the first to die because of seeking her, but
you are not likely to be the last!"			.

I saw that his intention was immovable, and
also that he was growing excited. The end was
drawing·near, but there was one last chance, and
I played it.

"Do you suppose My Lady will tolerate you
after she finds that you have murdered me?"
I asked.

"She will never know it," he returned, with a
terrible certainty.

"She will surely know that I am dead, and she
will want to know how and why."

"The manner will be evident, and that soon,"
he replied, with one of his expressionless laughs.
"An *accident* is going to happen which will be a
quite sufficient explanation; when everything is
over, she will only know that you have disappeared
— perhaps she will think you have run away from
her." The wretch would have grinned if it had
been possible; he seemed to be making super-
human efforts to bring some expression into his
features. He gloated over me as though he were

some beast about to devour me; he seemed hardly able to tear himself away from the contemplation of my hopeless condition.

"What do you mean to do?" I asked; and for my life I could not keep a tremor out of my voice. He noticed it, and laughed again.

"You will know soon enough," he returned; "quite soon enough for your own comfort."

He turned away and glanced at the shutters of the windows. They were wide open, except on the side toward the house. He closed them all, but did not take the trouble to fasten them; and when he entered the other room, I heard him close them there in the same way. Next I heard a sound of rending wood; then silence for a few moments, while my heart beat almost to bursting with the strain of waiting. I expected him to return shortly, and knock me in the head or cut my throat; it seemed the easiest and quickest way, and I supposed he was making preparations for the disposal of my body. I knew how far I was from any other dwelling on the plantation, and the uselessness of shouting for help. He knew it too; he was so certain of it that he had not taken the trouble to gag me. His failure to do so proved his absolute security against interruption. I felt the hopelessness of further parley

u

with him, and tried to make up my mind to die silently and courageously. But it was hard; I was young, and life and love were sweet.

Burton came to the door and glowered at me, taking a fresh torch and holding it high above my face. He stuck it in a crack between two logs, and disappeared for a moment, returning with an armful of broken wood that I recognized as the remains of the rough furniture of the outer room. This he proceeded to pile loosely against the partition, just outside the door. From where I lay, I could watch the whole proceeding, and though I wondered what he could have in mind, I disdained to ask him further questions. I was sure that, as he had said, I should know my fate very shortly.

At last the sticks were piled to his satisfaction, and he looked around at me.

"Good-by, my friend," he said. "I leave you free to cry out as loudly as you please; it will be music for me. I told you I intended to do the thing nicely; in an hour more it will be a sharp searcher who can discover even so much as one of your bones. I shall know where you are, but no one else will, and My Lady may perhaps think you have run away rather than face her and the explanation that she is expecting from me. Of course I shall give her an explanation, but it will be very different from the one I have given you to-night, and it will show you and your conduct in a vastly different and less complimentary aspect. Good-by, my friend! It is not a pleasant death that is coming to you; still, many others before you have travelled the same path, and they all seem to care very little about it now."

Keeping his eyes still fixed on me, to enjoy the expression of horror that must have come over my face, he stooped, and thrust his torch into the loose pile of sticks.

"Good-by, my friend! It will be slow, and it will be sharp, but far quicker and far easier than I could wish for you. Good-by!"

The jeering voice died away; the devilish face disappeared; and I heard the outer door close. I was alone in the hut face to face with death—and death by fire!

Only then did full realization of my situation rush upon me. The hope—almost the belief—that he could not be in such deadly earnest, which kept me up heretofore, disappeared in a single breath. My resolves to meet my fate manfully and in silence, if it did come, gave way, and I must confess that I was terrified to the last degree; nor am I in the least ashamed of having been so. If he had offered to shoot or stab me, or even beat out my brains, I could have faced it ; but such a thing as this had never entered my mind. I saw his plan : long before the fire broke through the windows or the roof, and brought the rest of the plantation on the scene, I should be only a charred corpse ; and when the last embers cooled off, I should be as thoroughly consumed as any old Roman on his funeral pyre. Meanwhile, he would stand in some convenient place outside, and listen to my cries as the fire scorched me.

The torch flickered and crackled in the light wood. From where I lay, I could see the flame beginning to creep upward, first slowly, then with a quicker rush. It caught on the framework of the partition, and climbed rapidly. A thick smoke began to fill the room, and I could feel the heat strike my face. The fire crackled and snapped ; sparks began to fly. One fell upon the coverlet under which I lay, and the coverlet was soon smoking.

The fire had fascinated and dazed me, at first ; when it began to climb, I seemed incapable of any thought except to wonder how soon it would reach me. I glared at it stupidly. My breathing was already a little difficult by reason of the smoke, which crept, too, into my eyes, and almost blinded me. I shook my head to dash away the tears and see more clearly. I saw the smouldering spark catch on my coverlet, and the creeping line of fire spread rapidly. Then my fortitude gave way when the thing came so close to me, and I shouted for help; I writhed and struggled desperately under my bonds, tearing the skin against the rope. I cried for help in a voice that would have moved to pity any one but a fiend like Burton. The rapidly increasing smoke blinded my eyes and stopped my lungs; I coughed and choked while I struggled, and at last lay still, utterly exhausted by my efforts, almost apathetic and half insensible.

And then, when the last hope seemed gone, I felt a sudden breath of fresh air that could only come from an open window. Just one breath, for the window swung back again; but that one movement brought my senses to me in some fashion, and I shouted again.

"Be still!" said a voice, and I felt the touch of a hand. The next moment most of the light of the fire died out. I learned afterward that it was because the door of the partition had been closed, shutting the body of the fire into the front room, for the time, though the partition itself was blazing in spots on the inner side.

Now that help had come, I was willing enough to be silent, knowing that Burton would not hesitate to commit another crime if necessary to insure my destruction. The rescuer apparently knew his danger also, for he spoke in a low tone that even I could hardly hear above the crackle of the flames.

Yet the next order was a contradictory one.

"Go on shouting at intervals. He must think you are still afraid!"

Stupid as I was from the smoke, I saw the sense of the command, and obeyed it.

I felt a hand run over me from head to foot.

"Where are the knots?"

"I don't know," I whispered. "Cut the rope."

"I have no knife," returned my new-found friend.

The hands began to feel again. "I have found one," said the voice, seeming to come from a great distance. The smoke in my lungs was suffocating me slowly, though I felt no inconvenience from it. Facts began to grow hazy to my mind, and I took no more than a languid interest in the proceedings, as though I were a mere spectator of a dull play. I could feel the hands tugging at the knots, and I felt only a faint amusement at the ineffectual struggles of the rescuer. I could hear him pant and gasp as he struggled; the smoke was in his lungs, too, I knew, and I wondered how long it would take him to reach the stage of apathy that had overtaken me. I hoped it would be soon, for I found it very pleasant, after the first sensation of choking was past. He was evidently a good fellow, and I hoped to see him rewarded for his efforts.

I heard the voice say, "Oh, my God!" and then the tugging at the knots ceased. Ah, he had become numb too, then I felt how he must be enjoying it. But no, he staggered to the window, and tore it open, the foolish fellow. I was inclined to call him names for not knowing when he was well off. The rush of air cleared the smoke somewhat, but it made the flames leap up fiercely. A vague figure leaned out of the window for a moment, while the smoke poured past him thickly.

Then my rescuer seemed to have discovered what he was looking for. Picking up something from the floor near my bed, he darted back to me and began slashing at the cords, which this time yielded, releasing my numbed legs. Later I learned that the flames had revealed my knife — the one that I had sharpened so carefully for my first attempt at escape months ago.

But my deliverance was as far away as ever. Indeed I anathematized my good friend for disturbing my comfortable lethargy. Without regard for my feelings, however, he rolled me over to the floor where the smoke was less dense. Then my senses came back, in part — torturing me, but bringing a fresh desire to *live*, to *breathe* once more. My deliverer tugged at my shoulders, encouraging me in low tones to make some efforts to save myself. Together — I know not how — we staggered to the low window which he had thrown open. Then, with a final shove from my helper and a last struggle on my part, I fell outward to the ground, a few feet below. I dropped heavily, and the shock revived me suddenly. I saw my rescuer leap through the window after me, and the shutter was closed with a quick jerk, shutting the smoke and the flame into the house. The fire was just beginning to break through the roof at the front of the hut, as I could tell by the faint glare on the tree-tops, but in the inner room the flames were still crawling slowly about the walls.

Out here in the open air, I revived rapidly; the wind blew the smoke in our direction, but most of it went over our heads. It served a good purpose, too, for it and the deep shadow in which we lay served to conceal us from the watcher that I knew must be standing somewhere close to the hut. My apathy was gone, now, and I was impatient for freedom. It seemed to me, however, that my limbs would never get life again. But at last they began to tingle, and what an unutterable relief it was to feel that I could stretch my arms and legs freely! All this time I had not dared to speak, for I could not tell how close Burton might be standing. My companion was silent also.

The last turn of the rope fell to the ground, and I rolled loose, free once more. I felt something cold and hard thrust into my hand, and my heart leaped as I recognized the handle of a dagger — the first offensive weapon I had held since my landing on the island. Now I felt myself a man once more; I was ready to meet Burton, or any one, and felt no doubt of being able to hold my own.

A hand clutched my arm, and a voice whispered, "Come!"

"Just a moment," I answered. I felt no fear of Burton, now that I was armed; besides, there were two of us. Even then I recollected the riding-whip that I had preserved so carefully. I had been handling it that evening, and had thrust it into my boot. The shock of my fall must have dislodged it. It certainly seemed worth looking for, and I knew that it would be buried among the ruins of the hut if it were left there. I stooped and felt on the ground, spending several minutes in the search. Again my rescuer's hand clutched me.

"What is it?" he whispered impatiently, and somewhat fearfully, it seemed to me. "We must be quick!"

Just then my hand fell on it. "All right, I am ready," I answered, straightening up and thrusting the whip into the bosom of my shirt.

He grasped my hand, and drew me forward. "Keep in the line of smoke," he whispered, "and follow me. It will help to conceal us."

I obeyed without a question. I was stiff in every limb from my long confinement, and each movement seemed more painful than the last; but the grasp on my hand never relaxed, and with my rescuer's help I managed to hobble forward, even to run in clumsy fashion.

We ran straight away westward through the grove; the darkness, even without the smoke, had been intense, but, just as we emerged on the farther side of the grove, a part of the roof of the hut fell in with a crash, and instantly the flames leaped skyward, lighting up the whole vicinity like day. Instinctively I turned to look at my companion, and broke out with a great cry that must have been distinctly audible above the noise of the falling timbers. While I had wondered who my saviour could be, my wildest guess had been wide of the truth.

"My Lady!" I cried, aghast, and stopped short where I stood.

By the light of the fire I could see her flush deeply. I still held one of her hands, and she pressed the disengaged one to my mouth. "Be still!" she whispered. "*He* is close by; come with me."

When she removed it, I raised the hand I held, and kissed it.

"My Lady and my love!" I whispered; but she made no answer, except to draw me onward.

Now that I could meet mine enemy on somewhat equal terms, I was loath to flee from him. If I had been alone, I should have hunted him like any other wild beast, as I had learned to stalk bears and Indians in their haunts, and have slain him with as little remorse. He would have hunted me down, if he had had the slightest idea that I was not lying beneath the burning logs of the cabin. But My Lady's hand was in mine,

and My Lady's safety was the first consideration.
I grasped the hand more closely, and we fled, like
a pair of frightened children, away from the
grove, now brilliantly illumined by the burning
cabin, across the rough fields, until we met a
cattle fence nearly a quarter of a mile away.
Along this we walked (not so carefully now)
toward the mansion. From the quarters of the
negroes we could hear excited cries, and by the
light of the flames, even at that distance, we could
see the slaves pouring out of their huts and hasten-
ing pell-mell toward the fire. It was too late for
them to succor me, if I had been still in the hut;
perhaps they had not even a thought of such a
thing. But a fire by night exercises a wonderful
power of attraction over even a civilized man;
he must follow it, and creep as close to it as he
can, just as I have seen horses, after being led to
safety, rush back into the flames they have just
escaped.

They hurried over the fields, shouting wildly
as they went, in a straight line from their huts
to mine. Our path lay to one side of theirs, and
though the light from the cabin threw us into
plain view (or so it seemed to us), not one of
them turned his head to notice us; perhaps, having that light in their eyes, they could not have

seen us if they had turned. At any rate, we went on unnoticed, until we had reached and passed the quarters they had just left, and were on our way to the mansion. And all our way thither, neither of us spoke so much as a word; she seemed to have nothing to say to me then, and my last words to her, with the tone of them, embraced all the speeches of love and gratitude that I could have spoken. I could say no more: if she understood them, nothing more was needed; if she did not, no floods of speech could explain to her what I felt. Sometimes I thought to express my thanks, but when I tried it I choked unaccountably, and held my peace for very shame's sake, fearing that a further endeavor at that time would make me burst into tears and break down entirely. Moreover, I could understand a part of what My Lady felt, and it was not for me to add to the strain.

The great house was dark and silent; every slave was at the scene of the fire, and doubtless they supposed their mistress was there too. The great door of the hall stood wide ajar, but My Lady would not enter it; instead, she led me to a side window that opened to the floor. It swung back at a touch, and we entered. The room was very dark, of course, but I knew it was the library where I had so often seen My Lady and the Master in those long summer evenings when I kept my lonely watch near them. So often had I watched them, so familiar had I grown with the aspect of everything there, that I felt as though I were revisiting a room in my own home. There was not a piece of furniture, hardly even a book, that I could not have laid my hand on blindfolded.

So when My Lady crossed the room, and I felt her sink into a chair, I knew it must be the chair in which she had been in the habit of sitting by the Master's side. I was sure that by stretching out an arm I could reach his own chair and draw it to her side. But I did not try to reach it; I thought it would seem a desecration to the girl who had never seen any figure in it but the one so lately lost.

She sank into the chair, and released my hand; and then, in the darkness, I heard the sound of great bursting sobs. She had given way at last; the only wonder to me was that she had not done so long before.

For some time I let her weep undisturbed. From my own sensations, I knew it must be a relief to her, for nothing would have suited my temper better just then than to give way to tears myself; indeed, I had some ado to prevent it. The last twelve hours had had a lifetime of emotions crowded into them. My nerves had been strained to the breaking point, and I knew that, if I gave way for a moment, my whole system must feel the crash that would follow. The only thing that sustained me was the necessity of caring for My Lady.

It was agonizing to wait there listening to her sobs in the darkness, even though I knew how they relieved her, and at last I could stand it no longer. Kneeling beside the chair (with much trepidation, I must own), I felt for her hands, which I knew were covering her face. To my vast relief, she yielded me a hand without resistance, and for some minutes I held it in both of mine without speaking. The silent hand-clasp of a friend often serves better than words; and if mine conveyed only half my thoughts, it is no wonder that it soon began to have its effect. Her sobs grew less explosive, though they still continued, and soon her failure to resent my advance emboldened me yet more. I slipped an arm around her and drew her toward me until her head leaned heavily against my shoulder, and still she made no effort to escape. Instead, she lay there quietly, as though glad of the rest and support, and her sobs came more easily and less frequently, until finally they ceased altogether; yet she did not withdraw from my embrace. I did not flatter myself that her confidence meant much. I knew it was merely due to exhaustion, and the longing for the support and sympathy of a friend, and any one else would have served the same purpose as well. She had forgotten who I was, except that I was a friend.

Yet it was a delight to me, even so, and I found it hard to refrain from putting some of my passion into my clasp of her. But it would not have been fair to take advantage of her momentary weakness; I kept myself well in hand, while thinking that the next time I held her, if such a time should ever come, it would be with her willing consent, and in my proper character of a man who loved her.

She was of too strong a nature to yield long to such an attack; gradually her sobbing ceased, and she withdrew herself gently from my clasp. Only an occasional trembling of her voice remained to show what trials she had so lately passed through.

"Mr. Darke," she said, as I rose and stood beside her, "I thank you sincerely for your forbearance. I know, now, how much wrong we have done you, and it is only by an accident that

you have escaped this last and greatest injury.
It shall be my business to see that no further
outrage—"

I could not bear to hear her accusing herself thus.
I dropped on one knee again, and felt for her hand.

"Oh, My Lady," I cried, "what has happened
has been no fault of yours or mine! Even your
father was deceived; and, with the light he had,
he was quite justified in defending himself in
every possible way. As for Burton's acts of to-
night, you could not be in any way responsible
for them. He is a madman, and if you could
have heard the story he told me—"

"I did," she interrupted. "I heard it all!"

"All?" I cried. "Were you at hand all that
time?"

"I had followed him," she answered, in a low
voice. "I could not sleep; I was sitting at the
window, and saw him steal out from the rear of
the house. I had bidden him stay in the house,
and he had never before disobeyed any command
of mine, that I knew of. From his secrecy, I di-
vined that his errand could not be a good one;
and after his conduct of yesterday, when he
showed his hatred of you so plainly, I felt sure
he had some design against you. I slipped on a
cloak and followed him."

x

"Followed such a man through the night! You have your father's courage, My Lady."

"I was armed," she returned. "I took my father's pistol. Besides, whatever else he might be capable of, he would never harm me."

After his late performances, I did not feel at all sure of that; his mania might easily take a sudden twist, and turn against the former objects of his affection. But I did not think it necessary to suggest this to her, at such a time; she had safely escaped for the present, and I resolved to take care that she incurred no more danger from him.

"Then you must have heard what we both said," I murmured absently, striving to recollect how much I had confessed of my own feeling for her.

The hand I held gave a slight involuntary pull, as though to withdraw itself, but I clasped it firmly, and she forbore to try further.

"I heard it all," she replied slowly, as though the words came in spite of themselves. "I did not know what he intended to do; but if he had attempted to strike you, my bullet would have found him. I should not have missed him, for I have practised shooting all my life. I know it is not a feminine accomplishment, but I have always been brought up like a boy, rather than as a girl.

I was unwilling to harm him unless I must, for
I was anxious to hear his story; and from what he
had said to you, I knew he was likely to tell more of
the truth than he would ever tell to me. Even
now, I should not like to see him harmed. Though
he brought disaster upon my father, except in that
single instance he has been wonderfully faithful
to us, and, after a lifetime of trust, it is hard to
change my opinion of him all in a moment. I
should be glad never to see him again, after what
has happened, though I suppose I cannot escape
it."

"I will see him first, and give him his dismissal,
if you authorize me," I said.

"Oh, no!" she cried, in quick alarm. "I must
do it myself!"

"At least, let me be near to protect you," I
begged.

She hesitated.

"You have every right. I had forgotten that
he murdered your uncle. You will have him pun-
ished for the crime?"

I hastened to answer the unspoken regret that
I detected in her tone. Perhaps I was wrong,
morally; I certainly did a very illegal thing. But
it seemed clear to me that no good purpose could
be served by having the old scandal of a quarter

of a century ago raked up and dragged through the mire of publicity again. For my own part, I felt no more interest in the matter than if Burton's victim had been a total stranger to me — as, indeed, he was, in all but name. The idea of vengeance at this late day did not appeal to me in the least. Only, her father's name must be cleared of the old disgraceful charge; though that could be done without necessarily bringing the real criminal to justice.

I paused to weigh my words.

"My uncle died before I was born," I said. "I had no thought of seeking his murderer when I came here. Let him go, if such is your wish. To be driven from your presence, knowing that you have learned his history and condemn him for it, will be a greater punishment than any law could inflict."

What a change in our relations during a few days! For a moment she did not speak or move; and then — then — her other hand sought mine, and held it firmly. What I felt is beyond description. For months I had been drawing closer and closer to her in my own mind, yet in hers I had been still afar off. That one instinctive movement proved to me that her mind had passed across the great barren distance that had lain between us, and that now we stood on common ground. We were friends, and more than friends; it would go hard with me if I did not draw her ever closer, until our two minds were as one.

And she knew that I loved her, yet she gave me both her hands thus! The hot words of love trembled on my lips; it was a hard fight to restrain them while those two strong hands were clasped so closely in mine. So we stood for a time, scarcely even thinking. The mere fact of presence was enough for me; for her, I could not tell, but I hoped many things, and with reason.

XVII

IN THE MASTER'S ROOM

FOR my own part, I felt quite willing to have this sweet companionship endure indefinitely. It did last for a long time, and during all of it I could think of nothing but of her and her presence. The sound of distant voices roused us at last; My Lady started as they struck her ear. The cabin must have been completely destroyed, and the negroes were returning to their broken slumbers.

"Come with me, quickly," she whispered, drawing me gently toward the door. So led, I would have followed straight to hell, if her path had lain that way.

"Where are you taking me?" I inquired, as we emerged into the great hall.

"Above stairs," she replied. "You must not be seen to-night."

"Why not?"

"Don't you see? Burton will return with them. I fear a fresh attempt against you, if he knows of your escape; and if he learned that I had been the means of it, and had heard all his confession, I dare not think what he would do, or attempt to do."

"Why should we not have him seized and placed in confinement to-night?" I asked, while we were ascending the stairs.

"Why should we run any unnecessary risks?" she rejoined. "If he does not suspect,—and there is no reason why he should,—he will be perfectly at ease. But to-morrow I shall question him; such an interview demands daylight, and plenty of witnesses."

"It may be better so," I said, after a little reflection. "But you must let me be near you; he may become dangerous when he learns the truth."

"He would never harm *me*," she answered, with certainty. "But you shall be near by; it is your right."

"There must be no question of rights between you and me, My Lady," I said, using the familiar title, to which my thoughts had grown accustomed. "The best of me is yours already, and I hope—"

"Here is your room," she interrupted hurriedly, as though afraid to hear the rest of my sentence.

As she opened the door, in spite of the darkness I recognized the room in which I had had that last memorable meeting with the Master.

"This room is yours, for the time," she explained. "After to-morrow we will see about other accommodation for you, — that is, if you care to stay with us for a short time longer. There is no compulsion, now," with a little tremble in her voice.

"If I care!" I exclaimed.

"I would like to make what reparation is possible for what you have suffered," she continued wistfully. "So I hope you will be in no great haste to leave us." The dear voice quivered suspiciously, and I hastened to put her at her ease.

"Once for all, My Lady," I said, with all the earnestness I felt, "there is no question of reparation between us, — I beg you to understand that. You had nothing to do with my detention. I tell you I am *glad* that it happened; and it has turned out for the best, since it has led to the knowledge of our relationship, and to —" I broke off my sentence, for it was leading to the thing that I was resolved not to say (if I could restrain myself so far) under the pressure of our late excitement. "And even if you had," I continued more quietly, "you are my cousin, and alone; and it will be a joy and pride to me to serve you however I may, — for that, and for other reasons."

"Your cousin!" she exclaimed softly. "I had

forgotten that part of it! It seems strange to think we are so nearly related."

"I hope we may be more closely related, some day," I ventured to murmur. The words were forced from me, and, as I feared, she took alarm at them.

"Here is the key of the door," she said, thrusting it into my hand, and ignoring my remark. "I beg you to lock yourself in, and do not let yourself be seen or heard until I come to call you myself. No one is likely to disturb you here, but it is best to be on the safe side. Use anything in the room as though it were your own. Good night; here come the servants. Good night!"

She gave my hand a friendly pressure, which I returned with warmth.

"Good night — Marjorie!" It was the first time I had ever used her name. She had never been addressed by it save by the Master.

I heard her give a little gasp, but she answered me never a word. She hurried away down the hall, and I entered the room and locked the door. I had no light; a candle, especially in that room, would have been the height of imprudence. I made my way quietly to the bed, and was soon asleep; the excitement of the night was past, and body and mind were thoroughly tired.

A gentle tapping on the door roused me from the sweetest slumber I had known for weeks; the first time I had lain down without a single care or doubt. I sprang from the bed and approached the door, being unwilling to answer until the caller spoke, for fear of betraying my presence prematurely. I would answer to no one but My Lady.

"Mr. Darke!" It was her voice.

"Yes; what is it?"

"Oh, are you awake so soon? I only wanted to ask you to dress as quickly as possible."

"I will be ready in a very few minutes," I answered.

"Thank you; I am sorry to have been obliged to waken you, for I know how tired you must be; but it was necessary."

"Yes, I know; there is no occasion for apology."

"Oh — and I meant to tell you not to forget that if you find any clothes in the room that you think might fit you, pray use them."

"You are very thoughtful. I will do so."

I waited a moment for another remark, but, hearing none, proceeded to put myself in order. There were at least a dozen suits hanging in the wardrobes, and I selected one of them that pleased my fancy and looked as though it might not be far from my measure. I also came across a case of razors (though the Master had worn a beard), and my first move was to make use of one of them. What luxury it was ! During these months on the island, my beard had grown long and thick. Somehow, I had never thought of what a difference it must make in my appearance; but as tuft after tuft of it dropped beneath the strokes of the razor, I seemed to take on a new life, to become literally a new man. Perhaps it was the last mark of my imprisonment dropping from me, like the broken shackles from the limbs of a released prisoner of state, that made me feel so. The face that I saw in the mirror when I first looked was almost the face of a stranger, so long had it been since I had seen it clearly; but, with the last scrape of the keen edge, I knew myself once more. It served to bring home to me the reality of the immense change that had taken place in my situation and prospects. Somehow, all that had gone before, especially the events of the last twenty-four hours, seemed to have been a dream ; but now I was awake, and myself at last.

Clean clothes and a clean face made another man of me inwardly as well as outwardly, and it was with a feeling of great elation that I heard a knock at the door, and My Lady's voice calling me. As I crossed the room, I noticed my precious relic, the little riding-whip, lying on the floor, where it had fallen from my clothes the night before; I picked it up and laid it on the table as I passed.

My Lady stood at the door, bearing a tray in her hands, laden with breakfast things. She kept her eyes demurely fixed on the tray as she entered and placed it on the table.

"I had one of the maids bring this up for my own breakfast," she explained, with a faint smile, beginning to arrange the things on the table in a nervous manner. "It seemed the only way to avoid a suspicion of any one else being in the house. Now I shall change my mind — like a woman — and breakfast downstairs as usual."

I closed the door behind her, and walked across the room, and stood with my back to the fireplace. My Lady still refused to look up, and I wanted to see her eyes. I thought I should never tire of looking at them.

"I hope you slept well," she continued, still toying with the dishes.

I made no answer, and there was a long silence, so long that she became uneasy.

"Why do you not speak to me?" she asked, raising her eyes suddenly.

I had expected her to be impressed by the

change in my appearance, but I was utterly unprepared for the effect of it. Her eyes fell on me, and then swiftly glanced above my head, and My Lady staggered back with a low cry of amazement — or was it terror? Without stopping to analyze it, I sprang forward to catch her; but she waved me off, while her gaze travelled backward and forward between me and the space above the fireplace.

"What is it, My Lady?" I cried, in lively alarm.

She could not speak, but her outstretched hand followed the direction of her eyes. I turned to look, and it was my turn to exclaim; for there, above where I stood, hung a portrait of the new face that had appeared in the mirror a short hour before. A little older, perhaps, but in all essential features the same, line for line. And not the face only; even the clothing was the same, for the coat that I had selected to wear was exactly the color of the one in the portrait. The likeness could not have been more precise if it had been finished that very morning. On the one previous occasion on which I had been in the room, the figure of the dying Master had absorbed all my attention, and this morning I had been too preoccupied with my thoughts and my preparations to notice my surroundings very carefully. It was no wonder that My Lady received a shock when she saw what seemed the original standing beneath the familiar portrait.

"Good heavens! Whose is the picture, My Lady?" I exclaimed.

She looked at me as though she thought me demented. Imagine a man asking to be told who was the original of his own accurate likeness!

"Whose is it?" I repeated.

"My father!" she answered, with the soft accent that always came into her voice whenever she spoke to him or of him.

I saw it at once. Why the likeness had not been noticed on my first arrival I do not know, unless weariness and exposure had somewhat altered my features. Then, too, the portrait and I had not been seen together before; and the clothing I had worn hitherto, plain in color, soaked with sea-water, and soiled by the ground on which I had slept after the storm, must have given me a vastly different appearance from the one presented by the gay cavalier in the maroon velvet coat that matched the costume of the portrait.

"It is wonderful!" I said, in a low tone. "No wonder you were startled, My Lady! No doubt it was painted when he was about my age."

"Yes," she said. "Just before I was born. My

mother wished it, and he could refuse her nothing."

"He was a younger man, then, than he looked,"
I said.

"Yes, far younger. I knew he had a trouble on
his mind that aged him rapidly, though until last
night I never guessed what it was, or how great.
When I first remember him, he appeared far from
young."

"No wonder! The thought of the unmerited
disgrace attached to his name, and the hopelessness of ever clearing it away, must have been hard
to bear, and wearing on his patience."

"Very hard," she murmured. "And I could
not help him!"

"Yet it seems to me," I went on, "that the consciousness of his own innocence might have helped
to sustain him, and take away some of the sting of
the disgrace."

She shook her head. "No doubt it did a little,"
she mused. "But he was so sensitive, so tender-
hearted! It even grieved him terribly that he felt
obliged to detain you — he told me so often; and
it was one more trouble added to those that have
been heaped on him through no fault of his own.
He trusted so in Burton's tale that your obstinacy
angered him. But he was often tempted to let

you go free, and trust to your honor not to betray him; indeed, I know that he would have done so long ago if he had not been quite certain that he had but a few months longer to live. He told me what he expected, but I did not believe it — I could not; I was sure he exaggerated the danger of his condition. I was wrong, and he was right, as he always was. Except in your case," she added bravely, after a pause. I honored her for her perfect justice. " But he said that a few months would be all he expected, and he wished to die in peace. He said, too, that a young man could well afford the time to ease the last hours of a dying old man."

"I do not regret the time, — now," I rejoined. " I am glad to know that those last months were as free from care as might be. But to think that all this might have been cleared up long ago, if he had only told me what his ideas were! I would most gladly have been a friend to him — and to you."

"He was so sure that you knew who he was, and that your denial was untrue! It was a most unfortunate misunderstanding altogether," she said sadly, "and you were not the only sufferer by it. But it seemed so evident that you had come in search of him, that he could suppose nothing else;

and Burton, of course, took all possible means of fostering the delusion."

"And yet Burton frankly explained the whole matter that could never have been understood without his help! We owe him some gratitude for that, at least, even though he intended the knowledge to die with me. What a surprise there is in store for him!" I said, with grim satisfaction, for the thought of the overwhelming punishment that was coming to him for his deceit and his murderous attempts was very pleasant. "What a surprise to find me still alive, and both of us in possession of his cherished secret!"

My Lady shook her head sadly. "I cannot bear to think of it," she said. "He has been so faithful for so many years, and we trusted him so implicitly! It is very hard to understand how a man could have two such opposite natures, and act according to both of them at the same time. Even now, I can hardly believe that it is not all a bad dream."

"It *is* only a bad dream," I responded. "At least it is all past and gone like a dream; and the dreams that I have dreamed were of happier prospect. If they are only fulfilled I shall ask nothing better of life!"

My voice trembled in spite of my utmost en-

Y

deavors. It was trenching on dangerous ground; ground that might — that must — be trodden ere long, but that was forbidden for the present. I felt like a soul standing at the gate of Paradise, seeing the happy walks and ways within, but not permitted to set foot on the threshold, as yet; not even sure that I would be permitted to enter at the last.

Again My Lady took alarm. After last night, she knew so well what thing I must say to her, sooner or later! But she fenced with the matter, tried to postpone it as long as possible. She rose from her chair quickly, and moved toward the door, but turned to speak again.

"I will leave you for a while," she said. "After the dinner hour I will have the great bell rung, and every soul on the island assembled below the porch at the front of the house. I shall confront Burton there, and he shall answer for what he has done. But before I speak to him, I will come for you."

She turned once more to leave me, but stopped suddenly, as though petrified. My eyes followed the direction of hers, and I saw her looking at the little riding-whip that lay on the farther end of the table. Slowly she approached it, and inspected it narrowly, without offering to touch it; and when she was assured of its identity the crimson mounted slowly to her face, until it was all aglow.

"Where did *that* come from?" she asked, without looking at me.

I hesitated.

"I found it — on the top of a dune."

She grew redder than before, if such a thing could be.

"How did it come here?"

"I brought it, last night."

"Why, you saved nothing from the cabin!" she exclaimed.

"You forget. When you bundled me out of the window so unceremoniously, that went with me; I had had it in my boot."

"Was *that* what you were searching for when I was trying to hurry you away?"

"Yes."

"Why? Was it so precious?"

I hesitated. The matter would take a long time to explain properly to her. I was not quite sure that I could explain it to myself.

"*Why?*" she repeated insistently, with her eyes still fixed on the whip.

"Because it was a sort of souvenir, and I had an affection for its — for it." I hastened to alter the form of my sentence. Again I had narrowly missed making the declaration she was so anxious to avoid. My unruly tongue seemed bound to get the better of me; my mind was so impregnated with my love for her that the words would start to my lips in spite of my efforts at restraint.

She seemed deeply mortified.

"Did you hate me so much as that?" she asked mournfully, looking down at the whip.

"Hate you!" I exclaimed. "How can you think such a thing? ... You told me you had heard *all* my conversation with Burton last night," I said slowly.

"I did, but—"

"Then you know how groundless and untrue such a supposition is," I continued.

There was a slight pause. "What are you going to do with it?" she asked.

"I don't know,—now. Still keep it as a souvenir, I suppose."

She thought deeply for a few moments.

"Will you give it to me?" she asked suddenly.

"To you?" I was taken aback by the request.

"Yes."

"I should be sorry to part with it," I said. "Yet it is already yours by right; I have no lawful claim to it."

She took it up, and moved toward the door;

and, as she turned the handle, " I shall make good use of it," she said. She raised her eyes as she spoke, and they were full of tears that were ready to fall; yet not exactly tears of sorrow, if her face told the truth. In another instant she had closed the door behind her, leaving me bewildered, to speculate upon her possible meaning.

I was sure that she would not care to carry the whip again. From what I had seen on the dune that day, I knew the associations connected with it must be painful, and I could not imagine why she should wish to keep the thing by her, unless to remind her not to be too hasty on some other occasion. Well, I thought if matters went on as I would have them, I should know all about it some day; and if not— I did not care particularly to think about that contingency, so I put it aside with commendable resolution, and sat down to breakfast. I was young and strong, and hope is a thing not to be put aside without the best of reasons. And it seemed to me, just then, that I had the best of reasons for clinging to all my hopes, even the wildest. Wherefore, I had an excellent appetite.

XVIII

THE RESURRECTION OF THE DEAD

WHEN My Lady first called me, I had glanced out of the window and observed the position of the sun, which was so well up in the heavens that I guessed it to be between ten and eleven. Evidently My Lady had felt the need of rest herself (and no wonder!), and had given both of us the full benefit of the time. By the time I had finished breakfasting it was nearly noon, and soon after I heard the bell rung to call the slaves to dinner. I watched them returning from the field, though I was careful to keep well back from the open window, that no wandering, casual glance might spy me. I was quite sure that My Lady had so laid her plans as to make the final settlement of Burton's account effective, if not actually dramatic; and I had no mind to spoil her design, though I could hazard only vague guesses as to what it was.

I had rather expected My Lady to call me when the first bell rang, for at that time all the slaves would, of course, come to their quarters.

But herein My Lady's mind was vastly better than mine, for she let them go to their huts as usual, without a sign; and I soon saw the good sense of the procedure. For when men are hungry, they think first of their stomachs, and have little mind or patience to spare for long statements, however interesting, or for abstract justice.

It had always been the custom to ring the bell when it was time to call the negroes from the fields, for the reason that, so used, the sound was carried to a great distance; and as there was almost always some one working in the woods, or perhaps well away toward one of the extremities of the island, such laborers could the more clearly hear the signal. But when they had all returned to their quarters, there was no need of any great volume of sound, and a couple of strokes of the bell were the signal to return to work.

Just here shone forth My Lady's genius. For, after they were all collected, and the hour allowed for dinner had elapsed, instead of tolling, as usual, the bell was rung violently. Every one on the plantation knew what such a signal meant; it was for the gathering of all the force of servants on the wide lawn that lay at the front of the house; a sort of general alarm call. So seldom was this signal used that during the months of·

my life on the island I had never heard the bell ring, except the regular noon and evening summons to meat. It can be imagined, therefore, what excitement, almost consternation, ensued among the negroes, and with what haste they poured on to the shady lawn before the house.

Even while the bell was still ringing, My Lady's dear voice called me at last, and as we descended the stairs together she laid her plan before me. All the house servants had already been sent out to the lawn, so that there was no danger of our being seen before the proper time came.

By her direction, I took my stand in the drawing-room. The curtains extended to the floor, and as the frames were cut from top to bottom, and hinged, they were often used as doors. In all of them heavy curtains were now drawn close, leaving but a narrow slit through which the light could enter. This arrangement afforded ample opportunity for me to view the spectacle, while it entirely concealed me from the view of the crowd outside; a single sweep of the arms would throw back the hangings, and three steps would bring me to My Lady's side.

The wild clamor of the bell ceased, and My Lady stepped forth from the hall door to the railing of the porch, and there she stood surveying the assemblage in silence for some moments. I wish I had the power to tell how sweet she looked, and withal so grand and stately, like a queen preparing to address her subjects. Yet there was in her face something of the judge, also; a certain grimness and menace that might have seemed natural enough on the Master's face, but that sat strangely on hers. An expression newly born of the occasion that called it forth, such as no one of them had ever seen on her before; a fixed determination that was strange to me also (though something like it had appeared the day she had saved my life at the quicksand), that sent a thrill of apprehension through the heart of many a poor slave who had no reason whatever for the trembling that seized him. The one man who had good reason to feel alarm was by an accident rendered almost incapable of displaying his feelings, though he was probably rejoicing in the belief that at one blow he had destroyed his enemy, his confessor, and every evidence of his guilt.

As My Lady scanned each face, the chattering died away, and a dead silence ensued.

"Where is Burton?" She had seen him, but affected ignorance of his presence. He came forward from the extreme edge of the crowd, and saluted.

"Here, My Lady."

"Let every one else stand back for a few yards. Do you remain where you are."

They left him alone in the midst of a great semicircle. I could see his eyes glance about furtively; he was not afraid, but he began to be uneasy, though he little imagined what exceeding cause for apprehension he had. This was not the sort of scene he had expected wherein to recount to her the false explanation that he had doubtless prepared to tell her.

My Lady looked all about her, as though searching for some one.

"I do not see Mr. Darke," she said, looking at Burton.

I could hear a sudden murmur sweep along the crowd, but only Burton spoke. He hesitated for a moment; then —

"Mr. Darke does not know the meaning of the bell, My Lady," he said.

"Ah, yes; I had forgotten that! Then send some one for him quickly; I wish him to be present."

Burton made no movement to comply with her order; the crowd around stood stock still. They knew — as they thought — what had become of me, but it was not their affair to tell of it unless they were asked.

"Well," said My Lady, with evident impatience, "why do you not send for him? I do not intend to spend the rest of the day waiting. Must I send one of the slaves myself?"

Burton seemed staggered at the demand. He knew the uselessness of sending to seek me, yet he did not know how to break the news to her.

"Mr. Darke, My Lady, —" he hesitated to put the thing into words. He could do the thing without a qualm, but to tell of it was something else. "Mr. Darke —"

"Well, where is he? Find him, some of you; I must have him here before I say what I have to say."

The negroes looked at one another, but no one moved. Burton was obliged to speak further.

"He is gone, My Lady."

"Gone!" I had no idea My Lady could be so good an actress. "Gone! Whither, and when?"

"I cannot tell, My Lady," said the miscreant, cowering under the stern, inquiring gaze she fixed on him.

"Did not my father give you strict orders to guard him with the utmost care, and to use every slave on the plantation, if necessary to the purpose?"

"Yes, My Lady, but —"

"Well?"

"Indeed, My Lady, it is no fault of mine, but I fear he is dead." He blurted out the last words as though they were forced from him.

"Dead!" My Lady was terribly shocked. "You *fear* it, you say; do you not *know*? Why was not the order obeyed?"

"Indeed, My Lady, it was obeyed as well as we knew how. I think it must have been his own fault."

She caught up the words on the instant.

"That was what you said when he was caught in the quicksand! You fear—you think—do you not *know* anything?" she exclaimed. "What had happened?"

He began to stammer,—that man of granite face and iron will and muscle—before her scornful eyes!

"He—I think—there was—"

"Stop! Think what you intend to say, and then say it plainly," she commanded.

"If you were awake last night, My Lady," he commenced, after he had collected himself, "you must have seen the fire."

"I saw it; one of the woodpiles, was it not? Some one must have been grossly careless to leave sparks so close to it. But that is not our business now. I want Mr. Darke."

"It was not a woodpile, My Lady."

"No? What then?"

"It was — a cabin."

"There is only one cabin in that direction. You do not mean to say — "

"Yes, My Lady, it was his." He looked as though he would rejoice to have the earth sink beneath him. He did not find it as easy to account to her as he had expected. Probably it might have been easier if she had not pointed her queries with an exact knowledge of the case.

"Mr. Darke's?" He nodded. "And where did you lodge him afterward?"

I congratulated myself that it was not I that had to undergo her cross-examination. Her apparent ignorance of the truth made her questions infinitely more searching and hard to answer.

"Nowhere, My Lady," abjectly.

Her eyes flashed. "You left him without shelter?" she demanded indignantly. He fairly writhed beneath her withering gaze.

"No, My Lady; he did not need it. He — he — we fear — "

"Go on!"

"We are sure he is dead!"

"Dead? I say it is impossible!" she cried incredulously. "How could such a thing happen?"

"The cabin, My Lady. He was in it."

"How do you know that?" Her questions followed his replies without giving him an instant for reflection.

"I do not know for certain, but where else should he have been — and we can find no trace of him anywhere."

"You have searched?"

"Every man on the island has been searching all the morning without avail. I put them at it instead of sending them to work."

"That was well done, at least! But perhaps he has gone away?"

"He could not. The boats have not been touched, and there is not a footprint on the beach that has been made within two days," he replied, gaining confidence as the worst of the ordeal seemed to be past. But she had another bolt in store for him.

"My father gave orders that, although he was to be detained, no harm was to come to him, and he made you especially responsible for ensuring this. How could this happen, then, — most of all, without your knowledge? Is this the way his orders have been obeyed? If he or I had a thought of such a thing, there would have been some great changes in the management of this plantation! I will see to it, for the future, that matters are otherwise."

It was a blow straight in the face.

"Indeed, My Lady, we did everything possible; it is no fault of mine," he stammered. "He was closely watched by day, and the cabin guarded at night. We did all that men could do to take care of him."

"Who watched the cabin at night?"

"We — we took turns on guard."

She stamped her foot with angry impatience. "You know what I mean! Who watched last night?"

He began to tremble. "I did, My Lady," he blurted out, with great effort. It was a fatal admission, and I was taken aback at his clumsiness.

"*You* did? Did I not tell you yesterday to go to the house and *stay there?*"

"Yes, My Lady."

Her voice took on a fine ring of scorn and anger.

"So you are not content with flagrantly disobeying my father's orders, but must also run counter to mine — to the very first I had given you since he died? This is your boasted faithfulness, then! The servant who will not obey in the lesser things will not obey in the greater, and such a man I will not have about me! What excuse have you for such a proceeding?"

The man cowered like a whipped hound, so that even I felt sorry for his evident distress.

"Because, My Lady, I had not given orders for any watch to be set last night, and I decided to watch myself," he groaned.

"You knew perfectly well that Mr. Darke was no longer to be regarded as a prisoner," she rejoined. "You know that my father's last words showed that he had been mistaken about him, and that Mr. Darke was really a friend."

"The Master was mistaken in that," he murmured. "I know he was an enemy."

"How do you know it?" she questioned sharply.

"I — I am sure of it," he answered weakly.

"Sure of it!" she repeated, with fine contempt. "Have you any proof of such an assertion? Do you pretend to know better than the Master?"

"No, My Lady." He seemed to quiver all over.

"I say he is a friend — a good friend — better than any of you could have imagined. He was a noble gentleman, persecuted and suffering from a terrible mistake; and he bore his hardships like a soldier, and forgave them like a gentleman.

He was not to blame in any way. The fault was wholly ours; it has been my intention to make what apology and reparation I could, ever since I learned the truth; and my father would have sconded me with all his power, if he had lived. Do you all understand this, or shall I repeat it?"

I vow that my very ears tingled at her declaration. It would have made me glad and proud at any time even to know that she could say such a thing if I had been really dead, or if she had supposed me so; but when she knew me to be almost within arm's length of her, the speech seemed to be addressed to me rather than to them.

There was a hoarse murmur among the crowd, which finally resolved itself into a common declaration of comprehension on their part.

"Very good," she proceeded. "I want that to be thoroughly understood, both now and hereafter." They could not see the significance of the declaration, but I could. "But your excuse is a lame one, Burton. Even if no watch had been ordered, and you thought one necessary, why did you not send one of the negroes?"

"I — they are apt to be careless, My Lady, and I thought I could keep better guard than they would."

"So you took such excellent care that you allowed the cabin to burn down, while the man who was confided to your care — our now honored guest, one to whom we owed more than you know — was asleep in it!" she said, with stinging sarcasm. "Why did you not discover the fire sooner? On my soul, I begin to believe that you were willing to let him die — if you did not actually cause the fire yourself. Did you?" she demanded sharply.

I began to fear she might overdo her appearance of ignorance of the facts. It seemed to me that such questions must rouse a suspicion in his mind; but he was so absolutely sure of his ground that it never occurred to him.

The miserable wretch saw her coming close to the truth, though he supposed it only a good guess. But his guilty conscience helped to terrify him; he had tied his own hands by his previous declarations and admissions; the tissue of lies that he had told was being twisted into a rope that was winding round and round him, ever tighter. He would risk anything rather than let the truth be known — to her.

"No, no, My Lady!" he cried, falling on his knees. The line of negroes around him gasped and stared with open mouths, as they saw their overseer, more the friend and equal than the servant of the dead Master, thus humbling himself. They did not understand what lay behind all this, but they knew it must be something fearful to bring this man to his knees. "No, no; I swear to God I had nothing to do with it!" He gazed at her with abject appeal, beseeching her to believe him.

My Lady looked down at him almost with pity. "Do you dare to take such an oath? Do you *dare?*" she asked solemnly. She seemed hardly able to believe her ears.

"Indeed, yes!" he cried eagerly. "I hated him, I confess, but I swear I never tried to harm him! If he could only come back from the dead, he would tell you the same!"

It seemed to him a safe enough appeal to make, and, despite my abhorrence at his wholesale perjury, I laughed to myself at the thought of what he would have to say when I appeared. But I had no idea how soon my resurrection was to come. My Lady, however, grasped the situation instantly, and her voice must have sounded to him like the trump of doom.

"You dare to appeal to the dead to appear and testify for you? Then the dead shall rise and speak!"

She took three steps to the window, and, tearing the curtains apart, she pointed where she knew I would be standing, though she kept her eyes fixed on him.

"Here is a witness from the dead!" she cried impressively. "Shall he tell what he knows?"

I stepped through the window on to the porch, and we stood side by side between the pillars.

XIX

EVEN AS KORAH

MY LADY had expected to create a sensation, but neither of us was prepared for the effect of my sudden appearance on the scene.

There was a wild shout of amazement and terror, and in an instant every human being on the lawn, except one, turned as if to flee, and yet remained rooted there, staring at me in a fearful fascination. The sole exception was Burton, whose jaw dropped, while his eyes dilated with an awful dread. For a moment he stood so; then a sort of froth came upon his open lips, and with a frightful, despairing cry of " Mr. Edward!" he fell forward on his face, mercifully insensible for the time.

We gazed at one another in wonder, unable at first to account for such a stupendous effect, until suddenly the solution flashed on us both simultaneously. My Lady had intended to make her impression by calling Allan Darke from his supposed grave. The flaw in the plan lay in the alteration in my appearance made by the razor and the change of clothing; and this alteration both of us had forgotten to reckon with. All the house servants were familiar with the portrait, and all the older negroes remembered the Master in his younger days. Burton, of course, recognized the likeness immediately, and it was too much for even his iron nerves. If My Lady, who knew of my living presence, had received such a shock at first seeing me, how much greater must have been the effect on the others, who supposed I was as certainly dead as was the Master. But, for the moment, my own personality was eliminated from the question ; no one thought of me — why should they ? To them I was the Master, risen from the dead, rejuvenated, to punish the wrong-doers who had violated his commands.

The panic might even yet have carried them away in flight, had they not been restrained by a voice that they were accustomed to obey without questioning.

"Stop!" cried My Lady, imperatively. "Stay where you are ; no harm shall come to you!"

Somewhat reassured, they turned again to face us, though there was craven fear depicted on many a countenance, and a very slight provocation would have sent the whole cowardly crew flying in a wild panic. They believed My Lady would protect them as far as she could; but how far did her power extend? Could the living stand against the dead who had returned to life?

"What shall we do about Burton?" I whispered, turning to My Lady.

"Let him lie there until he recovers," she replied, with a cruel fierceness that I had not expected from her. "It will not be long; there is too much to bring him back to life! Numa, get some water, and throw it on — that thing!"

He brought it, and dashed it over the prostrate man, still keeping a timid watch on my motionless figure. I believe if I had made the slightest movement, he would have dropped the water and fled helplessly.

The breathless crowd stood still. Their eyes were all upon me; My Lady's and mine were upon Burton; and we all waited.

In a very few minutes he began to recover. He sat up, and leaned heavily upon one arm, while his dazed eyes travelled around the circle of those who stood near him. He seemed to be trying to recollect what had happened. From them his gaze shifted to the porch where we stood — and then memory returned. With a weak cry of horror he began to creep backward, not trying to rise, but dragging himself upon one arm, while his staring eyes never left my face. He was incapable of a single thought but that he must retreat beyond the range of my accusing vision.

"Stop!" commanded My Lady. "You cannot escape." She fixed a stern gaze on him. "You called a witness from the dead to justify you," she said slowly. "Will you speak the truth, or shall he tell what he knows?"

"No, no!" cried the grovelling wretch. "I will confess. I will confess all! Oh, Mr. Edward!" His voice became a wail of grief and agony. "Pardon! Mercy!"

"Speak the truth, then — the truth!" commanded the accusing voice.

"I will confess. I did it! *You* know! Pardon!"

I let no change come over my features, but waited for My Lady to speak.

"What did you do?"

"I killed him — Allan Darke! He came to drag us back to imprisonment and disgrace. I killed him! I tied him fast, and set fire to the cabin."

The listening crowd drew long breaths of horror.

"Those previous attempts on his life that he told of — did you make them?"

"It is true! I tried many times to kill him, but each time he escaped — I do not know how. He seemed to have a charmed life, but the last time I succeeded."

"What other crime did you commit?"

"What other?" He seemed bewildered. He had really forgotten the older crime in the events that the new one had brought.

"That old one, thirty years ago!"

"Thirty years ago I killed Harold Darke, his uncle. I did it, and let you be accused of it. Pardon, Mr. Edward, pardon," he wailed.

The confession seemed sufficiently complete; he had owned to the main facts, and the details were not necessary, since My Lady and I both knew them. My Lady glanced at me uncertainly, and I took the glance as a hint for me to speak. What I said was boyish, foolish; perhaps the nervous tension under which I had lived so long was partly responsible for it. Certainly I repented deeply enough for the way in which I spoke.

"Thank you, Burton," I said ironically. "You have told us quite sufficient for the present purpose. But it is only fair you should know that not only I, but My Lady also, heard your very complete confession in my cabin last night."

I could not help the taunt. I had thought to overwhelm him with this new knowledge, but it was a monstrous mistake for me to speak at all (though neither of us could possibly have known that at the time). While I had kept silence he had

never thought but that I was the Master miracu-
lously risen to accuse him. But if he remembered
the Master's face so well, he remembered his voice
also — and he remembered mine, with the accurate
observation of deadly hatred. I saw the dawning
light of recognition come into his staring eyes, and
as I finished speaking he sprang to his feet with a
cry of rage, all his faculties and his strength restored in a moment. The supernatural appalled
him, but the real made him a maniac.

"*You!*" he shouted, as he regained his feet,
and ran toward the steps.

With a swift spring My Lady threw herself in
front of me. There was the sharp report of a
pistol, and My Lady fell backward into my arms.
As I laid her softly down, oblivious of all else, I
saw blood flowing from her shoulder.

"Oh, My Lady!" I cried, in agony. "This for
me!"

She was very white, and for a moment was near
fainting, but she smiled reassuringly.

"It is nothing! I am not much hurt. Take
care; he may try again!" She tried to turn me
to face him.

I began cutting the sleeve open to get at the
wound.

She submitted docilely. I found the place

where the ball had gone right through the fleshy part of her shoulder, and used my handkerchief — one of the Master's — for a temporary bandage. I was testing to see if the bone was hurt, when she spoke again.

"I tell you it is nothing! See!" She moved the arm freely up and down, to my infinite relief. I knew enough about such matters to be able to attend to a simple flesh wound as well as any doctor, but a smashed bone was beyond my ken. My Lady turned her head.

"Oh, see there!" she cried, and struggled to her feet.

The negroes had been spellbound by my appearance, even while I spoke to Burton. They did not at once recognize the voice as mine, and the influence of my mysterious appearance remained with them so far. But when Burton fired and My Lady fell, the spell was broken; the shot set every one in motion. They had loved the Master, but they idolized My Lady. In her cause, or to avenge her, they would have charged into a den of lions, every man himself a lion.

As though moved by a single impulse, every man, and most of the women, cast themselves upon the would-be murderer; even Theodore threw his single hand into the fray. Beneath the weight of the sudden onslaught Burton had gone heavily to the ground, but not tamely. As My Lady cried out to me, the great heap of struggling humanity parted with a mighty heave, and in the midst appeared Burton's powerful figure dealing fearful blows in all directions. A moment sufficed to free him from most of his assailants; before his sudden dash the crowd parted like turf before the plough. He was free, running like a deer eastward toward the seashore, with never a backward glance at the foes at his heels. In spite of the punishment his giant strength had inflicted, a dozen of the stoutest negroes set off instantly in pursuit of him, though apparently hopelessly distanced from the start.

I turned to My Lady, who was so absorbed in the spectacle that her wound was forgotten.

"Go into the house, My Lady, and rest until I return; then I will dress the wound properly." I turned again to the late combatants, who were investigating their cuts and bruises, which were many, and looking somewhat dazed — as well they might — by the suddenness with which one event had followed another. They had probably experienced more strange excitements during the last hour than in all their lives before.

"Catch me a horse, one of you!" I cried. "Do

it quickly.   Never mind the saddle; a rope around
the jaw will serve.   Hurry!"

My Lady came closer to me.

"What are you going to do?" she asked anxiously.

"Follow them!" I replied, pointing to the
figures flying seaward, fast becoming mere specks
in the distance.

"You must not! It is too dangerous!" she
cried.

"That is why I must go — to assist them!"

My Lady came close to me, and laid her un-
wounded arm across my shoulders. "Do not go
— Allan!" she pleaded, maiden fear and shyness
swallowed up by anxiety.

Who would not have been sorely tempted? I
was no more than mortal. Very tenderly I put
my arms about her and kissed the cheek that was
so close to mine. She made no resistance, did
not even color, but went on as though I had done
something perfectly natural and usual.

"He is armed!"

"So am I!" I answered grimly. I meant to
use my weapon to good purpose when the time
came. I had been willing to overlook my own
grudge against him for My Lady's sake, but I
could not forgive this injury to her, even though

the bullet had been intended for me. "I am armed, but the others are not. You see I must go, sweetheart." I kissed her again, it might be the last time, I thought to myself, for Burton was now doubly dangerous since he had been unmasked, and had nothing more to lose — or to live for, as it seemed to me.

"Good-by, Marjorie!" I released her, and sprang down the steps, not daring to look back, lest I should be too strongly drawn to return to her. I had a task before me that was hateful, but I was all aglow with happiness. In one so proud and distant as My Lady, her meek submission to that caress meant much, very much; if she did not yet love me, she could not be far from it.

Therefore I rode seaward in pursuit of mine enemy as gayly as a lover to meet his lass. The horse that bore me was a fine one, and the thunder of his hoofs on the hard road made sweet music. It was the first time I had crossed a horse since I left Cape May, some six months ago. The swift rush of the wind brought a wild exhilaration, and as we neared the sea I believed that I could ride out on its heaving surface, so ethereal did I feel. Presently the roar of the surf was in my ears, and I was riding up the beach.

A mile or so above me I could see a solitary figure, and far beyond that a dark spot that denoted a group of men. As I sped along, I made out that the lone man was running toward me, and as we neared one another he threw up his arms and shouted wildly. It was Theodore, the strongest, the best, the most sensible of the slaves.

I stopped my horse close to him. "What is it?" I cried.

"A rope!" he panted.

"A rope? To tie him? Have you caught him, then?"

"No, but he is caught — in the quicksand!"

Amazement dumfounded me for a moment. I knew how well he was acquainted with the place.

"The rope is needed to pull him out?" I demanded.

"Yes; quickly, too, or it will be too late!"

"Go back there," I said hurriedly. "Get logs, rails, anything that might float, and throw them to him. I will fetch a rope." I knew they could throw him nothing that would support him for any length of time, but I fancied that perhaps such things might serve to uphold him for a little while.

I had come fast from the house, but the speed

was slow compared with what I reached in returning. At the sound of the hurrying hoofs one of the maids ran out in alarm, and I reined up for a moment.

"Tell My Lady not to be alarmed; everything goes well!" I cried, for I knew my wild pace would excite apprehension.

It was no great distance to the barn, where I knew a supply of rope was kept. I leaped from the horse, and dashed into the building and out again with a coil that I knew would be ample for the purpose. As I neared the house again I saw My Lady on the porch, watching me anxiously; and though time was too precious to allow me to reassure her by stopping to explain matters, I held up the coil for her to see as I passed, and shouted, —

"No danger!"

Looking back, I saw her wave her hand as she turned toward the door.

Those miles at racing speed told heavily on the horse. Before we reached the sea for the second time he was panting violently; foam gathered on his jaw and dripped from his haunches, and when we turned up the beach his pace slackened, willing beast though he was. But there was a good two-mile run before him yet, and it was no time to spare horseflesh; with voice and blows I urged him on until the miles, interminable as they seemed, were covered, and I dropped to the ground on the edge of the quicksand.

I had been making a running noose on the end of the rope while we toiled up the beach, and when I sprang to the ground the coil was all ready to cast. I paused a moment to take a survey of the situation.

Burton was in the very centre of the treacherous area, so far from the edge that, knowing its nature as he did, he could only have come there by deliberate intention. He was already sunk more deeply than I had been when My Lady cast her anchor line to me, but I anticipated little difficulty in extricating him. My Lady alone had been able to save me, and here we had a dozen strong men.

He stood perfectly motionless, with folded arms, glaring fiercely at his late pursuers, who were running wildly about the edge calling all sorts of instructions to him. He was by far the calmest of all the crowd. Around him in all directions lay pieces of driftwood, a few fence-rails that they must have brought from considerable distances, some myrtle bushes that they had dug up with their bare hands from the top of the dunes, where they grew thickly in spots; even small twigs had been cast to him. They had flung everything they

2 A

could lay their hands on, without discrimination. I noticed that most of the things near him were piled up in small heaps, laid so regularly as to preclude the supposition that they could have fallen so. The negroes told me afterward that he had seized and piled up everything that fell within his reach, though at the time they could not imagine his object.

I bade the negroes hold the end of the rope and prepare to pull, while I cast the noose to him. It was a long throw, and the noose fell short; I gathered it up and threw again, and this time it fell close to him. I was mindful of My Lady's directions to me in a similar case.

"Put the noose beneath your arms!" I cried.

He stretched out his hand to it and held it for a moment while he glared at me.

"Fasten it beneath your arms!" I cried again, thinking he had not understood me, or was too dazed to comprehend my meaning.

He raised his arm and threw the rope far away with a bitter curse.

"Damn you!" he cried. "Shall I *never* be free of you?"

His hand went to his pocket, and I saw the flash of the sun on the steel barrel of a pistol. Before I could move he levelled it at me and pulled the trigger. There was a shower of sparks as the flint struck, but no report followed; the bullet from it had already struck My Lady, and he had forgotten that the barrel was empty.

"So! Even that fails me at the last!" he sneered.

He caught it by the barrel, and the next minute it came flying at me, impelled by all the force of an arm always abnormally powerful, and now strengthened by hate to a supreme effort. I dodged, but not quick enough to escape scot-free; the whirling missile touched my head, hard enough to cut the scalp, but doing no serious damage. He raised a savage scream as he saw the blood flow.

"At last!" he cried triumphantly, with a mad laugh.

"Not yet," I answered, recovering myself. "Don't be a fool, man; I am trying to save you! Catch the rope and keep it this time," and I cast it again close to him.

He seized it and gave it a powerful jerk that nearly tore it from the hands of the unsuspecting negroes.

"I nearly had it that time," he laughed shrilly, and again he cast it from him, making it only too plain that he would not be saved by his own will.

I saw that the man was mad and determined on

suicide; if he was to be saved, it must be in spite of himself. Whispering to the negroes to pull quickly when the noose caught, I gathered up more of the rope and extended the noose widely, hoping that it might fall over him; and after several vain attempts I saw it settle loosely around him.

"Pull!" I shouted.

If the man was mad, he had not lost all his reasoning powers. Before the negroes, quickly as they responded to my cry, could tighten the noose around him, he had seized it, shifted it to his neck, and drawn it close, so that it was impossible for us either to recover it or to tighten it without strangling him.

"Now, curse you, pull if you choose!" he jeered.

We were helpless. He was sunk nearly to his shoulders by this time, and even with his aid it was most unlikely that we could have rescued him. With his neck encircled by the noose, which we dared not pull, he was our master, and he had his own way at the last. Standing like statues, we watched him sink, inch by inch, until the creeping sand touched his chin; then I could stand it no longer, and, turning my face away, I stood horror-struck, waiting for the end, knowing that it must be all over in five minutes more. Presently there came a sort of spluttering sound, and a gasp from

the negroes, who had been fascinated by the trag-
edy happening before their eyes. I clapped both
hands to my ears to shut out the sound ; and
presently, when I dared to remove them, there was
silence.

I looked at the quicksand and turned away
shuddering. At the very surface of the sand, two
maniac eyes glared hatred and defiance at me, all
unconscious as they were. Fearless and unrepent-
ant he had lived, and in like manner he died.

I heard some of the negroes, overcome by the
horror of it, fall on their knees and begin to pray
— not for him, but for themselves. Presently
Theodore touched my arm. He was trembling
violently, and his face, like the faces of the rest,
had become of that dark ashen-gray color that in
a negro denotes paleness.

"Marse Allan, shall we pull him out now?" he
whispered.

It was terrible to look at the sand again,
but it had to be done. To my infinite relief,
the surface was as placid as it had ever been.
It was gone; even the bushes and driftwood had
disappeared. A few feet of rope, which some of
the negroes still clung to, was all that remained
to testify that a life had just gone down into those
depths before our eyes.

"Shall we pull him out?" repeated Theodore.

"No," I answered. "It cannot be done. We might tear him to pieces, but we could never bring him to the surface now."

"But the rope?"

"Fling it into the quicksand!" I said, shivering.

We watched it slowly sink, the last trace of the madman and of our unavailing effort to save him; and then we walked slowly away, and left him in the grave he had chosen.

XX

IF I had not reassured her when I rode away, my long absence would have made My Lady anxious; as it was, she had so much confidence in my statement that she returned quietly to her room and stayed there. Consequently, when our party reached the house, I was met by a maid with inquiries from My Lady. I told her to say that Burton was dead by his own act without doing further harm. Would My Lady see me? My Lady begged to be excused for this afternoon; her wound had been dressed by the maid, and she was resting. She would prefer not to come down-stairs again to-day. Would Mr. Darke consider the house and its contents as his own, and use them accordingly? Mr. Darke would and did — except the one thing among the contents of the house that he longed most to see. But it would have been worse than discourteous to insist on seeing her.

I had the wound in my head dressed, and bound

up with a handkerchief, and a very piratical-look-
ing craft I must have appeared. The servants
eyed me curiously; they knew my former be-
whiskered visage and my tattered raiment well
enough, but this smooth-faced gentleman, made
in the likeness of the Master's portrait, wearing
the Master's clothes, and treated as an honored
guest and trusted friend in the house of his
quondam enemies, was a stranger to them in more
ways than one. They did not. yet know of the
relationship between us, or they would have wondered still more.

What an afternoon it was! I felt centuries older
than I had been yesterday; the lives and deaths
of a half-dozen people had been passed in review
before me in that short time, and the little island
world had been turned topsy-turvy. Even I, who
held the key to the whole situation, felt giddy
from the swift rush of events; how much more
must it affect the slaves, who could only surmise
vaguely.

I could not rid myself of the feeling of excited
tension that had held me in its grip so long. I
was constantly looking for some further develop-
ment, some new danger to be faced, and would
have welcomed it for the chance it might give of
working off the nervous state of strained expecta-

tion that troubled me. It seemed impossible that all these things could have been accomplished already.

The hours wore away. I wandered aimlessly about the grounds; I was seized with a mighty restlessness, and could settle to nothing. The one thing that I wanted I could not have. One of the slaves, seeing my unrest, mixed a great bowl of bombo, and set it beside me in the hall, during one of my few quiet moments. I tried it, and found it excellent of its kind, though doubtless my long abstinence from all liquors made it doubly grateful; but not even that and a pipe sufficed to solace me.

Still, however impatiently I might drag through the long hours, they did pass somehow. Sunset was long past, and the darkness was gathering rapidly, when I strolled out again among the trees to smoke my pipe in the open air. Beneath the trees the shadows were deeper, and I could barely see my way.

A light sound, like the snap of a twig, not far away, caused me to turn in time to see a white-clad figure gliding rapidly off to the right, in the direction of the house. Even in the darkness, there was something familiar about the carriage of it. I dropped the pipe, and my foot crushed it into a dozen pieces as I sprang forward in chase of the hurrying form, and caught up with it at the edge of the grove.

"Ah, My Lady, do not fly from me now! If you only knew how I have been longing to see you!"

She saw that she was recognized, and stopped.

"I did not intend to meet you again until to-morrow," she murmured. "I thought you were in the house, so I slipped out by one of the side windows, not thinking you would find me here."

"I am sorry you should think it necessary to avoid me," I said, somewhat hurt; "and if my presence causes you annoyance, I will leave you."

"Oh, no," she replied quickly. "It is not that; only—" she hesitated, and I caught up the word.

"Then let there be no 'only,'" I said. "Surely, if you could come out to sit here alone, there is no reason why you should not stay for a time with me."

She moved uneasily, seeming at a loss what to say.

"You know that sooner or later we must have an explanation of certain things, and make some arrangements for the future," I began. "Why not commence to-night, if you feel strong enough?"

Still she made no answer, and I offered her my

arm. "There is a seat close by," I said. She went with me, barely touching my arm.

"Now, My Lady, I hope I have not offended you in any way. You seemed so cold, so distant, just now, I feared I had done or said something wrong."

"No, never!" she said emphatically, and stretched out her hand on a sudden impulse. I was not long in grasping it.

Her touch influenced me strongly, and served to concentrate all my ideas into one. I could not wait; for joy or sorrow, I must learn somewhat of my fate to-night. Holding her hand so, I knelt beside her.

"My Lady, you heard what I said to Burton last night; you know what my feelings have been in regard to you. Even during the later and darker months of my detention here, I loved you, in spite of myself. I loved you then; I love you now. To win you for my wife would make me the proudest and happiest man in all the Colonies. I know how you have been taught to think of me these many months, and the knowledge of how far wrong the lesson was has not been yours long enough to let you care greatly for me. But, Marjorie, sweetheart, is there not a chance that some day you may learn to know me better, and be willing to let me care for you while I live? I can be very patient, My Lady, if I have something to hope for, but I must have some knowledge of what my fate is likely to be. Dearest, may I have this hope? I will ask for nothing more until you are willing."

She sat very still and silent for a long time, and I waited as patiently as might be. Once or twice I heard a faint catch of her breath, like the commencement of a little sob. The longer she waited, the lower my spirits sank, and had she offered to withdraw her hand I should have despaired.

Presently she rose from her seat, still leaving me that little hold on life.

"Come with me, if you will be so kind," she said.

"But will you not give me some little hope?" I begged.

"Wait, before you say more," she said very gently. "But come with me now."

She led me to the house and into the library where we had sat alone last night. The place was dark, but both of us knew the room perfectly; she by a life's experience, I through my nocturnal vigils in the grove. It was very dark, and My Lady pulled the bell-cord.

"Bring candles," she said to the servant who answered the ring. "Light these that are here, and then bring all that are in the parlor. And send Theodore to me quickly!"

I knew she must have an object in all this, though I could not fathom it, and waited in silence. The servant lit the candles that were already there, and went for the others. Theodore came to the open door; My Lady went to meet him, and there was a whispered conversation. Theodore seemed to be protesting against something; My Lady grew imperative, and he finally succumbed.

The servant brought more candles, so that the room was flooded with light, and went back to her own place.

"Now, Theodore!" My Lady called.

He entered reluctantly. My Lady had not once looked at me since we entered. She stood in the middle of the room waiting for him, but as he drew near her she turned her face to me. What did that strange expression mean? — sacrifice, repentance — love? I hardly dared to hazard the last guess. Certainly not aversion! Her gaze fascinated me.

There was a swift motion of the negro's arm, and a livid streak sprang in sight across her cheek — the cheek that I had been suffered to kiss that morning when I rode away in chase of Burton!

My Lady caught her breath sharply from the pain.

With a great cry of rage, I leaped fiercely at the man, with murder in my heart, which was doubtless pictured on my face. That any one should dare to strike her — and he, of all others! Cripple though he was since his accident, I could have strangled him with the greatest content.

My Lady sprang between us; she must have expected some such action on my part.

"Stop!" she cried. "I ordered him!"

He fell back in affright at the look on my face, and his weapon dropped from his hand and rolled to my feet. I picked it up mechanically. I knew it well; I had seen it only that morning. It was a small green riding-whip with a silver handle.

"Go, Theodore!" said My Lady. The man glided away, stealing a curious glance at us both as he went, and softly closed the door.

My Lady sank into a chair and hid her face. The silence grew painful before I found my voice.

"Why did you do this?" I demanded, in a very unsteady tone.

"To show my repentance for what I did that day — to make reparation," she whispered.

"And did you think I could take pleasure in such reparation?" I asked, drawing nearer.

"I do not know. I did not think of that. I wanted to do what I could."

"Must there always be the question of rights and reparation between us, My Lady?"

"You have so many wrongs to forgive!"

"None to forgive *you!*" I said passionately. "But even if it were so, cannot love cancel such a score as that?"

She would not answer. I drew close to her and put an arm about her, and she did not shrink from me.

"If you are bent on making reparation for fancied wrongs, there is one way you could take that would leave me hugely in your debt. But I would not take it as reparation, My Lady; I ask it as a gift, to be given without any obligation whatever, except what is implied by the giving. I ask to be your debtor to that extent."

She raised her tear-stained face and looked at me, laying a hand on my shoulder.

"Pray do not call me 'My Lady,'" she said.

"Why not? It has become a habit that would be hard to break; it was so long before I knew your name."

"That is just the reason," she said. "It is a reminder of those wretched months when—"

"Not a word more about that!" I interrupted.

"If you wish it, I will call you Marjorie. But there is still another name that I would use."

She gave me a strange look, and then turned her eyes away and gazed straight before her, as though not to see my face. Her hand dropped from my shoulder.

"Long ago I gave my heart to a man who, it was shown to me, was unworthy of it. I love him."

So quietly said!

It was no wonder she avoided looking at my stunned face while she spoke my sentence of death, or worse than death. Why had I struggled to defeat Burton's treacherous ambushes? Why had she rescued me twice from his grasp? If she had only let me sink in the quicksand, or burn in the cabin! Surely the tender mercies of the — No, she was not wicked; her cruelty was done in ignorance! But it was none the less hard to bear for that.

Slowly, feeling like a man suddenly stricken with years, I withdrew my arm and stood up. I had no right to touch her. There was a ringing in my ears, and my voice sounded like the voice of another man far away. I saw a vision of long years of loveless loneliness and hopeless longing before me.

"You love him still?"

"Yes."

I turned my face away, lest she should look up and see it, and be hurt thereby.

"Does he know it?"

"Not yet, I think!" Her voice was very soft, with a note of tenderness that hurt me sorely.

"Is he worthy, now?" My own voice was harsh; I had to make it so to hide the pain that clutched at my heart and made me weak and sick.

"Most worthy!" very softly.

It was hard, very hard, to do; yet every day of my life I have given thanks that I found strength and courage to say it.

"You are my cousin. For that — and because I love you, and would see you happy —" how the words choked me! — "is there anything I can do for you — or for him?"

Very quietly her answer came.

"I do not expect ever to see him again."

So I was not alone in my wretchedness. Pray God hers was not as mine!

"I am sorry," I said; but I could not look at her yet.

I felt her come to my side. Her arm went about my neck, and the bruised cheek was pressed against mine.

"He was a prisoner, then, now he is free. I shall not see him, because he wore a beard, then, — but not now!"

Then I understood. What was the vision of the coming years I had seen? I lost all remembrance of it when I entered Paradise.

It was a long while before I ventured to ask a question that had vexed me for months.

" Marjorie ! "

" Yes, dear ? "

" Sweetheart, that day on the dune — why were you so angered at me ? "

" I was not ! "   She spoke indignantly.

" Then why did you — "   I got no farther, but I was not likely to resent being interrupted in that way!

" My father had told me that you were an enemy; he said that the story you told proved you a liar and a coward, whom I must distrust and despise."

" It was a natural enough mistake on his part. Thank God he knew the truth before he died. . . . But I only tried to save you when the sand crumbled. Could you not have forgiven my rudeness on that account ? "

She laughed nervously, and evaded the question.

"It was the only time I ever questioned his judgment. In spite of my trust in him and his positive assertion, I could not believe him. I *knew* there was some mistake."

"Even then? If I had only known. . . . But that does not account — "

"You put your arm around me that day," she went on hurriedly, as though to prevent any more questioning.

"Like this. Well?"

"It is hard to explain. . . . It was not you, nor what you did. . . . It was only that — you suffered because — I was angry at myself — because I could not be angry at you!"

It was a somewhat complicated statement, but I thought I knew what she meant.

"Then you were not angry, as I had thought, because I put my arm around you?" I asked slyly.

My dear Lady drooped her head and pressed her face close against my coat. She would not meet my eyes, but she answered my question in a very smothered voice.

"Oh, Allan! Angry? No. . . ." She summoned up her courage with a rush. "Why, that was just what was the matter with me! I — I *liked it!*"

HUGH GWYETH,

A ROUNDHEAD CAVALIER.

BY

BEULAH MARIE DIX.

12mo.   Cloth. $1.50.

WITH A STRIKING COVER DESIGN.

A story of the time of Prince Rupert, that dashing cavalry leader, the Prince in fact appearing on the scene. The young hero, having been bred in the puritanical household of an uncle, orphaned, lonesome, and forlorn, steals away under cover of the night to join a cavalier school-fellow who has already taken arms in defence of his king. A stranger in the royal ranks, Hugh is compelled to engage in menial duties about the camp, while perceiving that he is recognized and repudiated by his father, whom he has hitherto believed to be dead. At last, in the fortunes of war, Hugh is able to defend his sire. Reconciliation follows, and also advancement in the service. A love episode, in which a jolly Roundhead girl-cousin figures, closes the tale.

THE MACMILLAN COMPANY,

66 FIFTH AVENUE, NEW YORK.

THE PRIDE OF JENNICO.

BY

EGERTON CASTLE.

ELEVENTH EDITION.

12mo.   Cloth. $1.50.

"Picturesque in literary style, rich in local color, rising at times almost to tragic intentness, and bristling throughout with dramatic interest." — *The Record*, Philadelphia.

"Hardly since the memorable success of 'The Prisoner of Zenda' has there been published such a stirring, brilliant, and dashing story." — *The Outlook*.

THE MACMILLAN COMPANY,
66 FIFTH AVENUE, NEW YORK.